THE
ALPHA
DRIVE

KRISTEN MARTIN

BLACK FALCON PRESS

For information contact :

Black Falcon Press, LLC

http://www.blackfalconpress.com

Cover Illustration by Alisha Moore © 2015 Damonza

ISBN: 978-0-9968605-1-2 (paperback)

First paperback edition, 2015

10 9 8 7 6 5 4 3 2 1

To eight-year-old me—
I told you you could do it.

1

Bloodshot.

Emery Parker focused on her reflection in the hotel mirror. A pool of grey stared back at her, the usual whites of her eyes replaced with intersecting red and white lines. Gripping the edge of the sink, she turned the faucet on, watching the smooth stream of water as it circled down the drain. Her hands dove under the steady flow, cool water splashing onto her face. She reached for a towel and dried her hands, then patted her face dry.

Her index finger grazed the screen of her phone. Holoicons hovered in the empty space before her. Messages, contacts, email. But there was only one thing she could seem to focus on. The date.

June 1, 2055.

Emery eyed the holoicons for a few more seconds before smacking the phone to the corner of the bathroom counter. It teetered on the edge, begging to be saved from its inevitable crash-landing.

Her gaze met the distraught figure in the mirror. Dirt and ash matted her once rich auburn hair, and the dark circles under her eyes had shifted from a faint purple to a deep violet.

How had she gotten here?

Emery sighed, breaking eye contact with the pitiful image before her. Her knees buckled as she collapsed onto the frigid tile, the towel falling to the floor.

How had she let this happen?

Her head fell into her hands, fingers drumming against her temples in rhythm with her accelerating heartbeat. She focused on slowing her breathing.

One Mississippi. Two Mississippi. Three.

With a deep inhale, Emery hoped that she could somehow overcome the feeling of dread that had followed her for weeks. All she wanted was to go home. To see her mom and her sister. To know that they were safe.

But she couldn't go back. Not anymore. Her home— her world—was gone. Nonexistent.

She'd made sure of that.

Emery clasped her right hand over her chest, eyes closing as her heart calmed, the thud low and deep.

That was the thing about shattered hearts. Even in the midst of tragedy, they begin to heal.

+ + +

One year earlier.

Emery heaved the final box out of her palisade-blue bedroom, mesmerized by the sunbeams dancing on the walls like tightly wound ballerinas. Leaning against the doorframe for support, she lugged the box right in front of her younger sister's room. She knocked on the door and poked her head inside, scanning the room for any sign of Alexis. The room was vacant, aside from the television's weak attempt to break the silence.

Emery wandered down the hall in search of her sister's whereabouts. The den was empty. So was the guest bedroom. Alexis always seemed to disappear at the most inconvenient of times—not all that surprising for a thirteen-year-old.

"Emery," her mother called from the kitchen, "are you almost ready? If you don't leave soon, you're going to run into traffic!"

The time had finally come. Emery Rae Parker was about to transfer to boarding school at the prestigious Darden Preparatory . . . if she ever left and made it in time.

Over the ironclad railing, her sister's brown ponytail swayed as she climbed up the steep staircase. Alexis looked strung out and tired, or perhaps it was just the Arizona heat that had flushed her freckled cheeks beyond recognition.

"Please tell me this is the last one," Alexis said, looking down at the misshapen box.

Emery nodded with a sheepish smile. "It should be. I'll check one more time, just to be sure."

She jogged back to her bedroom, scanning the surfaces for any miscellaneous items that may have been left behind. A crinkled up photograph caught her eye, wedged in a corner underneath her desk. Pushing her chair out of the way, Emery crawled underneath the wooden structure, extending her arm as far as it would go. As her finger made contact with the edge of the photo, she tightened her grip and snatched it from the carpet.

She sat back on her heels, smoothing the photograph in her palm. It was a picture of her father, decked out in army gear from head to toe. He'd been deployed when she was just an infant, so memories of him were scarce. When she was just six years old, they'd received news that her father's assignment would be permanent.

She hadn't heard from him since.

Emery wiped a tear from her eye as she folded up the photo and stuck it in her back pocket. She pressed herself up off the ground and took a deep breath, pushing the thoughts of her father to the back of her mind, then made her way into Alexis's room, checking for the fourth and final time for anything her sister may have "borrowed" in the past and "forgotten" to return.

Just as Emery was about to head downstairs, something on the television caught her eye. The headline at the bottom of the news channel read: *Testing in Progress for New Biofuel.* She plopped onto the bed, turning up the volume as the director of the program gave his report.

"We're in the third and final phase of testing . . ."

Emery sat back in disbelief as the director and the reporter bantered back and forth. Nothing had moved forward in the way of science or technology for years and years. Twenty-eight years to be exact.

No advancements. No breakthroughs.

At just twelve years old, Emery had asked her mother about it, to which she'd simply replied that the government had stopped funding any and all exploration related to science or technology for tax purposes. Which meant that for over two decades, they'd had the same cars, the same medicine, the same phones and televisions.

Of course, Emery attempted to research the topic further, only to find that the internet was full of conspiracy theories and a whole lot of junk. Why the government had stopped the funding was the one overarching question of her generation.

And no one seemed to know the answer.

A deafening clatter sounded throughout the house. Emery clicked the television off and darted out of the room. From the landing, she could see her jewelry box and all its remnants splayed out on the tile. Alexis stood at the foot of the stairs, corners of a damaged box in hand. She looked as though she were about to burst.

Before her sister could make a scene, Emery rushed down the stairs to gather the array of earrings, necklaces, and bracelets that had spilled onto the floor. They each scooped up a pile and then headed toward the front door, their mother hot on their heels, surveying the house to make sure nothing had been left behind.

Alexis unlocked the doors of her sister's black Volkswagen Jetta and slid into the passenger's seat. Emery opened the driver's side door and dropped the remainder of the jewelry into the center console, then turned around to face her mom.

"Make us proud," Sandra fussed as she opened her arms for a hug.

Emery met her mother's warm embrace. "Do I really have a choice, being a Darden legacy and all?"

A wry smile crossed Sandra's face. "Ah, yes. Above all, I'll miss your sarcasm the most." She winked. "I can only hope that your experience at Darden will be longer lived than mine was." She paused, as if suddenly remembering something important. "Wait here just a second."

Emery watched as her mother scurried back inside the house. Through the window, she could see her rummaging through the drawers of the coffee table. A minute later, she returned, holding a small tin box with a yellow bow plopped on top.

"What's this?" Emery asked as she turned the box over in her hands. She didn't mean to sound ungrateful, but her family wasn't exactly the gift-giving type.

"Open it," her mother urged. She glanced over her daughter's shoulder, almost as if she were expecting someone.

Emery narrowed her eyes. "Are you alright?"

A wave of calm washed over her mother's face as she shifted her gaze from the street. "Yes, dear. I'm fine. Go on and open it."

Emery shook her head, trying not to read too much into her mother's behavior. She had her quirks, that was for sure, but Emery hadn't seen her this frazzled in a long time. She slid the bow off the box and lifted the lid to reveal a silver ring, an outline in the shape of a fish staring back at her.

"I've held onto that for quite some time, but I want you to have it now. It represents new beginnings." Sandra's lips curled upwards, but the smile didn't reach her eyes. "I want you to take good care of it."

Emery stared at her mother, trying to hide her confusion. "I will," she said as she slipped the ring over her right index finger, admiring the tiny diamonds embedded throughout. "It's beautiful."

A familiar look crossed her mother's face, one Emery hadn't seen since they'd received news of her father's permanent assignment. It was a look of uncertainty, confusion even, but there was something else laced in her expression.

Fear, maybe?

Sandra cocked her head to the side and stepped in for another hug. The embrace was longer this time, but Emery didn't mind. She wanted to soak up the moment for all it was worth.

"Go on now. I don't want you to be late for check-in."

Emery squeezed her mom's arm one last time before walking to the car. She lowered herself into the driver's seat and positioned herself in front of the steering wheel. Even though she'd had her driver's license for a month already, the freedom she felt when putting her hands on the wheel never got old. Emery reversed out of the driveway, then shifted the car into drive. Her eyes locked on the rearview mirror as her mother waved goodbye, the comfort and security of her home slowly disappearing behind her.

Alexis chatted away as she messed with the playlist, jumping from one song to the next, but Emery's focus was elsewhere as her mother's expression drifted across her mind. The furrow along her brow. The doubt lining her eyes. Why had she looked so frightened? The question plagued her as she drove along the freeway, the music humming softly in the background.

Alexis turned in her seat with a whimsical expression on her face. "You look nervous," she teased as she playfully poked Emery's arm.

"You caught me," Emery admitted with a smile, even though her nerves felt like ticking time bombs. As a transfer student, she had absolutely no idea what to expect.

After hearing so many conflicting things about boarding school, it was hard to choose what to believe.

During her two years at public school, Emery had joined the track team and chemistry club—the latter due to her mother's influence—but finding a group she fit in with had been almost impossible. Seeing as her mother was a single parent, it was no surprise that Sandra had taken a "mother hen" approach when it came to raising both of her daughters. And so, both Emery and Alexis's lives revolved around academics.

Social outings were limited to gatherings after track meets and homecoming dances. From what Emery had heard, boarding school was a sort of punishment—a place where the bad eggs went, yet she wasn't one of them. She was as good as they came, and yet, she was still being sent there. All because of her legacy status at Darden.

"Hellooo," her sister cooed as she waved one hand across her face. "You just faded out there for a good five minutes. Is something wrong?"

"No, not really. I was just thinking about you and mom and how much I'm going to miss you guys."

Alexis laughed. "It's just boarding school. You're only going to be three hours away. We'll still be here when you come back to visit. Nothing is going to change."

"Speaking of which," Emery started as she dug through the center console, "have you seen my phone?"

Alexis turned around and lifted her sister's purse from the backseat, then pulled her phone out. "Got it."

"I forgot to text Riley and Anthony. I said I'd let them know once we left the house."

Alexis swiped her finger across the phone to unlock it. "I'll text them for you." She began to key in a message, then stopped. "Hey, why didn't they come to the house to see you off? You'd think your best friend and your boyfriend would want to say bye before you left."

Emery sighed. "Anthony's at summer camp for football and Riley's on vacation with her family."

"That's cutting it kind of close, isn't it?"

Emery shook her head. "Public school starts two weeks later than Darden does, so they don't have to be back as early." A bout of sadness rose in her throat, but she quickly shoved it back down. "I do wish I could have seen them before I left though. Would have been nice."

"It'll be fine. I'm sure they'll come visit you as soon as they get back."

Emery smiled at the thought.

"Oh and before I forget, make sure you take the west exit and not the east one."

Emery gave Alexis a playful nudge, even though she was right. It was no secret that she had a tendency to get lost, sometimes even circling the same cul-de-sac multiple times in the same neighborhood. In her opinion, cardinal directions were a thing of the past. Wasn't that what technology was for? Luckily, she had a living, breathing GPS sitting in the passenger's seat.

Emery turned toward her sister, who was now rummaging through her own purse. "Hey, you have your plane ticket, right?"

Alexis rolled her eyes as she pulled the ticket out of her bag and waved it in the air. "Got it right here, *mom*."

Emery made a pouty face. "As your big sister, it's my job to check these things. I'm sure you wouldn't want to be stranded on campus after helping me unpack."

Alexis shrugged her shoulders. "It wouldn't be so bad. I'm sure I'll end up there anyway, just like you. Once a Dardenian, always a Dardenian."

"I'm pretty sure that's not what the students call themselves . . ."

"Well, I do," Alexis giggled. "And someday, I'll be a Dardenian just like you!" She clicked the next song on the playlist and turned up the volume, lowering her window even though it was a blistering one hundred and five degrees outside.

Emery briefly took her hands off the wheel to fasten her deep crimson hair into a bun, the strands whipping wildly back and forth. She was tempted to tell her sister to roll the window up, but one glance at her changed her mind. Alexis had her feet propped up on the dash with one arm behind her head, the other halfway out the window. She looked so . . . happy.

Alexis belted out the next few songs, her voice overpowering the vocals on the track. Emery couldn't help but laugh and join in, bopping her head to the beat. Her nerves began to subside as they continued to sing, laughing and poking fun at each other after each song ended.

The interstate stretched on for miles. The vast canvas of mountains highlighted the vibrant blue sky. Seeing as it was summer, there wasn't much greenery—mostly desert sand and tumbleweeds—except for the cacti dotting the edges of the mountains. Having grown up in Illinois, Emery was partial to forests, flowers, and shrubbery. Anything green, really.

But there was something to be said about the serenity of a still desert night. She'd done her best thinking in the wee hours of the morning out on her family's patio, gazing up at all the stars twinkling in the clear night sky. At least home wasn't too far away.

Out of nowhere, Alexis lowered the volume. Her expression turned serious. "Hey, Em? Do you think we'll ever see dad again?"

A knot formed in Emery's chest. She thought back to the crinkled photograph she'd found earlier that afternoon. "I don't know, Lex. It's kind of hard to say. I mean, I hope so." She glanced over at her sister, hoping her response didn't sound too indifferent. "You were only three years old when we found out he'd been permanently deployed." Her throat caught. "Do you, uh, remember him at all?"

Alexis sighed. "Not really. But from the stories mom's told us, I think I'd like him."

"Yeah . . . me too." Emery reached over the center console and squeezed her sister's hand. The only thing she remembered about her father was that he loved riddles.

"Maybe one day." Alexis yawned and leaned her head against the window. In seconds, she was fast asleep, leaving Emery to finish the drive in silence with her thoughts.

Three hours later, they finally arrived at Darden Preparatory. Traffic guards directed the flow of cars into the main parking lot near the sports arena, where maroon and gold banners lined the streetlamps and intersections. The line of cars was backed up for miles, all the way to the main street. After ten minutes of what Emery considered "patiently waiting", she rolled down her window and asked the nearest traffic guard where she could find her dorm, Rosemary Hall. The man opened his mouth to respond, then abruptly turned away from her and started pushing buttons on his headset. After a few moments, he turned back toward her with an apologetic expression on his face.

"Rosemary Hall will be straight down this road. Make a right, then make your first left into the parking lot," the guard instructed. Her eyes followed the direction of his arm, and she couldn't help but gawk at the dilapidated brick building he was pointing at.

"Lucky me," she muttered.

"You have a nice day now, Ms. Parker," he said as he turned on his heel to walk toward the next car in line.

"How did you know—?" she stopped, realizing he was too far out of earshot.

How had he known her name?

She sighed and took her foot off the brake, letting the car roll along the street. Emery eyed her rearview mirror, watching as the traffic guard spun the dial on his radio. Maybe her eyes were playing tricks on her, but she could have sworn she saw him mouth the words, "She's here," into his headset.

2

"Are we in?"

Torin Porter keyed in the final HTML code, his fingers flying against the virtual keyboard as the last sixteen digits blinked before him on the system's holostation. He lifted his hands and swiped his index and middle fingers across the air to make contact with the virtual screen.

As he scrolled through the numerous pages of code he'd written, he realized it was probably best to review it line by line. His successful hacks up to this point included TCP ports 21 and 25, but TCP port 22 was giving him some trouble. After so many attempts, errors tended to blur together, making them almost impossible to spot.

Halfway through the review, his vision grew fuzzy. Torin closed his eyes and shook his head in an attempt to refocus, but it was no use. The numbers and letters swirled together. He may as well just launch the program, errors and all.

With his index finger, Torin pressed the INITIATE button. The system beeped as hundreds of database screens appeared. He could only hope that he'd be granted access into each one. That last firewall was hard to beat.

"Porter, did you hear me?"

Torin swiveled around in his holopod, the rotation smooth and fluid, even though he was suspended about three feet in the air. He'd almost forgotten that someone else was in the room with him. His eyes locked on the one man he wasn't prepared to face just yet.

The Commander.

"I heard you, sir. I'm almost in." He spun away from the Commander's unnerving stare, the scar on his left cheek more prominent than the last time Torin had seen him. The history of the scar was a mystery, but everyone, including him, was too afraid to ask. So, he continued to walk on eggshells, just like every other employee in the building.

Torin diverted his attention back to the horde of flashing images as the final firewall for TCP Port 22 appeared. He shifted his pod closer to the screen. "This is it," he muttered under his breath.

He knew not to get his hopes up with all the failures he'd experienced recently. Breaking into the Federal Commonwealth's mainframe was a top priority for the Seventh Sanctum and, of course, he'd been the one tasked with the nearly impossible assignment. Although Torin was new to the organization, his credentials in "hackerdom" and holotechnology made him a prime candidate for this sort of work. So was the burden of being inherently tech-savvy.

Torin watched dejectedly as bright red letters appeared on the screen. **ACCESS DENIED.**

He clenched his jaw, his hands curling into fists. *I really thought I had it this time.* Sadly, the result wasn't all that surprising. Another attempt. Another failure.

The Commander sighed as he headed back toward the sliding glass doors. "We're running out of time. I don't know how many times I have to tell you—you're the best there is, but I'm starting to lose faith. You need to figure this out, and quick, before we lose our window of opportunity."

Torin lowered his head, hoping his shaggy chestnut hair would hide the defeat in his eyes. "Understood, sir."

"Let me know when you have something worth reporting."

The Commander stormed out of the room, leaving Torin to mull over his failure in silence. He gazed around at the stark white walls. *Government institution or mental asylum?* Lately, it'd started to feel like the latter.

Of course, with every failure came an inescapable time for self-reflection. The burning question he could never seem to answer? Why he'd joined the Seventh Sanctum in the first place.

Torin had been recruited four years ago, while he was still in middle school. Still a child. His real name was actually Sam Moore. His biological parents had given him up for adoption before he was even a year old. He'd transferred in and out of different orphanages, but at the lucky age of seven, his foster parents, the Porters, had adopted him. And so he became Sam Porter.

From that point forward, he was immersed in a world of luxury and technology—very different from the used toys and raggedy hand-me-down clothes at the orphanages. His parents loved him, but time never seemed to be on his side. They were always jet-setting off to another continent. With an empty house and a babysitter that didn't care, Torin taught himself how to use the one thing he never had access to in the orphanage. Computers. Or, more specifically, how to hack *into* computers.

He'd started with the basics—websites and small shop security systems—his knowledge only growing the more his parents were away. Then, on his tenth birthday, he'd received news that turned his entire world upside down. His parents' plane had crashed. And there were no survivors.

As a minor, he should have been placed back into foster care, but Torin didn't want to go back. He hacked into all of the government databases and erased any trace of Sam Moore and Sam Porter, then gave himself a new identity with a new name: Torin Porter.

He'd considered changing his last name for security reasons, but keeping alive the memory of his foster parents was more important. He couldn't give up hacking, not at a time like that, so instead of starting high school like everyone else, he found a job with the Seventh Sanctum. Torin started as a low-level hacker, but after proving himself time and time again, he quickly moved his way up the ranks to Corporal. His latest assignment required him to break into the Federal Commonwealth's mainframe and pull some information that would contribute to another segment of the mission. That was all he'd been told.

At first, it seemed as though he was just a pawn in a larger game, until one afternoon when he'd overheard a discussion between the higher-ups. Well, not so much *overheard* as *hacked into*. It was tough working day in and day out, not knowing if what he was doing would contribute to something worthwhile in the long run. Fortunately, his concerns were put to rest.

The discussion he'd eavesdropped on was one between the Commander and his subordinates. The military jargon was difficult to understand, but the overall message was clear: people were trapped and it was 7S's responsibility to get them out.

Where these people were trapped, Torin had not the slightest idea. Why they were trapped—well, that was an even bigger mystery. But at least his thirty-seven failed attempts weren't wasted on nothing. These people, whoever and wherever they were, needed him, and he wasn't going to give up that easily.

Torin cracked his knuckles and rolled his neck as a blank template appeared on the screen. Back to square one. He took a deep breath, hoping that maybe he would get it right this time around.

Thirty-eighth time's a charm, right?

3

The encounter with the traffic guard played over and over again in Emery's head as she drove down the narrow street. It was probably just a figment of her imagination. Maybe the traffic guard had informed the Resident Assistant that she'd arrived. Or maybe they'd met somewhere before.

Highly unlikely.

She shook off the eerie feeling and brought the car to an abrupt halt, looking out the window at the horrendous structure before her. Piles of faded brick lay desolately on the sidewalk. The doors to the entrance of Rosemary Hall were painted two different colors—one tan, the other a deep brown—and there were still strips of blue tape where the painting was unfinished. It was almost as if the administration had started some renovations and suddenly decided to stop halfway through.

Alexis's stunned expression mirrored her own. "Well, maybe it's not so bad on the inside." She climbed out of the car, peering into the deeply tinted windows of the backseat. "You're on the third floor, right?" she asked as she walked over to the main entrance. She opened the doors to the lobby, then disappeared from sight. After two minutes, she returned, the expression on her face dismal. "Oh, Emery. You're not going to like this."

"I'm not going to like what?"

"Your dorm . . . it doesn't have any elevators."

Emery groaned. Of course. She would be the one to get the outdated building with no elevators. "That's alright," she said, trying to hide her disappointment. "See all of those people in gold and maroon shirts?" Her eyes shifted to the horde of people bustling in the parking lot. "I'm pretty sure they're here to help. They have full-size bins with wheels and everything."

"If you say so." Alexis rolled her eyes and walked to the back of the car. She popped the trunk and began to unload box after box of clothes, muttering to herself why any girl would possibly need this many pairs of shoes and jeans.

Emery smiled, trying not to laugh, when a sea of students in maroon and gold shirts caught her attention. Many of their shirts were plain, but a number of them had large logos stitched on the sleeves. Her gaze shifted to a row of buildings across the street as more students appeared. They didn't look like residence halls, and she wondered if they were administrative buildings of some sort.

A deafening slam invaded her eardrums, causing her to jump like a horse that had been spooked one too many times. She couldn't help but direct a harsh stare at her sister.

"What?" Alexis asked, resting her hands on the trunk of the car. "Don't look so jolted. Grab some stuff from the backseat and I'll go find some bins."

By the time they'd filled up four of the bins, there wasn't a gold or maroon shirt in sight. As they rolled the oversized bins through the dorm lobby, Emery couldn't help but frown. The entire building looked like it was under construction. There were concrete and plaster-covered walls everywhere, paint chips scattering the floor amongst piles of overflowing garbage bags. But the smell was the worst, like multiple sewage pipes had sprung leaks and hadn't been repaired yet. How could they let students move in when the lobby was hardly even functional?

I pray to god this isn't what my room looks like.

They stopped at the front desk, a chipper woman greeting them for check-in. She jotted down Emery's information, then pulled a shiny black key card and a gold room key from her desk drawer. The woman scanned the card to activate it, then handed both items to Emery. "Room 319 will be through the door on the right on the third floor. Welcome to Darden."

Emery thanked her and proceeded to a glass door with a large paper cut-out of the letter C taped messily to the window, as if a kindergartner had been given too much leeway during arts and crafts time. She searched the door for a second, noticing a small black box next to the doorframe with a little red light above it. A faint beep sounded as she swiped the card over the access reader, the light turning green.

They maneuvered the bins into the dimly lit stairwell, cringing at the sound of screeching voices and echoing footsteps from the floors above. The yellowish-green lights emphasized the black scuffs on the walls from the numerous move-ins and move-outs the dorm had accommodated over the years, and the once white tile looked like it hadn't been scrubbed in centuries.

"So much for getting help," Alexis scoffed. "How are we going to carry all of this? And up three flights of stairs, mind you?"

Emery tried to stay positive, but the situation was progressively growing worse by the minute. "You stay here with the bins," she instructed. "I'm going to take a few things upstairs and unlock the door. I guess we'll just take turns. That way, my stuff won't be left unattended."

"Are you crazy? That'll take us forever to get unloaded!" Alexis whined.

"Well, if someone in a maroon or gold shirt happens to waltz down this marvelous staircase, feel free to ask them for help," she retorted. "I'll be back in a couple of minutes."

Emery grabbed her iron, a lamp, and a bag of cleaning supplies from the bin and started the trek upstairs. With aching thighs, she finally reached the third floor and pushed through the worn wooden door that led to the hallway corridor. The hallway was just as poorly lit as the stairwell, lined with the same yellowish-green lighting. The stench of stale pizza and moldy cardboard boxes filled her nostrils. *Gross.*

Her experience up to this point went against everything she'd heard about boarding school in general. She'd expected grand residence halls with new fixtures, and renovated dorm rooms with the latest technology. A building with elevators, at the very least.

This was the exact opposite of that.

As Emery continued down the hallway, she realized it was eerily quiet for what was supposed to be a chaotic move-in day. The door numbers increased with every step, the even numbered rooms on the left an odd numbered rooms on the right. She held her breath as she walked down the hall, exhaling once she reached her room, number 319. The door was slightly ajar, so she gently pushed it open with her foot. In the middle of the room stood a brunette, sporting a fitted black vest and jean shorts. Her bracelets and bangles jingled as she spun around excitedly at the sound of the door opening. At the same time, an older female and male poked their heads out from behind a closet door and smiled. Emery made a quick calculation, presuming that this was her roommate, accompanied by her mom and her dad.

"Finally!" the brunette exclaimed. "You must be Emery. I've been waiting to meet you all day. I'm Rhea." She rushed over and embraced her new roommate in a tight hug. Emery attempted to hug back, trying to balance her belongings in her already occupied arms.

Rhea pulled away, the smell of coconut and lime lingering in the air. She grinned, showing off her flawless, pearly white teeth. Emery felt overwhelmed and mesmerized all at once.

"Silly me, let me get that for you," Rhea offered as she unloaded Emery's arms and turned to place the items on a nicely polished desk. Emery was quick to notice a bed situated overhead, realizing it was actually all one unit. *A desk and a bed in one. How convenient.*

"Oh, I almost forgot. These are my parents. You can just call them Mom and Dad."

"Hi," Emery waved, feeling entirely uncomfortable. "It's nice to meet you."

At that moment, Alexis appeared in the doorway with not one, but all four of the bins. "What's taking you so long?" she huffed. "I finally found someone to help us." She nodded her head at the tall, lanky kid next to her. "Thanks for your help, Tyler."

Emery smiled at the boy as he walked away, then cleared her throat to indicate that they weren't alone.

Alexis peered around the doorframe, then nudged her sister, clearly wanting an introduction. Emery tried not to roll her eyes. "This is my sister, Alexis."

"Nice to meet you, Alexis." Rhea's attention shifted to the bins in the doorway. "It looks like you lugged a lot up those stairs. Did your parents help you?"

"Actually, our parents aren't helping me move in," Emery interjected. "Just my sister."

Rhea's parents exchanged quizzical looks, which made Emery feel even more uncomfortable, but Rhea was unfazed. "Is that all of your stuff? Or is there more?"

"I think there might be four more bags in the car," Emery replied, turning toward her sister for confirmation.

"Mom, Dad, would you mind helping them bring up the rest of Emery's things?" Rhea asked sweetly. "Alexis may never leave if it's just the two of you. Poor girl's probably tired already."

"Of course, sweetheart," her dad responded as he placed a hand on his daughter's shoulder.

Emery couldn't help but feel a twinge of jealousy. They seemed like the picture perfect family. A pit formed in her stomach as she thought about the conversation in the car with her sister. The question Alexis had asked repeated over again in her head. *Do you think we'll ever see dad again?*

Emery watched as Rhea's parents left the room with Alexis, immediately feeling more comfortable in a one-on-one situation. She surveyed the room, her displeasure diminishing more and more by the minute. Their room actually looked like it had been remodeled and repainted—a huge improvement from what she'd just witnessed downstairs in the lobby.

"What a day," Emery sighed, digging in her purse for the gift her mom had given her. *Now where to put this?* She walked over to the closet, noticing a pink silk pouch sitting in the back corner. *Perfect.* She picked up the pouch and dropped the tin box into it, then tucked it far back into one of the built-in drawers.

"What's that?" Rhea asked as Emery shut the closet door behind her.

She shrugged. "Just a gift my mom gave me. It's kind of weird, actually. My family never gives gifts. And it's even weirder that I already miss her."

Great, now I'm rambling.

"I know exactly how you feel." Rhea turned to her desk to look at a photo of her family. "It'll be weird not having my parents here. But I have you now." She smiled and turned back to a partially unpacked box of jewelry, make-up, and shoes.

Emery raised an eyebrow. *What exactly does she mean*

by that? Before she could ask, Rhea's phone rang. "Be right back," Rhea mouthed as she walked out of the room to take the call.

The bins sat in the middle of the room, begging to be unpacked. *Guess I should get started on that.* As Emery began to organize her shoes, her phone buzzed with a flight reminder. *It's time for Alexis to leave already?* It seemed like they'd only just arrived. A wave of sadness washed over her. Even though her sister drove her crazy at times, Emery was going to miss her. She pulled her keys from her pocket, then strode out the door, signaling to Rhea that she had to run a quick errand.

+ + +

Even though twenty-four hours had passed since Emery had dropped Alexis off at the airport, it felt longer. If there was one thing Emery hated, it was saying goodbye. Goodbyes always came too soon.

She stared up at the ceiling from her uncomfortable twin mattress. She and Rhea had spent all last evening, and this morning, getting acquainted with one another, but Rhea still seemed to be somewhat of a mystery.

Designer labels filled the room as Rhea unpacked the last of her jeans, shoes, and accessories. Emery wasn't sure why her roommate had packed so many nice clothes, seeing as they were required to wear their school uniform to class. She flipped onto her stomach where she had a direct view of Rhea's desk, noticing miniature bottles of whiskey and vodka protruding from her purse.

Rhea caught her staring. "I hope you don't mind. I brought some party favors—you know, to celebrate being roommates."

"Oh . . . um, that's cool." Warning bells sounded off in her head.

"Yeah. It wasn't easy to sneak in, but I always find a way. Even at my old school," Rhea gloated, "and they were way stricter there."

"You're new to Darden too?"

"Yeah. I got kicked out of public school in California, so here I am." She turned back to the half empty box and pulled out some light scarves and oversized derby hats. "I'm thinking we should decorate this little shoebox of a room."

Emery wanted to ask why she'd gotten kicked out, but figured her roommate had probably changed the subject on purpose. "How do you want to decorate it?"

"I don't know. Maybe we can ask our residential advisor if they have some fabric or stringed lights or something. It's just so drab in here."

Emery sat upright and looked over at the window where Rhea was standing. She seemed to be deep in thought, trying to visualize the room with whatever color and decoration scheme had appeared in her head.

"So . . . do you have any brothers or sisters?" Emery

asked in an attempt to keep the conversation going.

Rhea turned toward her, a boot in one hand and a necklace in the other. "Nope, it's just me. I'm an only child."

This was surprising. Based on what she'd seen so far, her roommate seemed like the kind of girl who'd have at least one sister. Emery scrunched her face, taking a minute to study Rhea. She wore cut-off jean shorts that were slightly frayed at the ends, an edgy band shirt, and red sneakers. Brown hair cascaded down around her shoulders into soft waves, her porcelain skin nearly flawless.

Emery felt her cheeks flush with envy. *Damn, she's pretty.*

Rhea waved her hand in the air. "Earth to Emery. Did I lose you?"

"Huh?" Emery replied, snapping out of her jealous trance. "I'm sorry. I zoned out there for a minute."

"Don't worry about it," Rhea smiled. She turned back to the window, then meandered over to her closet. "God, this is a mess. There just isn't enough space for all of my shoes."

As Rhea pondered over her underwhelming closet space, Emery's phone rang. She grunted and hopped off the bed, landing with a soft thud onto the floor. She ducked her head and reached across the desk, knocking over a picture frame and coffee mug in the process. Even though she didn't recognize the number, Emery decided to answer it anyway.

"Hello?"

"Hello. Is this Emery Parker speaking?" The voice on the other end was raspy. A male's.

For a brief moment, she considered hanging up, but decided otherwise. "Yes, it is. Who is this?"

"I'm with the Darden administration. We need you to come down to the lobby of Rosemary Hall to discuss your class schedule. A couple of changes need to be made."

Feeling confused, Emery thought back to the check-in process the day prior. "The girl at the front desk said everything was fine—"

"—we need you to come downstairs at your earliest convenience."

She hesitated. "Um, okay. I guess I can come now. Whom should I ask for?"

"When you get to the lobby, take the south elevator to floor B2," the voice instructed. "Knock on the door at the end of the hallway. I'll meet you there."

Emery was about to ask him to repeat the information when she heard a click on the other line, followed by the dial tone. She drew the phone away from her ear and stared curiously at the blank screen. Tucking it into her back pocket, she turned to tell Rhea about her confusing conversation with the mystery caller, but her roommate was nowhere in sight.

Emery tried to ignore the wave of uneasiness washing over her as she jotted down a quick note for Rhea. She stuck it to the screen of her roommate's laptop, then grabbed her things, locking the door behind her. Padded footsteps echoed in the empty space as she made her way down the stairwell. She swiped her key card and pushed the door to the lobby open, jumping as it slammed shut behind her.

The lobby was unnervingly quiet. The front desk was unoccupied and there wasn't a soul in sight. *Where is everyone?* She searched desperately for any sign of movement, but there was nothing.

It was entirely deserted.

Emery tried to ignore the peculiar atmosphere as she strode toward the south side of the lobby. She made her way over to the silver-paned elevators and pressed the button, jumping as the elevator doors shot open almost immediately. With caution, she stepped into the elevator and pressed B2, watching as the doors closed in front of her. Emery glanced at the walls around her, the hair on the back of her neck rising as she recalled what her sister had said yesterday.

Rosemary Hall didn't have elevators.

4

Panic-stricken, Emery looked over at the button she'd just pressed, realizing that it was a one-way ride.

There was no option to return to the lobby.

She shuddered and took a deep breath, her mind racing with every horrible outcome imaginable. The elevator chimed and the doors opened slower than a sloth scaling a tree. Emery peered at what lay before her: another dimly lit hallway, one that led to a single door.

With no option to return to the lobby, she stepped out of the elevator and cautiously made her way to the looming, maroon-shaded door. Swallowing the lump in her throat, she knocked twice, then stepped back a few feet. When there was no answer, she knocked again. The door rumbled as bolts and locks underwent their rickety rhythm on the other side.

The unknown side.

Emery's eyes grew wide with fear as she watched the

door open. Much to her relief, a young girl with a blonde, pixie haircut stood on the other side. The girl held a black tablet, and an elaborate earpiece jutted out from her right ear. "She's here," the girl stated into her headset, flashing an award-winning smile. "I'm Naia. It's so wonderful to meet you. Please come in."

Emery stepped into the room, comforted by the fact that a normal human being had been on the other side of the door. What else would it have been? A robot?

"Please have a seat," Naia instructed as she gestured to a gold-trimmed, leather chair. "Theo will be right with you." She turned on her heel and walked to a smaller door within the room. The door closed gently behind her, leaving Emery completely alone.

The room itself was of decent size, but it wasn't overwhelming. It was brightly lit, unlike the hallway she'd just been in, and the walls were painted a crisp gold with maroon and black embellishments. The marble crown molding was a spectacular swirl of black, grey, and white specks.

Emery peered over the edge of her chair, looking back toward the door from which she had just entered. It was the same color as the exterior—a deep shade of maroon. Standing on either side of the door were two exquisite white, marble columns that had clearly been influenced by Roman mythology.

Emery turned in her seat to face forward, noticing

that the only other chair in the room was the one sitting in front of her. They were almost identical—massive and made of leather—except the one across from her was adorned with maroon trim instead of gold. There was an emblem on the seat of the chair that was difficult to make out, but the letters looked like F-C-W.

The door creaked open, causing Emery to straighten her posture immediately as a lanky, male figure sulked toward her. He was dressed in black from head to toe, wearing a sharp blazer, dress pants, penny loafers, and a suede fedora with petty feather accents. His face was jagged and worn, as if he'd spent many sleepless nights pondering philosophical arguments.

"Emery, it's so wonderful to finally meet you," he drawled as he extended his hand for her to shake. "I'm Theo Barker. Welcome to the Headquarters of the Federal Commonwealth."

Emery couldn't help but notice his square jawline and the way his mouth pressed into a harsh line as he spoke. She hesitated before standing to shake his hand. "It's nice to meet you, too."

"I hope your trip down here wasn't too uninviting."

"No, but the elevator—"

"I know this meeting may seem out of the blue," Theo interrupted, "but we're so thrilled you came."

Out of the blue is right. He's definitely not a school advisor.

"I bet you're wondering who I am and why I've

brought you here," Theo continued, as if he could read her mind. "What I'm about to tell you may seem hard to believe. In fact, you may choose not to believe it at all." He paused, attempting to read the expression on her face. "I highly encourage you to keep an open mind. Can you do that for me?"

"Sure . . . I guess," she stammered.

"Please have a seat."

Emery obliged, her eyes locked on the mysterious man in front of her. As Theo fluffed his blazer and took a seat, a tiny patch at the bottom of his jacket caught her eye. Trying not to be too obvious, she craned her neck for a better look. The patch looked like some sort of emblem—likely the same emblem she'd discovered on the seat just moments earlier.

"Miss Parker," Theo began, "I've brought you here today because I want to extend to you an opportunity. One that has the ability to change the course of your life and the lives of those around you." He stopped for a moment, the corners of his lips curling upwards.

"What I'm about to tell you here must not be repeated outside of these walls. If you accept our offer, we will move forward as planned. However, if you decline, you will have no recollection of this encounter once you've left. Your memory of your time here will be expunged. Do you understand?"

Emery hesitated before answering. She was certain

the look on her face was one of complete and utter horror. She nodded, hoping that it would suffice in place of a verbal agreement.

"Lovely," Theo remarked. "Now, where to begin?" He cleared his throat before continuing. "I'm the head chairman of an organization called the Federal Commonwealth, or FCW. Before you can understand why the FCW was created in the first place, there is something very important you'll need to wrap your head around." He eyed her warily, waiting for a cue to continue.

Emery scooted forward in her chair. "And that is?"

"This whole world . . . it isn't real."

"Pardon?" Emery tilted her head. "I'm sorry, I don't think I caught that."

"This world isn't real," Theo repeated, his expression serious.

Emery's expression matched his until she couldn't keep a straight face any longer. "Ha-ha. Very funny," she laughed. "Now what are we really here to talk about?"

Theo narrowed his eyes. "Exactly what I just said."

Emery eyed the exit as she lifted herself from the chair. "Right, okay. Well, I have a lot that I need to do, seeing as it's my second day at Darden and all." She shook her head, disappointed. "You know, if this is some sort of joke for freshman initiation, I highly recommend you rethink it."

Theo sighed. "I should have guessed that this would be your reaction. Allow me to approach this from a different angle. Ms. Parker, have you ever wondered why technology hasn't advanced in twenty-eight years?"

Emery stopped dead in her tracks.

She turned back around to face Theo. "The government . . . they stopped it . . ."

Theo shook his head slowly as soft tisks slipped from his mouth. "Or is that just what they want you to believe? Twenty-eight *years*, Emery. Surely if it had been a question of funding, it would have been resolved in a year or so. But twenty-eight *years*?"

Emery stifled a yelp of disbelief as her body went rigid with shock. He was right. She looked down at her trembling fingers, then squeezed her hands into fists to calm her nerves. After taking a deep breath, she slowly gazed back up at Theo.

"Good. Now that I have your attention, let's circle back, shall we? This conversation we're having right now technically isn't real. Your years growing up in elementary school, middle school, and high school, thus far, haven't been real."

"Of course they were real," Emery shot back, feeling offended. "I'm sitting right here in front of you. I am the product of those years in school. I am the product of my life thus far." She could feel her anger rising. "I am living proof that my life is real!"

"Emery," he soothed, "I need you to calm down and keep an open mind." He raised his eyebrows, the lines in his forehead creasing. "Remember?"

Emery circled the chair, then paced back and forth, running her nails along its plush surface. After taking a deep inhale, she sat down, her heart seconds away from exploding out of her chest.

Theo waited for her to calm down, tapping the tips of his fingers together. "Ever since democracy was founded, mankind has assumed that the government is the most powerful entity in the world. Unfortunately, this assumption is profoundly incorrect. Some odd years ago, an organization called the Seventh Sanctum, or 7S, successfully invaded every continent on the planet and overthrew the governments. They couldn't stand the idea of free will—it disgusted them. In 7S's eyes, the laws previously enforced by the world governments were not stringent enough. Crime rates were rising, birth rates were dropping, and chaos ensued. We were living in a world of exploitation, degradation, and corruption. The Seventh Sanctum had a plan to end it all, so they did." His eyes gleamed with malevolence. "By inducing a worldwide coma. You're living in their fake world—in *Dormance*." Emery looked at him with a bewildered expression. She opened her mouth to speak, then closed it again.

A comatose world? It was impossible. No one in their right mind would do something like that . . . would they?

"Have I always been in this," she struggled with the words, "fake world? In Dormance?"

Theo nodded. "That is correct. You've always been a dormant."

Emery took a deep breath. *I've been in a coma ever since I was born.*

She was silent a little while longer. "I guess I'm confused. If mankind was so terrible, what was the point of rendering everyone comatose? Why didn't they just kill us all?"

A clever smile touched Theo's lips. "I knew you were a smart girl. You see, the plan entailed that 7S's new society be built from scratch. But, as with everything, there are limitations. There is no way for them to make this strategy a realization without *us*. We may all be in a comatose state, but our cells—our *DNA*—are still needed to create new life. Without our DNA, 7S has no way to create new life."

"Hmm," Emery murmured as she processed the information. "And what happens to all the people living in Dormance after 7S finishes building its new world?"

Theo looked down at his hands before responding, then whispered, "7S will kill all of the dormants. The new population will be able to reproduce, so there won't be a need for the previous inhabitants."

Emery shook her head. "It doesn't make any sense.

What will 7S's new world have that ours doesn't? What will it look like?"

"That, my dear, is something we're still trying to figure out," Theo clucked as he licked his lips. "I suppose it'll be a world with more order, more stringent rules, and less freedom." He waved his hand in the air in a sarcastic, huzzah motion.

Emery bit her lip. Something didn't feel right. It wasn't fitting together. "Hold on a second. How do you know all of this if you're supposedly in Dormance too?"

"Simple," Theo responded. "We have a source on the outside. Or, I suppose I should say, on the *inside*." He chuckled, the sound almost inaudible in the vast, marble chamber.

Emery raised her eyebrows. "You've made contact with someone in the Seventh Sanctum?"

He nodded. "Once our source was able to provide proof that the world is completely comatose, the Federal Commonwealth was born. Our inside-source wants to end the 7S reign as much as we do."

Emery squeezed her eyes shut as she desperately tried to make sense of it all, but there were still so many questions that needed answering. "If Dormance was *induced* by the Seventh Sanctum, then isn't there a way we can break out of it?"

"Bingo," Theo chimed. "Do you see where I'm going with this?"

Emery blinked as the realization hit her. She felt like her eyes were going to fall out of their sockets. "You're building an army to free the dormants."

A wide grin spread across Theo's face, his teeth crooked and unsightly. "Right you are. We're calling this initiative, The Alpha Drive. Now, if we don't defeat 7S, we'll be doomed to live our lives in Dormance until we're eventually killed off." He brushed away an imaginary piece of dust from his blazer as if what he'd just said was of little to no importance.

Emery stared at him blankly, her mouth agape. It was all too overwhelming for words.

"You're probably wondering how this involves you," Theo chortled. "This may sound strange, but we've kept tabs on you for quite a while now. We know everything about you, from your birthday to your favorite color to where your family vacations in the winter."

Not creepy at all.

"Which is why you, Emery Rae Parker, have been selected as a candidate for The Alpha Drive."

5

Emery gripped the armrests as Theo made his last statement. She closed her eyes, her mind spinning in eighteen different directions. *An army. They want **me** to join their army.* This was not at all how she'd expected her first week at Darden to go.

Should I feel flattered? Confused? Terrified?

"What exactly does participation in The Alpha Drive entail?" she managed to ask.

"Ah, yes," Theo mused. "Essentially, you'll be living a double life. You'll keep living your life as an unsuspecting dormant while simultaneously training for The Alpha Drive."

Emery couldn't help but frown. She felt as though she were on an emotional rollercoaster that would never stop. At first, she'd felt pure shock. Awe, even. But in that moment, all she felt was anger and resentment toward the

Seventh Sanctum. How could anyone believe that rendering the world comatose and starting anew was a good idea? How could anyone be okay with taking millions of lives? Had mankind really been so terrible that it needed to be completely wiped out?

Theo interrupted her thoughts. "Of course, The Alpha Drive isn't without its limitations. After all, we are talking about a life and death situation."

"This is unbelievable," Emery muttered, her confidence wavering. "I'm sorry, it's just . . . it's just a lot to process." She drummed her fingers against her temples. "How are we . . . I mean, how do we defeat the Seventh Sanctum?"

Theo gave a reassuring smile. "Well, let's get right into the nitty gritty of it, shall we? Candidates are hand-picked by the FCW after careful deliberation and many years of observation. Candidates are brought to an underground location, similar to the one you are sitting in right now. Candidates, participants, and members of the FCW are the only ones who are able to access these underground locations. To everyone else, they do not exist."

"That explains why I could see the elevator," Emery murmured.

Theo nodded, then shifted in his chair. He cleared his throat before continuing. "Once chosen, candidates are introduced to their consultant, who, in your case, is me," he paused, gesturing to himself.

"In addition to meeting me, you are also introduced to my assistant. I believe you met Naia earlier."

At the mention of her name, Naia appeared in the doorway, her hair bobbing as she walked. She approached them with a serving dish, atop of which sat glasses of sparkling water and a plate filled with cheese and crackers. She gave Emery a comforting smile before turning to Theo to confirm he didn't need anything else. Theo shook his head and, with that, Naia retreated back to the door.

Emery reached for a glass of sparkling water, accidentally spilling some of the liquid onto the table. She wiped the droplets away with her hand, then raised the glass to her lips, meeting Theo's steady gaze. Something about his expression was disconcerting. She tilted the glass away from her face and set it back down on the table. "This is just water, right?"

Theo smirked. "So, you've met me and you've met Naia," he continued, ignoring her question. "You should also know that each participant is required to have a microchip embedded into their skin on the nape of the neck or on the heel of the foot. Your choice."

Emery looked at him with wide eyes. "Are you serious? You have the technology to do that?"

"You look surprised. Of course we do."

"But how? Technology hasn't advanced in twenty-eight years?"

Theo waved his hand in the air. "Never mind how. What's important is that we have the technology."

His sudden brashness caught her off-guard. "Does it hurt? The microchip embedment, I mean?"

"Technologically speaking, the embedment process is quite advanced. Most claim that they feel a pinch and that's it," Theo assured.

"Why on the nape of the neck or heel of the foot?"

"Your question brings me to my next point," he answered. "These chips must be hidden—out of sight. Dormants are unable to access the office locations, and they can also never know about the Federal Commonwealth or The Alpha Drive. Knowledge of any of these by external patrons will result in memory purge."

Emery shifted uncomfortably in her chair. "Meaning what exactly?"

Theo scratched his chin. "Meaning we erase their memories."

Harsh.

"Similarly, if one participant discovers another, the one who has been 'found out' will be removed from training and their standing will be revoked. Their memory and any information regarding The Alpha Drive will be erased," he explained.

"But why?"

"We need the very best soldiers. If a participant is careless enough to let the chip be seen, then there's really no telling what else they'll reveal."

Emery nodded as she picked at her cuticles. "So, how do I avoid that?"

"Simple. Keep your chip hidden."

Emery narrowed her eyes. "How can anyone see the chip if it's embedded into the skin?"

"The chip will blink a faint shade of purple when two participants are within twenty feet of one another and will continue to blink until one participant has cleared the proximity. If you see that blinking purple light, it's game over for the other participant."

Emery knew she was asking a lot of questions, but she needed to know what she was getting herself into. "But how—?"

"How do we know what you see and don't see?" His telepathic nature grew more impressive by the minute. "Your chip acts as a second set of eyes. We see everything that you see. You can't hide anything from us." A sly smile touched his lips. "In order to build the best defense and increase our chances of defeating the Seventh Sanctum, we can't have anyone hide anything from us, now can we?"

Emery considered this. "No, I suppose not."

"Good. I'm so glad that we're on the same page," he confirmed as he licked his lips. "So, like I said, you'll be disqualified and your memory will be erased if you're identified by another participant. Failing your training is also grounds for disqualification."

"There's training?"

Theo sighed, clearly annoyed by all of her questions. "Of course there's training. We wouldn't just throw you out there and expect you to come out on top."

Emery nodded her head to indicate that she understood. "Look, I'm sorry for all the questions. I'm just trying to understand."

"Is there anything else you'd like to ask me?"

"Yes, actually." She paused. "I understand what happens if I'm found out by a fellow participant, but what happens if a *nonparticipant* sees the chip?"

A flicker of doom crossed Theo's face. "If a nonparticipant sees the chip, their memory will be erased as well. You can lose all of your relationships in the blink of an eye. Again, these microchips *cannot be seen.*"

Emery sat there, motionless, as she tried to process this last bit of information. She blinked a few times, hoping to rattle her brain for a response, but found that it was lost in a sort of hell there seemed to be no escape from.

"Right, well, I'll leave you to it. The choice is yours." Theo lifted himself up off the chair and walked toward the door. "I'll be back momentarily while you contemplate your answer."

And just like that, he was gone.

There she was. Entirely alone. Left to ponder this. *All* of this.

Emery sighed, placing her head between her hands. She closed her eyes, trying to sort through everything Theo had just told her. Her bottom lip quivered as reality set in. *The world is in a coma. Nothing is real. My entire life has been a lie.*

It dawned on her that if she wanted to, she could just leave. She could leave without any recollection of what had just happened and go on living her life. When comparing the two choices, this seemed to be the sensible thing to do. Ignorance was bliss, right?

Or . . . she could take a huge risk and participate in The Alpha Drive for a chance to free the dormants. To give everyone a second chance. To make life *real* again.

Emery squeezed her palms against her temples, but the voices in her head only grew louder. Why couldn't they have given her a heads up? Why now? This time in her life was already stressful enough, what with boarding school starting and moving away from home.

In that moment, all Emery wanted to do was call her best friend. Riley would know what to do, what to say, what questions to ask. She would also probably think Emery was out of her bloody mind for even considering something like this.

And then it hit her. She couldn't discuss this with anyone—she had to sit in this room and contemplate her future without any advice. From anyone.

Emery snapped out of her daze. *Focus.* Theo wasn't going to let her leave until she came to a decision.

THE ALPHA DRIVE

Her gaze fixated on the table in front of her. A tablet, the screen glowing a bright white, sat next to a black stylus, both anxiously awaiting her attention. Emery scooted forward in her chair, thumbing through the pages on the tablet. After scanning the first few sentences, she decided it was best to be thorough and read the document line by line.

THE ALPHA DRIVE RULES AND REGULATIONS

1. Microchip embedment is required for each participant. Any tampering or attempt of removal will result in disqualification and memory expungement of all things related to The Alpha Drive initiative.

2. Participation in The Alpha Drive will remain anonymous. If a participant discovers another, the participant who has been discovered will be disqualified and their memory will be expunged. If a nonparticipant discovers a participant, the nonparticipant's memory will be expunged.

3. Training is mandatory.

4. Failed training will result in disqualification and memory expungement.

5. Participants who succeed in the training will be deployed to the 7S world for battle, where Statute 2 above becomes null.

WELCOME TO THE ALPHA DRIVE

Emery sat back in her chair, letting the tablet fall into her lap. She put her hands beside her temples and gently massaged her pounding head, her heart thumping at the same pace. Her eyes landed on the glass of sparkling water

Naia had delivered earlier. She grabbed it and took a swig, coughing as the carbonated bubbles tickled her throat.

Her body slunk into the armchair. Half of her felt invisible and unseen, like she was underneath a magical cloak; the other half felt like she was under a microscope, her every thought no longer private, her every move scrutinized and documented for further research.

Ten minutes went by until her headache finally subsided. Emery snatched the stylus, tapping it noisily against the table. *I could give it a shot*, she deliberated. *If it's not for me, I could disqualify myself and go back to my normal life in Dormance. My fake life.*

Just the thought was enough to make her cringe.

And what about her mom and sister? Riley and Anthony? If she chose not to participate, could she live with herself knowing that she'd refused her loved ones the life they deserved?

Emery tapped the stylus a few more times, watching the text glide smoothly up and down the screen. She analyzed the document twice more before getting up and walking around the room. *I must be going insane. Only someone who's completely lost their mind would consider something like this.*

The conflicting voices in her head weren't making it any easier to decide. Emery made her way back toward the table and planted herself in the chair once again. She glared at the tablet as the screen flickered, taunting her.

Oh, what the hell.

She pressed each of her fingers into the square boxes on the tablet, watching as her prints filled the empty spaces. The door in the back creaked open as Theo appeared, an expectant look on his face. His phone buzzed, and he switched it off as he ambled over to where Emery was sitting. He sat on the armrest of the chair, directing his full, undivided attention at her. His eyes met hers.

"So?"

Emery locked eyes as she pushed the signed contract across the coffee table. "Count me in."

6

Theo watched as Naia escorted Emery to the door, his heart pounding faster than usual. For a split second, he'd been worried that Emery would decline participation in The Alpha Drive. Luckily, it hadn't come to that.

He walked down the dimly lit corridor, past the four training rooms, until he reached his office. A blinking blue light on the monitor caught his eye. One missed call. He strode over to his desk and called the number back, anxiously waiting for the other line to pick up.

"You didn't answer when I called."

Theo gulped, eyeing the shadowed figure on the holostation. "My apologies, President Novak. I just finished meeting with Emery—"

"What did she decide?" the President interrupted.

Theo bit his tongue, trying to keep himself from chastising his superior. "She's in."

A long sigh of relief filled the airwaves. "Have you decided what her first training session will be?"

Theo guessed that this would be one of the first questions he'd get. Fortunately, he'd given it some thought. "Aquam training, sir."

"Do have everything you need? Has everything been prepared?"

Theo rolled his eyes, insulted by the President's lack of confidence in him.

"You may not be able to see me, Mr. Barker, but I sure can see you."

Theo half-smiled at the shadowy figure on the screen. "We're all set, sir. I'll keep you updated as her training progresses."

"Wipe that stupid smirk off your face. Why you were chosen to lead this initiative is beyond me. Unfortunately, my vote didn't count, but I assure you, I would have chosen *anyone* else." He grunted. "Don't mess this up for us."

Theo hesitated as the insult sunk in. His mouth pressed into a harsh line. "You have my word, sir."

The line clicked. Theo glared at the blank screen, hoping that one day, he'd muster up the courage to give the President a piece of his mind.

7

Rhea pushed through the heavy, oak door that led to her dorm room. *Where is she?*

Emery was nowhere in sight, but there was a note stuck to the screen of her laptop. After reading it, Rhea took it upon herself to go look for her unpredictable roommate. She ventured over to the parking garage, wondering if maybe Emery had journeyed downstairs to grab something out of her car. With no luck, she'd passed back through the lobby to the grassy lawn outside their dorm.

Rosemary Hall was situated in between two other residences, Bishop Hall and Dorsey Hall. All three of the buildings were old and rundown, but unlike the others, Rosemary Hall was only three stories tall. A coat of faded, red brick adorned the outside. It looked like something out of a cheaply-made 1950s film. *Why in the world did I leave California for this?*

As Rhea entered her dorm room, she dropped her purse on the floor next to an unopened box that had "Emery's Books" scribbled along the side. She kicked off her shoes and plopped onto her desk chair, staring at the yellow post-it note still stuck to her laptop before crumpling it up and throwing it into the metal waste bin. All it said was, **Be back soon**. No mention of where Emery had gone, when she'd be back, or even a phone number she could be reached at.

I'm an idiot for not getting her number, Rhea scolded herself, feeling like a teenage boy after a failed first date.

It was the first time in a long time she'd felt this way. As an only child, Rhea was used to having all eyes on her—but now, sitting alone in the dorm room, away from her parents, friends, and new roommate, she couldn't help but feel incredibly lonely. Is this how she'd feel every time she was left alone? Sad and depressed?

Her pity party was interrupted as the door handle jiggled.

Emery bolted through with a frazzled look on her face. She'd only known Emery for a day, but she could immediately detect that something was different. This was not the same girl she'd met yesterday.

"Hey," Emery said hurriedly. She shuffled through some items on her desk, sat down in her chair, then stood back up and began to pace back and forth.

What's wrong with her? Rhea wondered as she brushed

her hand nervously across the back of her neck.

Emery stopped pacing, her eyes fixed on the floor. "Hey, I'm sorry I left so suddenly."

Rhea shrugged. "That's okay. It was nice of you to leave a note. Where'd you go?"

"I went for a walk around campus," Emery said as she shifted her weight from one foot to the other. "I met up with an advisor."

Keep her talking. "Oh. I was sort of hoping we would do that together." The hurt in her voice was loud and clear. "But no big deal—I can do it tomorrow."

Emery looked up from the floor, eyes drooping like a puppy that had been stranded on the side of the road. "Oh geez, I'm sorry. I guess I wasn't thinking." She shook her head, clearly disappointed by her actions.

"Don't worry about it," Rhea quipped, trying to lighten the mood. Her intention hadn't been to make her roommate feel worse. "It's only our second day here."

"How about I go with you tomorrow? To make up for being so inconsiderate," Emery offered.

"I'd like that." Rhea tilted her head sideways. "Hey, wanna grab a coffee?"

Emery shrugged her shoulders. "Sure, I could go for some coffee."

Rhea grabbed her things and headed for the door with Emery close behind her. They trudged down the stairs in sync, then pushed through the double doors of Rosemary

Hall. The mesmerizing sight ahead brought them both to a halt. The once empty lawn had suddenly turned into an enlarged mating ground for new students.

Out of nowhere, a familiar voice called Rhea's name. She grabbed Emery's arm mid-step, stopping both of them in their tracks.

"Ouch," Emery muttered, stumbling over her own two feet. "Why are we stopping?"

Rhea held up her hand, as if to silence her roommate. Her ears perked up as the voice shouted again.

"Rhea! Is that you?" a male voice called out a second time.

I know that voice. She stood on her toes, scanning the dense crowd. A hand landed on her shoulder, causing her to jump.

"Rhea Alexander, it is you!"

She spun around to find herself immersed in a tight bear hug, her chin chest-level with a striped navy and white shirt. As she caught her breath, Rhea inhaled a familiar scent. *I know that cologne.*

The mystery guy released his grip, allowing her to finally see his face. *No way.*

"Mason!" Rhea's mouth dropped open in disbelief. "What are you doing here?"

"I go to school here. And I'm guessing . . ."

"Yeah, I go here too," Rhea grinned, holding his steady gaze. It was hard to turn away from those enticing amber-lit eyes.

"So, how'd you end up here?" he asked as he adjusted his hat. His hair shifted with the movement, waves of sandy blonde lying unevenly beneath the brim.

He's still so attractive and . . . She stopped mid-thought, realizing she hadn't answered his question.

"Uh, well," she stammered, "I mean, I didn't really have a choice. My parents sent me here."

Mason grinned, revealing a perfectly-aligned set of fluorescent white teeth. "Looks like we have that in common." He averted his gaze as something caught his eye, then stepped to the left, looking a few paces behind Rhea.

She followed his gaze to see what had caught his attention.

"Emery?" Mason said in shock.

For a minute, Emery's face was blank, not registering who he was. Then, as if a light bulb had turned on, she flashed a smile of recognition.

"Hey, Mason. Good to see you again." She stepped across Rhea to give him a hug.

"Wait, how do you two know each other?" Rhea asked, doing her best to mask the confusion in her voice.

Emery smiled. "I could ask you the same thing, roomie."

"Wait a minute. Roomie?" Mason looked at Emery, then back at Rhea.

"Alright, let's figure out this little friend triangle that we've got going on here," Rhea said as she cleared her throat. "Mason and I went to elementary school together in California. Our parents were really good friends. I think we actually even dated in, like, third grade." She chuckled, sneaking a look at Mason to see if he remembered.

He nodded and laughed.

"But then his family moved to Arizona, leaving me all alone," Rhea continued, making a pouty face. "As for Emery and me, we were randomly assigned as roommates this year, so we share a dorm room." She gestured toward Rosemary Hall. "How do you two know each other?"

"I know Emery's best friend, Riley," Mason answered. "Over the summer, Riley brought Emery over to a mutual friend's house. Come to think of it, I actually haven't seen or talked to you since then."

Emery blushed. "It was a busy summer. I wanted to spend as much time with Riley as possible before leaving for Darden."

"I'm just giving you a hard time," Mason teased. "What a small world. We should all get together sometime. My friends and I are actually thinking about going out tomorrow night before classes start."

"Really? How are you going to manage that?" Emery asked. "I've heard the Headmaster is pretty strict when it comes to letting students go off campus."

"We'll figure something out," Mason winked. "Are you guys in?"

"Definitely," Rhea said, answering for the both of them. "We'll see you later. It was nice running into you."

"Likewise." Mason smiled as he left to join a group of friends at the far end of the lawn.

"Well, that was random," Emery laughed. "So, are we still getting coffee?"

After waiting in line for what seemed like three hours, the under-caffeinated barista finally took their drink order. "I'd like a tall, vanilla latte," Emery said as she scrambled through her purse for some cash.

"You're aware that it's over one hundred degrees outside, right?" Rhea teased.

Emery shrugged. "What can I say? I've never been a huge fan of iced coffee."

"I'll take a grande, iced, chai latte," Rhea said to the barista.

Emery continued to scramble through her bag, pulling out crumpled receipts and tubes of chapstick.

"Hey, don't worry about it," Rhea said as she slid her hand into her back pocket and pulled out some cash. "This one's on me."

Emery smiled. "Thanks. I'll get the next one."

They retrieved their drinks from the counter, spotting an empty table over by the window. Emery carefully removed the lid of her cup and blew on the steamy liquid. She took a sip, jumping a little as she burnt her tongue.

Rhea took a quick swig of her drink, feeling immediately refreshed before setting it down on the wobbly, wooden table. "How's your coffee?"

"Scorching. I think I burnt my tongue."

Rhea laughed. "I know I already said this, but you're crazy for ordering a steaming, hot beverage in the middle of this desert heat."

"I'm used to it, I guess. I've lived here almost my whole life."

"Really?" Rhea asked, her curiosity peaking. "Where did you live before?"

"I was actually born in Boston, but my family lived in a lot of different places on the east coast."

Rhea took another sip of her coffee. "Army family?"

Emery's breath caught as she lowered her eyes.

Looks like I struck a nerve.

"Something like that. My family moved around a lot when I was younger," Emery recalled as she set her drink down. "I don't really like to talk about it."

As tempted as she was to pry further into her roommate's early childhood years, Rhea thought better of it, and decided to bring up something a little more recent. "So, you went to middle school in Arizona?"

"Yeah," Emery replied, fidgeting with the cardboard holder wrapped around her cup. "Middle school wasn't my favorite. I had really frizzy hair, round glasses, bushy eyebrows, and braces for most of it. The kids were really mean. Riley was my only real friend." She smiled at the thought.

Rhea took a minute to really look at Emery. Her deep crimson hair fell in sleek waves just below her petite shoulders and her olive skin highlighted her light grey eyes. Come to think of it, Rhea had never met anyone with her combination of looks. It was difficult to imagine her roommate with frizzy hair and glasses. She was pretty, in an understated sort of way.

Rhea gulped down the last of her coffee, wishing she had gotten the larger size. "What about high school? Has it been any better for you?"

"High school hasn't been my favorite so far," Emery admitted. "At my public school, I joined the track team and chemistry club, but I never really found a group I fit in with. I sort of just . . . floated." She blushed, looking down at the bracelets on her wrist. "Not to mention my upbringing, which was super strict. I was never really able to go out. Surprisingly, I was allowed to have a boyfriend. So, I became known as the girl who always had a boyfriend."

"The girl who always had a boyfriend, huh? So what, do you have one now?"

Emery turned her head to the side and placed a hand on her neck as if she were about to crack it. "Um, yeah, actually, I do," she confessed.

Rhea looked at her inquisitively, waiting for her to continue.

"His name's Anthony. He's a couple of years older than me. We've been together for a little over a year," Emery said hurriedly.

Rhea furrowed her brow, wondering why she felt the need to rush through her answer. "Does he go to Darden?"

"No, he goes to the same public school I went to before I transferred here." Emery took another sip of her coffee. "But enough about me. I want to know more about you—where you grew up, how school's been . . ." She waved her hand, clearly wanting to change the subject.

"Well, I was born and raised in California with a great family and a lot of friends," Rhea began. "Unlike you, I was sort of a wild one in middle school. I actually started drinking in sixth grade—"

Emery nearly spit out her coffee. "Did you say sixth grade?"

Rhea laughed, amused at her reaction. "Yeah, nothing too heavy though—mostly beer and wine coolers." Her train of thought broke as her phone buzzed noisily against the table.

"Are you going to answer that?" Emery snooped.

Rhea looked down at her phone as a message lit up the screen. Her stomach turned as she skimmed the contents. She tried as best she could to keep the expression on her face neutral. *Don't freak out.*

Rhea's neck tingled as she gazed back up at her roommate, praying that she wouldn't ask questions. Fortunately, Emery's focus seemed to be somewhere else entirely.

8

Emery moved her hair to the side as her fingers grazed the back of her neck. Her thoughts drifted back to the microchip embedment from earlier that day.

After signing the contract, Theo led her out of the common room to a daunting hallway. Running along both walls of the corridor were numerous steel doors, unlike the wooden door at the entrance. Emery stayed right on Theo's heels, managing to read a few of the labels plastered next to each door, until they stopped at one labeled **Embedment.**

Theo scanned his retina and fingerprints, the nuts and bolts click-clacking within the door. A buzzer sounded to indicate that the door was unlocked. With a deep breath, she'd followed him into the blindingly white room, shivering at the air blasting from overhead. In the middle of the room sat a smooth, marble table with an open, circular area at one end that was surrounded by grey cushion.

Directly above the table was a terrifying contraption she'd never seen before, and Emery could only guess that it was the embedding device. At first glance, it appeared it would be more painful than Theo had let on.

Theo instructed her to lay face down and shift her hair to the left side of her body. A high-pitched buzzing sounded as the contraption lowered and slowly bridged the gap between it and her neck. Much to her surprise, the press of the machine was gentle, and just as she'd reached for the grips attached to the underside of the table, it was over.

Theo was right. It was painless. A small pinch, a moment of stillness, and it was over.

Emery snapped back to reality, realizing that Rhea had been talking the entire time. She nodded her head, pretending like she'd heard the whole thing.

Rhea swiped her finger over her phone. "Ready to go?"

Emery nodded again and followed her roommate out of the café. "So, are we definitely going out with Mason and his friends tomorrow?"

Rhea turned to look at her as she opened the door to Rosemary Hall. "Do you want to?"

Emery considered this for a moment as she trudged up the stairs behind her roommate. "Yeah, I think so. I mean, it'll be fun, right?"

Rhea laughed. "Of course it'll be fun."

Emery followed her roommate down the hallway, not sure how to bring up what she wanted to say next. "What you said about drinking earlier . . ." Emery hesitated. "I think you should know that I've never had alcohol before. Not even a sip."

Rhea stopped mid-step. "Never?" she asked in disbelief. "What are you, a nun?"

"Sheltered upbringing, remember?" Emery pulled her keys out of her pocket and unlocked the door to their room.

"Well, do you want to try it?"

Emery bobbed her head from side to side, contemplating her response. "I've never really thought about it. I guess it wouldn't hurt to try."

"Maybe tomorrow night then." Rhea walked into the room and opened her closet door, analyzing her clothes for their upcoming outing. After a few minutes, she gave up and headed into the bathroom. "I'm gonna shower. I'll be out in a few. Don't get into any trouble." She winked, then disappeared behind the wooden door.

Emery collapsed into her desk chair and leaned her head back. She sat there, motionless, enjoying the soothing sound of running water and overall stillness of the room.

The feeling didn't last long as her phone vibrated, buzzing noisily against the desk. She picked it up and looked at the screen to see who was calling. It was her boyfriend, Anthony. Part of her wanted to let it go to voicemail. The other part told her to answer the call. Using her better judgment, she decided to go with the latter.

"Anthony, hey," she answered as she swiveled away from her desk.

"Hey babe, how's it going?"

"Things are good. How are you?"

"I tried calling you yesterday to see how the move went, but you didn't answer," he said, sounding a little hurt.

"Yeah, sorry about that. Things have been pretty hectic, but I'm almost all moved in."

"Well, that's good to hear. I'd love to come and see you sometime. Oh yeah, and meet your roommate. Have you met her yet?"

"Yep. Her name's Rhea and she's from California."

He laughed, sensing some tension. "Do you like her?"

Emery paused for a minute. "Well, I've only known her for a day. We have pretty different backgrounds, but yeah, I guess I like her."

"What do you mean different backgrounds?"

"She's just really easygoing and her life doesn't revolve around academics like mine does. Maybe she can show me how to have fun." Emery rolled her eyes, realizing how dumb she sounded.

"That's good, I guess."

"Yeah, I think we're going out tomorrow. I'm actually kind of looking forward to it."

"You? Go out?" He laughed. "Meeting Rhea might be the best thing that's ever happened to you."

Emery was quiet. In all honesty, his comment stung a little. It was no secret that Anthony was incredibly well-liked in high school. He was on both the football and baseball team and had a strong connection with basically everybody he met. He'd consistently mocked Emery for having only one close friend, saying that she needed to put herself out there more. She'd tried this a few times and quickly found out that she had absolutely nothing in common with the majority of the girls at her public high school.

"Well, I'm sure you'll have fun tomorrow," he assured. "Don't forget about me, alright?"

"I won't."

An awkward silence filled the airwaves.

"Alright, well I'll let you get back to it," Anthony said. "I love you."

Emery hesitated. "Love you too."

"Bye," he whispered before ending the call.

Emery removed the phone from her ear and tossed it onto the desk. As much as she wished to deny it, her feelings for Anthony had shifted over the last couple of months. No longer did he make her feel carefree and exhilarated. Now, talking to him left her feeling exhausted and overwhelmed. Why couldn't things still be the same as when they'd first met?

Memories of track and football season filled her mind. As a freshman, Emery had made the Varsity Track & Field Team at her public high school. A few weeks into practice, she noticed some cramping in her quadriceps, so she started seeing the on-site physical therapist on a regular basis, about three times a week. One day, about halfway into her sessions, a muscular, dark haired football player had stumbled through the door, his hand wrapped in wads of blood-spattered towels and athletic tape. She'd immediately known who he was. Everyone knew him.

Anthony Bolero.

The look of excruciating pain on his face was almost unbearable to look at. The physical therapist immediately turned his attention to Anthony, instructing him to lay down on the table opposite Emery. She'd watched as the therapist unraveled the athletic tape and towels to reveal a crushed, misshapen hand.

She and Anthony had never really spoken to one another, except for a brief passing or two in the hallway. Emery knew her place since he was older and held a certain status in the school—but in that moment, none of that mattered. She saw someone in severe pain, someone who was in need of comfort. So, that's exactly how she'd behaved.

She'd laid her hand on his shoulder until his gaze met hers. "They really got you good there, huh?"

He winced as the therapist injected something into his arm for the pain. "My hand . . . crushed . . . between helmets," he mustered through clenched teeth.

She'd stood there for a few minutes, waiting for the expression on his face to soften.

When the pain had finally subsided, he'd looked up at her and said, "I'm Anthony."

"Yeah," she'd replied. "I know."

From that moment on, they were inseparable. Not only had he wooed her, but he'd also wooed her mother. He took Emery on new dates every week, and he never failed to shower her with thoughtful gifts every month for their anniversary. He knew everything about her and vice versa.

But his tendency to judge her and try to change her had gotten old. He cared too much about what other people thought. Putting on a show for everyone was tiring and she wasn't sure how much longer she could parade around pretending to be someone she wasn't.

Emery snapped back to the present as Rhea emerged from the bathroom, the wooden door clanging behind her. "Did my phone ring by chance?" she asked, searching for it underneath a pile of clothes.

"No, but mine did," Emery replied as she spun her phone on the desk.

"Oh?" Rhea turned toward her, eyebrows raised. "Who was it?"

Emery hesitated before answering. "It was Anthony. He was just checking in to see how the move went." She stopped, waiting for Rhea's reaction.

"Do you think I can meet him tonight?"

"Tonight?" Emery picked at her cuticles. "Tonight's probably not going to work out."

Rhea shrugged, then disappeared behind the closet door. After a couple of minutes, she reappeared wearing a white t-shirt and jean shorts. "Well, I'm sure I'll meet him soon enough," she said as she walked over to her desk and began searching for her earbuds.

Emery didn't have it in her to tell her roommate that their relationship was going downhill. And fast. "Hopefully not too soon," Emery mumbled. She looked up to see if her roommate had heard her, but Rhea was already in the zone, tapping her feet to the beat of the music buzzing from her headphones.

9

I give up.

Torin hopped down from the floating pod, pressing a button on the side of the machine to power it down. The blue lights underneath the white oval structure blinked, then faded into black. The pod lowered to the ground, locking itself into place with the four bolts protruding from the steel floor.

Torin trudged over to the exit and leveled his face with the retina scanner, then swiped his hand over the identification reader. The sliding doors opened without hesitation.

"Good morning, Corporal Porter," a friendly, female voice greeted him over the intercom.

Morning? He pulled his phone from his pocket and looked at the time. It was 3:15 A.M. Another twenty-four hours gone trying to crack the Federal Commonwealth's code. *Another twenty-four hours I'll never get back.*

Torin's stomach erupted in frenzied hunger growls. He couldn't remember the last time he'd eaten, or even thought about anything else besides writing code, revising code, wanting to *murder* code.

He strode through the doors and walked over to the nearest teleportation platform, digging in his pockets for the circular, crystal dials. He dropped one onto each wrist, watching as the crystal morphed to become one with his skin. The cafeteria was his only option, but since the food was sub-par, his best bet was to head to his apartment and order a decent meal from there.

Torin stepped onto the platform, instructing the machine to take him to the main floor. The tingling came first in his toes, then his legs, and worked all the way up to his chest, shoulders, and neck. He closed his eyes as the machine's familiar gust of wind transported him from the fifty-sixth floor to the first floor. He opened his jaw, ears popping from the ride down. No matter how many times he teleported, his ears never seemed to adjust to the changing pressure.

Voices echoed in the hallways from above.

Who's still here? And at three o'clock in the morning, for that matter?

Shadows danced along the walls of the seventh floor—the same floor as the Commander's office. Torin hid behind the back panel of the T-Port, the clever name scientist Thompson Porter (no relation) gave his invention after defying the laws of physics and gravity when he discovered teleportation was possible. Torin poked his head out from behind the T-Port, watching as the shadows entered one of the main conference rooms.

He'd hacked into that room before.

Wavering between his hunger pains and his curiosity, he stepped back onto the platform and whizzed up to the seventh floor, then tiptoed across the hall until he stood just a few feet away from the conference room. Reaching into his back pocket, Torin pulled out his phone and logged into the 7S database. He'd learned the hard way that for this particular room, he had to be within range in order for the hack to work.

Torin tapped in the code from memory, then waited for the green light to flicker across the screen.

He was in.

A square-shaped hologram hovered over his device. Three people stood in the room—the Commander, Sergeant Griggs, and Sergeant Botlek. They spoke in hushed tones, forcing Torin to bring the hologram close to his ear in order to hear their conversation.

"This whole situation has gotten completely out of hand," the Commander declared as he paced back and forth across the room.

"Sir, we're doing everything we can to remain in control—"

"Well, it's not working, now is it?" he snapped.

The sergeants bowed their heads in shame.

"More than half of the world has been rendered comatose. They're living in an alternate reality with no knowledge that their world *isn't real*. We're the most technologically-advanced organization in the world and we can't figure out how to stop it?" He was yelling now. "Do something! Break them out!"

Torin held the device away from his face, eyes wide. *Half of the world? In a coma?*

"We're doing everything in our power to solve this as fast as we can," Sergeant Botlek stated. He took a deep breath. "Are you sure you're not letting your familial ties interfere with the strategy?"

The Commander's eyes narrowed, his lips pressing into a firm line. "Pretty soon, everyone's family will be trapped in Dormance, not just mine."

"But you can see how it could be viewed as a conflict of interest—"

"Enough," the Commander barked. "I've heard enough from you."

Sergeant Griggs spoke up. "The young corporal—Porter, is it? Has he had any luck breaking into the Federal Commonwealth's mainframe?"

The Commander grunted. "Every time I ask him, the answer is 'almost'. Almost doesn't cut it. We need to get in. Now."

Torin had heard enough. He clicked off the device and darted over to the platform as newfound adrenaline coursed through his veins. It was time to prepare himself for another long night in his office. He wasn't an "almost" sort of guy. He was an "all the way" kind of guy.

And it was time for him to prove it.

10

For the first time in years, Emery dreamt. She'd crept down an elongated hallway that looked familiar, but she couldn't quite place where she'd seen it before. Passing room after room, she'd finally arrived at a secured door of a private chamber. Rhea's voice had echoed in the halls as she stood in front of the door when suddenly, a gunshot fired—and then she'd woken up.

Emery racked her brain, trying to remember more, but that was all she could seem to recall. She glanced at her phone. Eight o'clock in the evening. It'd been a while since she'd taken a decent nap, and this one left her feeling surprisingly refreshed.

Rhea had just returned from the campus gym, beads of sweat dripping from her forehead. "Hey, did you have a nice nap? I hope I didn't wake you."

Emery nodded as a yawn escaped from her mouth.

"Good. I'm going to rinse off," she called out, grabbing her towel from the rack. "I'll be out in fifteen minutes. You better wake yourself up before we go out tonight."

Emery hopped down from her bed and opened her laptop, browsing through the countless emails that had accumulated while she'd been asleep. Syllabi, welcome email, more syllabi.

Fifteen minutes passed and, like clockwork, Rhea emerged from the bathroom, her towel wrapped loosely around her body. She stepped behind her closet door, her foot poking out from the side. A few hangers clattered to the floor, followed by a few swear words. Finally, Rhea stepped out from behind the closet door wearing tan high-waisted shorts, a black crop top, and black heels embellished with gold studs.

"Wow. You look . . ." Emery paused, searching for the right word.

"Fierce?" Rhea finished, her expression hopeful.

Emery flashed a sincere smile. "You read my mind."

"I'll take any opportunity I get to wear something other than that atrocious school uniform," Rhea murmured as she opened the door to Emery's closet. "Now, it's your turn. We need to find an outfit for you."

"Oh, I was just going to wear jeans and a shirt—"

Rhea looked at her with disapproval. "Emery, dear, this is our first night out together as roommates. You're wearing something other than jeans and a shirt." She rustled through Emery's closet for something worthy of being seen in.

"Aha!" she exclaimed. Rhea pulled out an old band t-shirt and a pair of high-waisted red shorts and handed them to her roommate, instructing her to change.

Emery gazed at the mirror hanging on the back of her closet door and examined the outfit she'd just put on. She tugged the shorts down a little, trying to cover more of her thighs, and adjusted her shirt with a glum expression.

"Something wrong?" Rhea asked.

"No," Emery muttered. "I guess I'm just not used to dressing like this."

"Well, get used to it," Rhea said, her eyes twinkling. "By the way, you look perfect."

Emery tried to hide her smile. "Thanks. I guess it's not that bad." She tugged on her shorts again. "Can you pass me my make-up bag and straightener?"

Rhea shifted her weight from one foot to the other, leaning across the counter to grab the straightener and teal, zippered bag. "Here you go," she said, tossing them across the room.

A couple of hours later, Rhea and Emery were putting the final touches on their ensembles. Emery gathered her money and I.D. cards and tossed them into her leather clutch. She reached behind her laptop for her cell phone, noticing that Anthony had sent her an unusually long text message. It was best not to read it, since he'd probably sent something that would make her feel guilty for going out. Not surprising.

"Ready?" Rhea asked as she fastened her necklace.

Emery nodded, throwing her phone into her clutch. They exited through the front doors of Rosemary Hall onto the grassy lawn, keeping an eye out for any Darden personnel that might be patrolling the campus. Luckily, there wasn't a soul in sight.

"Where exactly are we going?" Emery asked. She realized they probably should have explored the outskirts of campus ahead of time so that they wouldn't be walking around aimlessly.

"We went out the wrong door," Rhea said, looking down at the map on her phone. "Come on, this way." She swiped her key card to get back inside Rosemary Hall, then headed toward the door that led to the parking garage.

"Wait, are we driving there?" Emery asked as they neared her car.

Rhea turned to face her. "Yeah, why? Is that a problem?"

"Sort of. Darden has ridiculous rules when it comes to leaving campus. You should have seen what I had to go through when I took my sister to the airport."

"Walking it is, then," Rhea sighed. She quickened her pace with her phone in hand, Emery following closely behind. They walked through the four-story parking garage and across the street, passing Darden's football field. The next street was the same one Emery had driven down earlier that week during move-in. She focused on the brick buildings that lined the street, a familiar observation floating across her mind. *Those can't be administration buildings.*

She tapped Rhea on the shoulder. "Do you know where we're going?"

Rhea ignored her question as she placed a buzzing phone to her ear. Emery could hear a male voice on the other end and assumed that it was Mason.

"Yeah, we're heading that way now," Rhea said into the phone. "We'll be there soon, okay? We can't drive, so we're walking. We'll probably be there in about ten or fifteen minutes." She hung up the phone and threw it back into her clutch.

"Mason?" Emery asked.

"Yep. He's wondering where we are."

After waiting at the crosswalk for what seemed like a century, they finally reached the mysterious buildings on the other side. Overgrown plants and shrubs surrounded the outside of the buildings while dead grass and tumbleweeds crunched underneath their feet. Even in the dim lighting, Emery was able to spot a crooked sign at the end of the street. She squinted for a few seconds until she was finally able to make out the words. **ALPHA DRIVE**.

How ironic.

Her discovery was interrupted by Rhea's shrill voice, who had somehow gotten a few yards in front of her. "Oh my god, no way! You have got to be kidding me."

At first, Emery thought they were about to get busted by Darden security for sneaking out of their dorm. She ran toward her roommate, remnants of tumbleweeds whirring around her in a frenzy. "What is it? Are you okay?"

"Would you take a look at this?" Rhea exclaimed with both arms extended toward the buildings. "They're club buildings!"

Emery looked at her, confused. She turned her attention to one of the many drab, brick buildings standing before them. It took a minute for her eyes to adjust, but they finally settled on placards inscribed with different names: Drill Team, Sychem, Club Med.

Rhea's eyes lit up. "We just hit the jackpot," she beamed, spinning around to face Emery. "I've heard that these buildings are used for student clubs and organizations during the day, but at night, students come here to hang out."

Emery's curiosity peaked, but was immediately replaced with apprehension. "Let's keep walking. We shouldn't keep Mason and his friends waiting."

Rhea pouted like a little kid who'd just been grounded. "Fine."

They walked further down the row of buildings, then

came to a stop to adjust their shoes. *Whoever invented high heels was an idiot*, Emery thought, as she leaned against the door of a dumpster.

"Hey!" a brusque, male voice called out.

Emery looked up from her shoe, trying to discern where the voice had come from. A few buildings down the street, on the second story balcony, stood two seemingly tall guys. It was hard to tell in the lackluster lighting.

"Hey!" Rhea shouted back.

Emery looked at her incredulously. "What are you doing?" she whispered. They watched as the two guys came down the stairs and walked over toward them. Indeed, they were tall, standing at about six feet, and they were somewhat attractive.

Correction: **very** attractive.

A musky scent wafted through the air. One of the guys had dirty blonde hair, the other a shade of dark auburn. "Where are you two ladies off to?" the blonde guy asked.

Emery piped up. "We're on our way to—"

Before she could finish, Rhea chimed in. "Here. We were on our way here." She stole a glance at her roommate, a hint of a smile touching her lips.

The guys laughed, immediately sensing that Emery and Rhea were new to Darden.

"I'm Jason," the brunette said.

"Drew," the blonde added, waving at the girls. "Come on, let's go inside. Things are just starting."

Rhea and Emery looked at each other and shrugged, then followed them into the building. The interior was nothing spectacular—cracked, disjointed crown molding lined the ceiling and the maroon paint on the walls was chipped and faded.

Jason and Drew walked them around the first and second stories, introducing them to the people in each room. There were already quite a few people there, which was surprising since it was only half past ten. Rhea and Emery walked into the main common area, wooden tables and plush leather couches sprawled out in the large space.

Lining the tables were bottles of alcohol, an array of juices—from cranberry to apple to orange—and oddly shaped cups that were small at the top, narrow in the middle, and bulbous at the bottom. They resembled an hourglass shape, but with a few nuances. Emery picked one up, examining the mysterious object with both hands.

"That's a jigger," Jason stated, recognizing the look of confusion on Emery's face. "You pour the juice into it first so it sits on the bottom, then you pour the alcohol in the top section." He smiled and kneeled down at the coffee table to face them. "So what's your poison?"

Rhea leaned forward seductively, putting her chin in her hands. "I'll take vodka and cranberry," she purred.

Jason poured her selection into the funny, little glass and handed it to Rhea, then turned his attention to Emery. "And for you?"

"I actually think I'm okay for now," Emery said, hoping that her cheeks weren't blushing an embarrassing shade of red.

Rhea rolled her eyes. "Oh, don't listen to her. She'll have what I'm having."

Emery opened her mouth to protest, quickly realizing that it wasn't worth it. *Okay, I guess I can have just one.*

More people filed into the room. A lanky girl, who reeked of whiskey, sat down on the edge of the couch next to Emery. Jason left the coffee table to mess with his laptop and speakers in an attempt to get the music started. After a minute or two, a song with heavy bass thumped from the speakers, the walls of the room vibrating.

Emery's eyes shifted from Jason to her roommate, who had been sitting across from her the entire time.

"Are you okay?" Rhea asked, holding a jigger in each hand.

Emery shrugged. "Yeah. Just taking it all in, I guess."

"Well, take it all in while drinking *this.*" She handed Emery one of the jiggers as a devious grin spread across her face.

Emery hesitated before taking the drink from her roommate's hand.

"Now, make a toast."

Emery raised her eyebrows. "Um, okay. To . . . boarding school." She glanced at Rhea for approval.

"Kind of weak, but I'll drink to that." Rhea winked as she raised her glass.

Emery watched as her roommate tossed hers back with ease, then slammed the jigger down onto the table. She looked down at the red liquid and tilted her head back as she brought it to her lips. The mixture burned her throat a little, but she finished it with no problem.

Rhea clapped her hands. "So what do you think?"

Emery shook her head from side to side as if weighing her answer. "Not too bad."

"I knew you'd enjoy it." Rhea laughed. "Hey, Jason!" she called out.

Jason looked up from his post at the speakers and nodded, then walked back over to where they were sitting.

"Another," she commanded, as he reached the table.

Emery tried to hide the bewildered look on her face. *Already?*

Jason smiled, clearly amused by her authoritative tone. "Yes, ma'am. Whatever you say."

Emery sat back, watching in shock as her roommate took shot after shot, pressuring her to do the same. Even though she'd never been intoxicated herself, Emery knew that Rhea was drinking too much too fast. She needed to get her roommate away from the alcohol.

It took over an hour before Rhea finally slowed down.

"I'm going to look for the restroom," Emery interjected, hoping that enough time had passed where Rhea would need to go with her.

Rhea let out an exasperated sigh as Jason poured another drink. "Hold on, I'll go with you."

They walked crookedly down the hallway when, out of nowhere, Rhea stopped, bursting into a fit of laughter. She positioned her body against one of the grimy walls, arms outstretched in both directions. "This is so fun. Isn't this fun?" she slurred, pressing her cheek against the wall.

Her roommate looked so ridiculous that Emery couldn't help but laugh. "Are you okay?"

Rhea released herself from the wall, almost losing her footing. "I've always been a lightweight. You think that I'd be used to it by now."

Emery walked alongside Rhea as she stumbled down the hallway, intervening a few times to keep her from face-planting into the tile. When they made it to the restroom, Emery pushed the door open, blinded by a brightly lit room. She wrinkled her nose as the stench of urine and beer filled her nostrils. *Gross.* Plastic, red cups circled the perimeter of the sinks and wadded up paper towels littered the floor.

Rhea didn't seem to notice her surroundings as she flung her clutch at Emery and bolted toward an open stall. "I can't hold it!" she declared as she slammed the door shut behind her.

Emery chuckled as she walked over to the sink. She fixed her hair in the mirror, stopping as Rhea's clutch began to buzz. She opened it, digging through the wadded up dollar bills and tubes of lipstick. A missed call flashed on the screen.

Mason.

Emery considered stepping out of the restroom to call him back when she heard the toilet flush. The handle jiggled, and it was clear that Rhea was struggling to unlock the stall door. Emery quickly tucked the phone back into Rhea's clutch and set it on the counter, pretending she hadn't just gone through her roommate's things.

"I don't know about you, but I need another drink," Rhea slurred. She ambled toward the exit, moving at a much faster pace than expected.

"Are you sure you need another drink?" Emery called out as she grabbed both of their bags and chased her roommate into the hallway.

"Of course I do." Rhea grabbed Emery's hand as she led the way down the hall. They squeezed their way back into the overly crowded room and ducked underneath an overhang, then made their way to the center of the chaos. Emery gazed at all the people dancing and flirting with one another. She spotted Jason, who was mixing more drinks, from across the room.

Here we go again, Emery thought as Rhea dragged her through the crowd.

"Jason!" Rhea called out over the deafening bass. They slipped past multiple moving bodies over to where Jason was happily playing bartender.

He grinned as they approached. "There you are. I was wondering if you'd left us."

"We'd be crazy to leave this early," Rhea flirted.

He turned toward the windowsill and grabbed another bottle of vodka and cranberry juice. "Well, now that you're back, I'm sure you're just dying to have another drink."

"I don't know if that's a good idea," Emery interjected.

Rhea waved her hand in the air. "Sure it is. Pour 'em!"

Jason poured two drinks, handing one to Rhea. Emery watched as they drank, feeling like a babysitter who was about to be fired for not doing her job. Emery panicked as he poured another one, trying to think of any excuse to get Rhea away from the alcohol.

The mood in the room shifted and a higher energy took hold as a dubstep song boomed from the speakers. The room suddenly broke out into a crazy dance orgy. Seeing her opportunity, Emery grabbed Rhea's hand and dragged her out into the middle of the room. She wasn't really the dancing type, but it didn't matter. She needed to get Rhea to slow down before she hurt herself.

They danced for what felt like hours, letting the music move them in whatever way it desired. The room maintained its exuberant energy level as more and more people filed in. It was as if they could go all night—never stopping and never sleeping. Except they couldn't.

Out of nowhere, a bout of nausea hit Emery. She stopped dancing and closed her eyes as the room started to spin around her, feeling dizzy and disoriented. She squeezed her eyes shut and opened them again, confused by the sudden sensation. She'd only had one drink. One drink wasn't enough to affect her. Was it?

Doing her best not to panic, she eyed the nearest seating area and ambled over to it, kicking the trash that littered the floor along the way. When she reached the couch, she sat down and fell onto her back immediately. Her neck began to tingle, the microchip buzzing with serious intensity. *What's happening to me?*

It crossed her mind to sit up and search for Rhea, but her body acted as if it were made of stone. Emery opened her eyes slowly, squinting at the ceiling. Another bout of nausea hit her as her eyes began to blur. A faraway voice echoed in her head. It belonged to a male, but she couldn't understand what he was saying.

Tiny black and white dots filled her vision, taunting her with their unrecognizable patterns. Emery tried as hard as she could to stay conscious as her fingers gripped the undersides of the couch. Theo hadn't mentioned anything like this. *Is this a side effect of the chip? Is it malfunctioning?*

She needed something—anything—to keep her conscious. Just as she was about to black out, Rhea's voice sounded from a distance.

"Emery!" she shouted, rushing over to the couch where her motionless roommate lay. Rhea grabbed her shoulders and pulled her up frantically, using her fingers to pry open her roommate's sealed eyelids.

Feeling her body being jerked upwards, Emery regained some consciousness. Her neck felt like it was on fire. She managed to open her eyes and focus on Rhea's face. "Please. Get me out of here."

+ + +

With her hands on Emery's shoulders, Rhea glanced behind her and nodded at Jason, who was still standing across the room. He let out a gasp with just one look at Emery's face as he knelt down next to Rhea. "Is she okay?"

"I don't know," Rhea gulped. "She doesn't look good."

"You don't look so great either."

Rhea swallowed, trying to keep her own feelings of nausea at bay. She took a deep breath, trying to formulate a coherent sentence. "I'm sorry, but I think . . . I think we need to leave."

They threw Emery's limp arms over each of their shoulders and walked her out of the room, pushing through the heavy door that led to the street outside.

"Do you think you can get her home?" Jason asked as he removed Emery's arm from around his shoulder. "I would walk you guys back, but all of my stuff is inside."

Rhea took on the rest of her roommate's weight as she looked at him, dumbfounded. "Your stuff? You mean, your alcohol?"

He shifted his weight from one foot to the other. "Yeah."

Anger coursed through her veins, sobering her up for a brief moment. "Wow, some gentleman you are," she scoffed. "I can't believe—"

But before she could finish, Jason had already darted through the door, disappearing from sight.

"Unbelievable," she muttered.

Rhea attempted to move in conjunction with Emery's movements, but whenever she tried to move forward a few feet, she ended up dragging her roommate like an unwanted rag doll. Who was she kidding? Emery was a tiny thing, but asking Rhea to carry someone in the same weight range was downright ridiculous.

They moved a few steps forward, Emery's feet dragging over a crack in the pavement. Almost tripping, Rhea let out a frustrated sigh and set Emery down on the curb, watching as her head fell back and made contact with a large rock.

"Oh, shoot!" Rhea gently pulled her roommate back into a sitting position, noticing that her eyes were still closed. A ping sounded from inside her clutch. Followed by another. And another.

"Gee whiz, who in the world is trying to get ahold of you?" Rhea said to her unconscious roommate. "We're busy!" She swiped the clutch from the ground and pulled out Emery's phone. Five missed calls from Anthony.

Not really a good time, Rhea thought as she silenced the phone.

She knelt down to Emery's level. "Hello? Is anybody in there?" She shook her roommate's shoulders, then lightly swatted both of her cheeks.

No movement.

Rhea checked for a pulse. It was slow, but it was there. Relief washed over her. *She's still alive.* She gazed at the empty street around her, hoping that someone would magically appear. But there was no one.

They were alone.

11

Theo yawned as he leaned back in his chair and kicked his feet up onto the desk. He'd hardly slept a wink after his last conversation with President Novak. To say the man was intimidating was an understatement.

Just as he was about to doze off, beeping sounded from the monitors stationed in front of him. Sighing, Theo dropped his feet to the floor and rolled his chair over to the main station. He swiped the screen, watching as Emery's profile appeared in red. Her vitals were low.

She'd been fine just a minute ago.

He rushed over to the cabinet, checking to see how much serum was left. "Naia!" he called out, panic lining his voice. "Please tell me we have more sanaré!"

There was shuffling outside the door as Naia appeared with a tray full of syringes. "These just arrived from the lab today."

He motioned for her to come closer as he observed the dismal number of syringes on the tray. Thirty in total. "Is that all we have?"

"We have enough of the components to make one more batch, but that'll be the last one." Naia glanced up at the screen. Her eyes widened with fear. "Is that—?"

"Emery will be fine," he assured. "Please keep this to yourself. We don't need to alarm the President."

She nodded, lowering her eyes from the screen.

"What is the status of the other participants?" he asked. "Any improvement?"

Naia shook her head. "All participants over thirty-five years of age show signs of decreased activity. They're not as quick or as agile as our younger participants."

"Do we know the cause?"

"While we can't be certain, it's likely that the lethargum has negative long-lasting effects. Being in a comatose state for an extended period of time may be causing their bodies to deteriorate at an accelerated rate."

Theo scratched his chin. "Well, it looks like you and I only have a couple more years before we deteriorate as well. Best our work be finished as soon as possible. We'll focus on our younger participants then. I'm guessing our teenage participants are the most promising?"

"Yes, sir."

"Very well then. Please make sure we expedite production in the lab to make the last batch of sanaré. It is our livelihood, after all." He took one of the syringes from the tray and, with the flick of his wrist, dismissed Naia. He keyed in Emery's microchip I.D. to access her file, noticing something odd. A piece of her chip had been deactivated, almost like someone had tampered with it. Theo pulled up the history of her chip, searching the records for any recent activity, but there wasn't any. Her embedment procedure was the only activity listed. Theo grazed his chin with his fingers, trying to recall Emery's embedment. The chip had tested positive with zero defects.

Something wasn't right.

He shifted gears and emptied the syringe of orange liquid into the fixed, oval capsule on the main station. The sequence initiated. The serum fused with the holochip, then merged with Emery's actual embedded microchip. Emery's vitals steadied, but the monitor still blinked red. "Come on, come on," he muttered through gritted teeth.

She had to pull through. She just had to.

President Novak would murder him if they lost Emery within the first week of her participation in The Alpha Drive. He'd also be displeased to learn that someone or something had tampered with her microchip. It was probably best if Theo kept that last part to himself. He wished that there was more he could do to help Emery, but he knew from experience that the sanaré would do its job. It'd just take time.

12

Hi, you've reached Rhea's voicemail. I can't come to the phone right now—

Mason looked down at his phone and sighed before clicking it off. He and his friends had been waiting for over two hours. *What's taking them so long?*

He strolled back inside the café and sat down on a slightly deflated bean bag. His friends eyed him questionably, and Mason had a feeling the interrogation was about to begin. He leaned forward, swiftly running his hand through his hair.

"Talk to those girls?" one of his friends asked.

Mason could sense the frustration growing amongst the group. "Not yet, but I'm sure they'll call me back. Hey, since we've been here for a while, why don't we head over to Alpha Drive? I heard there are a couple of things going on at the Sychem and Club Med buildings."

"Without the girls?" one of the guys teased, slapping Mason playfully on the back.

"Yes, without the girls," he retorted, forcing a grin. Mason threw his plastic, coffee cup into the recycling bin and walked toward the front door, his friends following suit.

"Appreciate it, man," Mason said, tossing some bills onto the counter. The clerk nodded with gratitude as he swiped up the change and placed it in the tip jar.

A hot gust of Arizona wind greeted Mason as he stepped outside. He pulled his phone from his back pocket and dialed Warren's number. The call was answered on the second ring. *If only I could get that type of response from Rhea.*

"Hey man, it's Mason. How is it over there?" He walked a few steps away from his friends who had started a loud discussion over some incident he'd missed earlier that day. Something about a dog, a skateboard, and a blonde girl—he wasn't too sure where they were going with that one.

Mason focused his attention back on the call. "I've just got a small group with me." He turned to look at his friends, hoping he wouldn't have to give them bad news. "Awesome. Thanks, man. We'll see you in a few."

Mason gathered his friends and they crossed the street, passing some billboards for new housing communities that were being built a couple of blocks away. There really wasn't much to do outside of Darden Prep—

a coffee shop inside of a bookstore was the only other establishment for miles. They passed a few abandoned structures as they crossed over to where the club buildings stood. Mason stopped at the front of the Sychem building, recalling some of the history he'd read on the Darden Prep website.

Sychem was originally a group of fifteen of the most brilliant scientists at Darden, both students and alumni. They were responsible for some of the greatest innovations in science to date, until one year, when one of the scientists took a chemistry project too far. The government ordered Darden Prep to shut down the organization, classifying every detail as confidential. And that was the end of that.

The Sychem structure was built entirely of red brick and stood two stories high. A large cement fence surrounded the property, probably constructed after it'd been shut down in order to keep trespassers out. Unfortunately for Darden, its students were smarter than that.

Mason knocked on the door, feeling surprised as it opened almost immediately.

"Yeah?" a tall, burly guy grunted.

"Hey, I'm Mason. I'm friends with Warren—he invited us over," he said, extending his hand.

The guy took Mason's hand and shook it firmly as he scanned over the group. "Hang on." The guy closed the door halfway and called Warren's name.

A few minutes passed until Warren appeared in the doorway. "Mason, my man!" he greeted, slapping his hand and pulling him in for a hug. "Come on in."

It truly was a sight to be seen. To the right of the doorway stood a long, rectangular hall consisting of bedrooms, a restroom, and community showers. The floors were scuffed and dirty, the walls painted with different class dates and members' initials from each year. Adjacent to the hall was a set of stairs leading to the second floor of rooms, as well as the balcony. Half of the rooms on the second story were in a long corridor similar to the first floor—the remaining rooms were outdoors, situated along the balcony. It was then that Mason realized the Sychem building was actually an old residence hall. The scientists had actually *lived* there. It hadn't been just their laboratory, but also their living quarters.

On the other side of the stairwell stood the entrance to a massive, indoor courtyard. Half covered in cement, the other half golf-course grass, it extended for the length of a football field. To his amazement, the courtyard was completely hidden by the walls of the building, and those walls were covered in weird, foamy material. *It's completely soundproof. What a genius idea.*

Group after group of Darden students filled the dozens of tables, chairs, and couches in the area. Mason noticed a large chalkboard hanging limply from a rusty nail on the far wall. Game tables were lined up underneath it.

Judging from the stains on the cement and the cracked ping pong balls scattering the perimeter, it was apparent that Darden students had been coming here for a while. It was hard to believe that Darden administration hadn't discovered their secret yet.

Mason and his friends continued to follow Warren into the courtyard as he led them to an open table. "I'll go grab some cups so we can get started," Warren offered, digging around in his pocket. He pulled out two ping pong balls and tossed them over to Mason. A few minutes later, Warren reappeared through a sliding glass door from the main room. In one hand, he held a bag of red, plastic cups, and in the other, a case of beer. He swung the case onto the table, making a loud thud as it landed. "You and me—we're a team."

How'd he get that in here?

Mason nodded as they began arranging the cups into a triangular shape at their end of the table. They played for a few hours and, after Mason and Warren won all three games, decided to call it quits. Mason guzzled the last of his beer, smashed the can, and threw it into the nearest garbage can. He eased into an uncomfortable patio chair, allowing his head to tilt back against the cold, hard plastic. The sounds of people laughing and yelling filled his ears. Dots clouded his vision.

Mason pulled himself up from the chair, eyeing the exit at the far end of the building. Realizing his sudden urge to break away from the noise, he walked toward it, scrambling for his phone along the way. The hinges creaked noisily as he pushed open a gate that led him into a dimly lit alleyway. He leaned against the brick wall alongside the exterior of the building, and let out a long sigh.

Just as he was about to return the phone to his pocket, it lit up. Mason glanced at the screen, trying his best to focus on the bold, illuminated letters.

It was Rhea.

He thought twice about taking her call—especially since she'd ignored him all night—but decided it was best not to hold a grudge. After fumbling with the finicky touch screen, he finally answered. "Hello?"

"Mason?" Rhea responded, her voice distant and far away.

"Hey, Rhea. What's up?"

There was a pause on the other end of the line as music filled the airwaves. It was hard to hear her response.

"Something's happened."

Even in his current state, Mason could tell something was wrong. He'd known Rhea for quite some time and she wasn't one to panic easily.

"Mason, I need—" her voice broke off as the line went dead.

"Rhea?"

No response.

"Hello?"

His phone flashed a few times, indicating that the call had been disconnected. Mason stood still for a minute, trying to clear his head. On one hand, both Rhea and Emery had bailed on him. On the other hand, he'd known Rhea for a long time and considered her a close friend. Not to mention, she seemed to be in trouble.

He repeated Rhea's last words in his head, and dialed her number again, hoping that she would pick up, but it went straight to voicemail. Frustrated, he hung up and knocked his head against the wall. *Think, Mason.*

He'd heard music in the background of the call, which meant that that she was probably out somewhere. Mason hit his hand to his forehead as he realized that there was only one place she could be.

On Alpha Drive.

All of the club buildings on Alpha Drive were known for hosting socials the week before classes started for one obvious reason: to allow new students to get acclimated to their favorite clubs. The more students to show up at one building, the more likely word would get out around campus.

Mason pushed open the alley gate that led to Alpha Drive, his vision blurred as he made his way along the outside of the building. The streetlights swayed back and forth, an orange halo of light shimmering around each lamp post. He paused briefly, focusing on the cracked pavement beneath him. *Pull it together.*

A strained yell of frustration sounded from the opposite end of the street. His gaze moved from the pavement to the end of the alleyway, his pace quickening as he focused on the sight in front of him. Two female figures entered his view. He could immediately tell that they were struggling—one of the girls was leaning heavily on the other, slowly slumping to the street with each step.

He was almost there. Just a few more feet.

Without thinking, Mason called out Rhea's name. One of the girls spun to face him, her hair whipping around the side of her head.

"Mason," she breathed, half thrilled, half panicked. "You found us."

He finished his last few strides, noticing that Emery was slumped over on the curb, her body motionless. Mason looked from Emery to Rhea, noticing her hands were shaking. He took her hands in his and squeezed them tightly. She was out of breath and looked seriously disheveled, but still beautiful as ever. As he looked her in the eyes, he tried to project his calm state of mind onto her. "Everything is going to be okay," he assured.

Rhea met his gaze and nodded, her breath slowing with each inhale she took.

"I need you to tell me what happened, from the beginning," he instructed as he knelt down to check

Emery's vitals. Her pulse was slow, but she was still breathing.

"We were on our way to meet you, but we were invited inside one of the club buildings for a few drinks." Her eyes shifted to her roommate's immobile body. "We were only going to stay for about thirty minutes, but I guess we lost track of time." A wave of guilt washed over her face.

Mason listened attentively as she finished her story. His instincts kicked in, his adrenaline overpowering the alcohol. "My first thought is to call 9-1-1."

Rhea's eyes filled with fear. "Mason, she only had one drink. I'm sure she's fine. No hospitals," she insisted as she scratched the back of her neck. "Please."

As much as Mason disagreed with her, he knew this wasn't the time to argue. "Okay, this is what we need to do. We need to get Emery back to your room and sit her upright, making sure her head is propped up. We can try to give her some water and maybe get some food in her system. Got it?"

Rhea nodded, her head moving up and down like a bobblehead on the dash of a car.

"Good. You walk in front, okay?" Mason glanced down at Emery's motionless heap of limbs. He leaned down and put his left hand under the back of her neck for support. He slid his right arm underneath her knees and, in one swift motion, lifted her off the ground. Surprised by his own forcefulness, he stumbled back a little. It took him a second to balance his footing and adjust to the dainty, yet noticeable, weight in his arms.

Mason trudged down Alpha Drive behind Rhea, one step at a time, until he reached one of the two crosswalks that led to Rosemary Hall. He set Emery down and propped her up against a nearby streetlamp, checking her pulse for good measure. As he straightened up, Mason noticed a motorcycle sitting a few stoplights away. His stomach turned.

It was campus police.

He froze, unsure of what to do. Maybe the cop wouldn't see them. If he picked Emery up now and ran, it would be too obvious—but if he just stood there and acted like everything was normal, the cop would probably still approach him. Either way, he was screwed.

Mason gazed at his surroundings, noticing an oversized, electrical box sitting just a few feet away from the sidewalk. "Rhea," he whispered as he grabbed her arm. "I need you to hide behind that electrical box."

Rhea's eyes widened. "What? Why?"

"Just trust me."

As she scurried to hide behind the box, Mason picked Emery up and shuffled over to where Rhea was kneeling. He gently placed Emery on the ground, then put his finger to his lips. It crossed his mind to stay crouched in hiding, but it was likely that the cop had seen at least one shadow.

He motioned for Rhea to stay put, then walked back over to the sidewalk.

The light turned green and Mason watched as the motorcycle inched closer and closer to where he stood. He let out a sigh of relief as the cop rode past him, but that feeling was quickly replaced with dread as the officer made an abrupt U-turn. He took a deep breath as the cop parked his bike, his grim expression suggesting his night had been anything but pleasant.

"Good evening, son."

"Evening, sir," Mason stated, doing his best to sound sober.

"Are you a Darden student?"

"Err—uhh—yes," Mason stammered, immediately regretting the words as they left his mouth.

The officer eyed him suspiciously, his mouth curling into a smirk. "All Darden students must obtain permission to be out after 10 P.M. Do you have said permission?"

Mason looked down at his shoes. "No, sir."

The cop took a step closer. "Have you been drinking tonight?"

Just be honest, Mason thought to himself. He was royally screwed either way, so he may as well tell the truth and hope the cop would go easy on him.

"Yes, sir. I have been drinking tonight."

The office pointed his flashlight over at the electrical

box, then shifted the light back onto Mason's petrified face. "Identification, please."

Mason's hand retreated into his back pocket as he pulled his driver's license out of his wallet.

The cop shook his head, clearly debating what to do. "Is this your first offense?"

"Yes, it is," Mason answered, wishing he'd just let him off the hook. He bowed his head as the officer scribbled furiously on his pad.

The officer handed the ticket to Mason. "Get home safely," the officer instructed as he hopped back onto his bike. The motorcycle roared as he restarted the engine, then sped off down the road.

Mason looked down at the ticket and, much to his surprise, smiled. **PLEASE STATE THE NATURE OF OFFENSE: JAYWALKING.**

13

Everything was upside down and spinning. Emery's eyes fluttered open briefly before shutting again. Her pelvic bone moved rhythmically as it hit up against what felt like the top of a shoulder. Opening her eyes again, she realized she had been slung over someone's shoulder like a bag of laundry. The carpet on the floor below turned tricks like a kaleidoscope as her mystery captor trudged along. The pattern was vaguely familiar. It was then she realized that she was back in her dorm, in Rosemary Hall.

Emery lifted her head slightly and extended her arms, hoping to get the attention of whoever was carrying her. Muffled voices surrounded her and she faintly recognized Rhea's laugh, but she couldn't figure out who her roommate was talking to.

They came to a stop and Emery heard a key slide into the door. It creaked open as her head brushed against the doorframe. In seconds, she was on the floor, a fluffy, goose down pillow acting as her only support. She lay there, motionless, looking up at the blurry images floating in space above her. An unrecognizable face moved closer to hers, and a hand rested on her forehead. Recognition took hold. *Mason.*

"Emery," Mason whispered, his hand still resting on her forehead.

"Hey." She winced as her stomach turned.

"You're awake," he breathed, letting out a long sigh of relief.

Rhea's face appeared overhead next to Mason's. "There you are!" she yelled in a volume far too loud for the time of night. "I thought we'd lost you. What in the world happened?"

That's a good question. Emery felt one shoe come off, then the other. She wiggled her toes, the rest of her body feeling numb and tingly.

"Do you have this under control?" Mason asked.

"I think so," Rhea responded.

"Okay, call me if you need anything." Mason smiled as he bowed out of the room, closing the door securely behind him.

Rhea took hold of both of her roommate's arms and yanked her upright to a sitting position. Emery sat there like a limp rag doll as her shirt came up over her ears and finally over her head. "We need to get you in the shower," Rhea demanded. "You were sweating profusely during your . . . episode."

"That's a good idea," Emery murmured.

"Of course it is." Rhea said as she turned on the faucet, then tugged her roommate up from the floor.

With Rhea's help, Emery stepped over the ledge into the tub. Just when she thought she had her balance, her right foot slipping away from her. She squealed, her body hurling forward into the ceramic, tile wall. Immediately, Rhea's hands were on her shoulders to steady her. She felt a push and collapsed as her legs gave out.

"Just sit and stay sitting," Rhea instructed as she walked out of the bathroom.

Emery did as she was told and closed her eyes, willing the faucet to stop the cascade of spinning water droplets that were pounding onto her head. Her eyes opened when she felt a nudge on her shoulder, a water bottle dangling in front of her face. As the image of the misshapen bottle came into focus, Emery looked down, realizing that she was still half dressed.

Rhea shook the water bottle again. "Drink up. You need to hydrate."

Emery grabbed the bottle, eyeing her roommate as she took a giant swig. "If you ask me, you're the one who should be drinking water."

Rhea waved her hand in the air. "I've had years of experience. Besides, I'm not the one who blacked out after one drink." She situated herself on the edge of the tub, her feet hitting the water with a splash, knocking things over as she reached for the shampoo. "We just moved in and already the shower looks like a bomb went off. How many bath products can two girls own?"

"A lot more than I imagined," Emery replied as she tightened the cap on the water bottle.

Rhea squirted a quarter size of shampoo in her hand and began to lather her roommate's hair.

Emery abruptly turned away. *The chip. Don't let her see the chip.* "You know what, I got it," she said as she batted Rhea's hand away.

Rhea gave her a funny look. "I was just trying to help."

Emery didn't want her to get suspicious, so she changed the subject by recapping the night. About five minutes into the conversation, they were laughing hysterically. It was their first real bonding moment as roommates.

As Rhea leaned over to turn off the faucet, there was a knock at the door.

"Emery?" a raspy voice called out.

Rhea looked at her roommate's face for recognition of the voice on the other side of the door.

Emery's face paled. "It's Anthony," she whispered.

"What should we do?"

Emery took a deep breath. "Hand me a towel."

Rhea threw her legs over the edge of the tub, pulling

a towel from the rack, quickly drying off her legs before tossing it over to her roommate. Emery dried herself off, squeezing the water from her hair, then walked out of the bathroom, grabbing her shirt along the way. She pulled the shirt over her head and opened the door, only to find an empty hallway. She gazed down the hall to see Anthony trudging to the stairwell with his head down.

"Anthony," she said in a low voice, not wanting to wake her neighbors.

He turned around and hurried over to her. "What happened? Why are you all wet?"

She ignored his question. "What are you doing here?"

"You haven't answered any of my calls or texts, so I was worried." He raised his hand to stroke her hair.

Emery took a step backwards, not wanting to be touched. "I'm not really in the mood," she said as she crossed her arms over her chest. "Look, I've had a long night and I'm not feeling well. I need to get some sleep."

Anthony lowered his arm, eyeing her suspiciously. "Oh. Well, can I at least come in and meet your roommate?"

The hurt in his voice ripped through her. She unwillingly grabbed Rhea by the arm and stumbled back toward the door. "Here she is."

Rhea looked at Emery with a confused expression, then shifted her attention toward Anthony. "Um, hi. I'm Rhea," she said as she extended her arm.

Anthony shook her hand to be polite, but his attention was entirely focused on Emery. She could feel him observing her. Judging her. The thought made her stomach turn. Her hand shot up to cover her mouth, the color draining from her face.

"I thought we were past this phase," Rhea grunted as she helped lead her roommate's shuddering body back into the bathroom.

"Can I help with anything?" he offered.

"Yeah. Grab another water bottle from the fridge," Rhea suggested. "And some bread. She needs to eat something."

"So, you two went out drinking." He paused. "Emery's not really into that whole scene."

"She only had one drink."

"Then why—?"

"Why is she shuddering and heaving?" Rhea looked down at her roommate. "I think that's the one question we all wish we had an answer to."

Anthony sighed as he scoured the mini fridge for water bottles. A loaf of bread sat atop one of the desks, so he grabbed it, then meandered back to the bathroom. He handed both items to Rhea, plopping his rear down outside the door.

Rhea tried to coax Emery into eating, but she could barely lift her head. She waited patiently until Emery was well enough to stand up. Anthony jumped to his feet and helped guide his girlfriend through the dimly lit room, pushing her up the ladder onto the bed.

As Rhea walked to the sink to brush her teeth, Anthony stopped her. "Listen, I know you just met me and all, but I'd really like to stay with Emery tonight."

She turned her head toward the sink, spitting some of the foam down the drain. "I get that and I know you drove a long way to see her—but we have class tomorrow and Emery needs to rest."

Anthony sighed, disappointment written all over his face, but he didn't argue. Instead, he sulked toward the door like an abandoned animal. "Okay. Well, thanks for taking care of her."

Rhea couldn't help but feel bad. "Hey, even if you did stay, I don't know how the two of you would fit in that twin size bed anyway. Talk about uncomfortable," she joked through the bristles of her toothbrush.

"Will you let me know how she is tomorrow?"

Rhea moved the toothbrush to the side of her mouth. "I'll have her call you first thing in the morning." She walked him over to the door and shut it behind him, stealing a glance at Emery, who was lying face down on her pillow. Rhea stepped up onto the bed's ladder and rolled her roommate's body over, positioning her so she was flat on her back.

Rhea could only hope that her roommate's episodes

wouldn't be a recurring thing. Unfortunately, she had a feeling that this was only the first of many.

14

Emery awoke to a pounding head and a screaming alarm clock. She clambered out of bed and down the ladder, reaching across the desk to hit the off button. A note was stuck to her laptop. Frustrated by her dependency on contact lenses, she brought her face closer to the jumbled handwriting. Went to the gym before class. Hope you're feeling better! Love, Rhea

How late had she slept in? Emery glanced at the clock again, the glowing white numbers coming into focus. It was 10:07 A.M. She moved her index finger across the touchpad of her laptop and quickly retrieved her course schedule for the fall semester. A sigh of relief escaped her lips. Her first class wasn't until 11:45 A.M.

A shower sounds perfect right now, Emery thought as she trudged over to the bathroom.

As the water trickled down her hair, memories of the

previous night flooded back to her. *Why had she suddenly lost consciousness? Had Rhea seen the chip? Had Anthony actually shown up at her dorm last night?*

She'd dreamt the same dream from earlier in the week—except this time she'd been dressed in a uniform and carrying a gun. The dream ended suddenly, like it had the first time—with a scream and a gunshot—but she still couldn't make any sense of it.

By the time Emery had gotten dressed and ready for the day, it was a quarter past eleven. She grabbed her notebooks, laptop, and purse from a pile on her desk and headed toward the door, letting it slam behind her on the way out. First up: Latin II, or as Darden called it, Advanced Latin. Learning languages came easy to Emery, almost like it was second nature. And thank god for that because she was in no shape to take on anything difficult today.

After listening to her teacher, Mr. Roberts, drone on and on for fifteen minutes, Emery came to the disappointing conclusion that Advanced Latin would be harder than she'd originally thought. The students seemed to be leagues ahead of her, something she wasn't used to at her old school. Normally, starting school was exciting, but her start at Darden was more daunting than anything else. Fortunately, that day's assignment involved writing in Latin instead of speaking it. Her pounding head appreciated the fact that she didn't have to hear twenty other students reciting phrases in another language.

An unpleasant growl rumbled low in her stomach and, to add to her misery, Emery could hardly focus on anything her teacher was saying. Her mouth was dry, her hands were shaky, and while she knew she should eat something, the thought of food was utterly repulsive.

A muffled buzzing broke the silence in the classroom. Mr. Roberts gazed up from his desk, searching the sea of students for the source of the noise. Emery waited until he shifted his focus back to his computer before pulling her phone from her bag, pushing aside packs of gum, crumpled up receipts, and tubes of chapstick. The screen lit up with a text from an unknown number. *Common Room. 1PM.* There was only one person that text could be from.

Theo.

Emery tried to hide her eagerness as she slid her phone back into her purse. There were forty more minutes until class ended, which meant forty drawn out minutes of mulling over what her meeting with Theo would hold. Maybe he would be able to tell her what had happened last night. Had her chip malfunctioned? Had he forgotten to tell her something?

The remainder of class was one of the most grueling times of her life. Finally, the sound of rustling notebooks and papers filled the room as her classmates packed their belongings.

As Emery rushed back to Rosemary Hall in the sweltering heat, her eagerness turned to fear. She couldn't shake the feeling that something bad was about to happen. Her anxiety rose as she pushed the elevator button, her foot tapping as the doors opened. One swift move into the elevator and she was headed down to what felt like her own funeral.

The doors opened and Emery walked down the hall, following the same routine as last time. As per usual, Naia greeted her at the massive door and led her into the main room. Emery took a seat and adjusted her posture, knowing that if she allowed herself to sink into the chair, she would surely fall asleep before Theo even entered the room.

She shivered as a draft swept through the room. *Where is he?*

As if he'd read her mind, Theo appeared, clad in all black. "Emery, how nice of you to join me." He took a seat in the chair across from her and looked her square in the eye. "Oh my. Please forgive me, but you look like you haven't slept in days."

She grunted as she rolled her eyes. His observation definitely didn't warrant a response.

"I'm aware that you had quite a riveting evening. I was hoping that we could discuss it, if that's okay with you?"

"Yes, please. I'm actually not sure what happened last night." She grimaced as the memories resurfaced. "Was there anything about the chip that you forgot to mention?"

Theo drummed his fingers against the chair. "I told you everything you need to know. We spent all evening and all morning trying to figure out what caused the abnormality in your chip's behavior."

Emery perked up and moved to the edge of her seat. "And?"

"We couldn't find anything, which is odd." He waved his hand in the air. "No need to be alarmed though," he reassured. "This sort of thing happens more often than you'd think."

Emery could tell he was lying. Just as she was about to respond, a wave of nausea hit, causing her to crumple into her lap. Her head fell between her knees as she clenched her teeth, stomach turning.

"Naia!" he called out. "Bring the serum, now!"

Emery slinked off the chair onto the floor, her body curling into the fetal position. *Serum? What serum?* She squeezed her knees tighter to her chest and tucked her chin down toward the floor.

"I would offer for you to stay as long as you need," Theo began, "but then you'd miss your first day of training."

Emery groaned as she attempted to lift herself up to a sitting position. It took her a few tries until she finally made it upright. "You've got to be kidding me. My first round of training is right now?"

"Indeed. But first, you need to recharge," he observed.

"What I need is sleep." Her eyes shifted from Theo to the doorway, where Naia stood with an oversized syringe, the end of the needle dripping with a bright orange liquid. Before Emery could process what was happening, Naia approached her and pierced the overly sensitive flesh on her upper arm.

Her mouth opened as she cried out in pain, her eyes watering as the serum entered her bloodstream. She felt her body slump to the ground. The last thing she heard were Theo's harsh whispers to Naia, the sound of their voices fading off into the distance.

Then everything went black.

+ + +

When Emery finally woke up, she had no idea how long she'd been out for. Her surroundings were familiar—she was still in the FCW's common room. Propping herself up on her elbow, she reached for the glass of water sitting beside her. Beads of perspiration lingered along her hairline.

Before losing consciousness, her body and mind had felt completely imbalanced, as if she were teetering on the brink of some unknown oblivion. But now, she felt alive, awake, and clear-headed. Emery sprung to her feet, half expecting the nausea to resurface, but it didn't.

A faint hum in the background caught her attention. She turned around to face the coffee table. A holodevice displayed her training schedule, and next to that was a neatly folded pile of clothes. She picked up the pile, skimming through each piece—a black long-sleeved shirt, a pair of black nylon pants, and black shoes that appeared to be a combination of soccer cleats and hiking boots. Emery thumbed through the tags, noticing that each one was water resistant, bullet proof, flame retardant, and aerodynamic. How could these clothes hold each of these properties at the same time?

Emery undressed and pulled the training shirt over her head, making sure to zip the front. The pants were more difficult to get into than she'd anticipated—they weren't as stretchy as they looked. The ensemble was complete as she slipped her feet into the sleek training shoes and threw her hair up into a tight bun.

Her eyes flitted over to the holoschedule. The room listed was Aquam. Emery waited for a few minutes, thinking that eventually either Naia or Theo would come get her. But they didn't.

Guess I'm supposed to find the room on my own.

The door at the back of the common room led to a long hallway with multiple doors on either side. To her delight, the first room she stumbled upon just so happened to be Aquam. Seeing as the door was slightly ajar, Emery stepped inside, blinking rapidly to adjust her eyes to the darkness of the room.

As she took another step forward, her foot suddenly plunged into a deep pool of water, her body catapulting forward. Goosebumps rose all over her body as water seeped into her ears and mouth, the taste saltier than ocean water. She flailed her arms frantically, gasping for air as her lungs desperately searched for oxygen. Spitting the liquid out, she forced herself to take a deep breath before plunging under the surface when, out of nowhere, a force-field type helmet materialized around her head. Before she knew it, her head and neck were encased in white and blue currents.

Emery tried to stop herself from going under, realizing that she'd probably be electrocuted once the helmet hit the water, but to her surprise, nothing happened. She surveyed the area through her helmet, a sea of deep blue staring back at her. Holding her breath seemed like the logical thing to do, but Emery quickly discovered that she didn't need to. The helmet enabled her to breathe regularly underwater.

Nothingness surrounded her. Not knowing what to do, she began to swim. Her arms glided through the water with ease as she propelled herself forward, her feet kicking with little effort. It was like she was flying, but through water instead of air. As she delved deeper into the water-filled underworld, Emery noticed a dark figure at the bottom. It looked like the shape of a human.

A woman.

She swam closer, worried that maybe it was another participant who had been left behind during a previous round of training. Theo had said that passing training was a requirement for The Alpha Drive and at the time, she hadn't thought to ask exactly what happened to those who failed the training. Hopefully it wasn't this.

Ten feet away. Her eyes widened as the face came into view. Same deep crimson hair. Same grey eyes.

It was her mother.

Emery screamed, the sound reverberating through the helmet, as she swam closer to her mother's lifeless body. Her face was pale and puffy, like she'd been floating at the bottom of this underwater abyss for weeks.

Oh my god. She's dead. She's not moving. Oh my god, they killed my mother.

Emery grabbed her mother's arm, using all of her strength to pull her to the surface, but try as she might, it felt as though they were both pinned down to the sand by an invisible force.

"Mom!" she screamed through hurried breaths. "Mom, wake up!"

Her eyes darted back up to the surface. *What do I do?* Out of the corner of her eye, Emery noticed that her mother's right hand was clenched into a fist. Her panic ceased for a moment as she pried her mother's fingers from her palm. A small orange capsule floated up into the water.

What is that?

Emery extended her arm to catch the floating capsule when, out of nowhere, water engulfed each and every one of her senses. Her hands flew up to her head as salt water stung her eyes.

The helmet. It was gone.

She fought to keep what little breath she had in her lungs. As much as she didn't want to leave her mother, Emery had no choice. *I can't breathe.*

She swam as fast as she could to the surface, bobbing every which way, her lungs on the verge of exploding. Reluctantly, she opened her eyes, trying to get a sense of how much further until she reached the surface. A light shone a few feet away.

Almost there.

Emery broke the water's still surface, thrusting her arm upward in an attempt to grab anything that might be floating nearby. As if by some miracle, someone grabbed onto her arm and pulled her up out of the water. She was hoisted stomach-down onto a flat, level surface, a pair of black leather shoes pointed at her face.

"Well," Theo commented, bending down to help her to her feet, "thanks for waiting for me."

"What the . . .?" Emery sputtered, her legs shaking uncontrollably. "What was that?"

"*That* was your first aquam training." He gestured toward the vast sea of water before them. "Because we don't know exactly what the 7S world looks like, we need to be prepared for any situation. Which is why your training covers the four main elements: earth, air, fire, and water."

Emery coughed, droplets of salt water spewing from her throat. "A little warning before being plunged into the watery depths of hell would have been nice."

A light chuckle escaped Theo's lips. "Do you think 7S will give you a warning before they strike? I don't think so."

Emery shivered as her body attempted to return to its normal temperature. "Warning or not, that training was dangerous. I could have died! And my mom," she said through rapid breaths, "what about my mom? Is she dead? Did you kill her?"

Theo's body tensed. "Your mother? What about your mother?"

Emery hesitated before responding, noticing his shift in body language. Something told her not to say anymore. "Nothing. It must have been my imagination. Forget it."

He eyed her curiously, then pursed his lips. "Well, for the record, you can't die in training."

Emery crossed her arms, rubbing her hands up and down her shirt to warm up. "What if I had drowned? I'm pretty sure I would have died then."

"If you had drowned, then we would have revitalized you." He pulled out a syringe of orange serum, the same one that Naia had used on her just before she'd blacked out. "With sanaré."

Emery immediately recognized the word. It was Latin, meaning "to heal".

"Sanaré repairs all internal and external wounds and even has the ability to bring you back to life, with certain limitations of course."

Emery eyed the syringe with a dubious expression. "That's physically impossible. Isn't it?"

"Not anymore. The power of science and technology is truly marvelous, don't you think?" He beamed like a third grader who'd just won the state science fair. "Unfortunately, not all the kinks have been worked out just yet. It can repair all wounds, no matter when they happened, but it can only reverse deaths that occur within a twenty-four hour period."

Emery was silent, waiting for him to continue.

"I digress. Back to your training. You must follow your schedule to a tee. If you miss a training session, the rest of the program will have to be pushed back since other participants are also using the rooms. So again, please respect your schedule. Do you understand?"

"Yes," she paused, "but won't I run into other participants if we're all training in the same rooms?"

Theo shook his head. "Not if you follow your schedule most precisely. You don't want to see them and trust me, they don't want to see you. That would result in disqualification for both parties."

Emery stopped him before he turned to walk away. "What will my next round of training be?"

He smirked. "You'll find out soon enough."

15

Torin had finally done it. He was in.

It had been forty-eight hours since he'd cracked the code and hacked into the Federal Commonwealth's mainframe. And in that time, he'd learned ten times more about the FCW and its initiative than he'd ever learned about the Seventh Sanctum and its mission. There had been an opportunity to learn even more about the FCW, but since he'd chosen to go the quick and dirty route, he was only able to gain access through a single device: a tablet that seemed to stay in one area, a common room of sorts. He'd overheard conversations about some of the participants, but when it came to who was truly in charge of the FCW, Torin had absolutely no idea.

The most intriguing conversations he'd happened to eavesdrop on were those about a participant named Emery Parker. From the constant buzz about her and late night phone calls, it was obvious that she was important to them.

He just didn't know *why*. So, he'd attempted to reach out to her by hacking into her microchip, but much to his dismay, the coding hadn't worked. For a brief time, he actually thought that she could hear him, but he'd thought wrong. He'd backed out of the system after thirty minutes, worried that if he stayed any longer, he'd leave a trace.

Torin decided it was best to keep this information to himself. Once the Commander found out he'd cracked the code, he'd most likely be kicked off the project because they wouldn't have a need for him anymore. They'd go back to treating him like an intern, which meant that he'd be completely in the dark. He'd receive no updates. No information.

I'm more valuable than that.

Torin knew that this decision could ultimately make or break him, but he was willing to take the risk. The more he could find out about the Federal Commonwealth, its initiative, and how 7S was connected, the better off he'd be. Or so he hoped.

Torin spent the last thirty minutes of his workday watching a holoscreen of what he assumed was the FCW's common room. After a long period of no movement, he decided it was time to log off and call it a day. But just as he was about to shut the system down, a girl with blonde hair appeared on the screen. She darted across the room and began searching for something, rummaging through every nook and cranny.

With his index finger, Torin drew an L-shape on the virtual screen, watching as the image zoomed in. The girl looked frazzled, like she was about to pull every strand of hair from her head. *What is she looking for?*

Torin watched as the girl pulled up a file—Emery's file—on one of the FCW's monitors. There was so much text written under Emery's name that Torin could hardly read any of it. He craned his next closer to the screen as she scrolled through page after page of notes, until the girl finally found what she was looking for. He tried to zoom in even closer, but it was no use. The text was too blurry. Torin refocused his eyes one last time, straining them to make out a letter . . . a word . . . anything.

The girl jotted a quick note onto her tablet, then pulled two small balls from her pocket. As she typed in another code, a drawer holding black clothes popped out from underneath the main station. She dropped one ball into each of the boots, then closed the drawer.

What was that?

Just as she was about to shut down the system, her phone rang. Torin's fingers flew across the virtual keyboard as he quickly hacked into the other side of the conversation.

"Where are we at?"

"Still on track, Mr. Barker," the girl responded. "Once testing is complete, we can use the device to render the rest of the world comatose."

"Good work. Please keep me informed of any setbacks."

"Roger that, sir."

Torin finished listening to the conversation, wishing that it had revealed more, especially since he was still no closer to reading the information in Emery's file. He watched in defeat as the girl shut the system down, then walked out of view.

Torin threw his hands over his head and leaned back in his chair.

I have to know what's in that file.

He could try to hack into the particular database where Emery's file was stored, but given the time it took for him to hack into the mainframe alone, he couldn't even imagine how long that would take. Pinpointing and decoding the location of one single file seemed impossible. That would have to be his next project. In the meantime, Torin knew what he had to do.

He had to get in touch with Emery.

16

Rhea slammed her history textbook shut. Two months into school and she was already close to failing the majority of her classes. She sighed impatiently, tapping her pen on the cover of her textbook, eyeing Emery as she typed away on her laptop. She was probably writing some paper for her Latin class.

How was it that Emery was able to stay on top of her classwork and she wasn't? Sure, Rhea attended some of her classes, but not all of them. She figured her time was better spent doing other things, like socializing. Not to mention, Emery didn't have as much to worry about as she did; Rhea had more pressing issues to deal with.

It was Friday afternoon and Rhea was in dire need of some retail therapy. She stood in front of her closet, combing through the piles of clothes that lay helplessly in plastic bins on the floor. Just as she was about to ask Emery if she wanted to sneak off campus to the nearest mall, her phone buzzed.

The noise caught her roommate's attention as well. "Who is it?" Emery asked as she closed her laptop.

Rhea hesitated before answering. The text was from Mason, but she wasn't sure she wanted to share that. The truth was that Mason had reached out to her multiple times over the past couple of weekends, wanting to hang out with them. She hadn't told Emery, simply because a better option always seemed to surface. Why make it difficult by having her roommate weigh in, when Rhea could make the decision for the both of them? It was just easier that way.

Unfortunately, Rhea was beginning to realize she couldn't continue lying to her roommate every time Mason texted her. She'd gotten to know Emery pretty well in the past two months, and an eye for suspicious behavior seemed to top her list of ingenious qualities. Emery consistently sensed when Rhea was lying or when information was being withheld. But if Rhea told her roommate the truth, she could risk damaging their friendship, and she wasn't quite ready to take that fall just yet.

"Oh, weird," Rhea said, trying to sound surprised. "It's Mason." She looked up at her roommate, trying to assess whether her acting skills were as good as she'd made them out to be. After all, she had spent the majority of her adolescence in Hollywood.

"What do you mean weird?"

Rhea shrugged. "I just haven't heard from him since we all went out."

"You mean he hasn't texted you for two months? Since that first night we went out on Alpha Drive?" Emery asked, suspicion lining her voice.

Rhea's eyes flitted at the mention of Alpha Drive. Oddly enough, she noticed how Emery's body language shifted at the exact same moment. *Was that just a coincidence?*

Ignoring her better judgment, Rhea decided to lie. Again. "Yeah, I haven't heard from him in a really long time."

"Well, what did he want?" Emery pressed.

"He actually invited us to hang out at Sychem. They're throwing a black-and-white social and he needs a date."

"A date? As in singular?"

"No, not singular. He invited both of us. Obviously, the more girls he brings, the better he'll look."

Emery considered this, then turned back to her laptop. "Nah, you go ahead. I should probably stay in and work on some homework. Maybe give Anthony a call."

Rhea could tell by the look on her face that talking to Anthony was the last thing Emery wanted to do. It was obvious they'd been having trouble as of late.

Anthony had only come over a few times since school started and every time he called offering to take Emery to dinner or hang out, she'd make up some excuse as to why she couldn't go. Rhea could see that their relationship was spiraling downwards quickly, and she couldn't help but think that maybe she'd influenced Emery's behavior for the worse. Her roommate wasn't exactly a social butterfly, but the more time the two of them spent together, the more Emery had come out of her shell. Rhea had seen this as a positive shift in behavior, and it was nice having someone to go out with for a change. She just hoped that it wasn't negatively affecting any of Emery's other relationships.

With this thought in mind, Rhea opened her mouth to agree with her roommate's plan to stay in, but was quickly interrupted.

"You know what? Screw it," Emery said as she popped up from her chair. "Let's go to Sychem. It'll be fun."

+ + +

Emery and Rhea walked into Sychem fashionably late, precisely as planned. Rhea led the way, noticing that Emery was a few paces behind her. She squeezed her roommate's arm reassuringly, then searched the courtyard for Mason, spotting him in the far corner with a group of friends.

"Mason!" she yelled as she pulled Emery across the lawn.

Mason approached them and extended his arms to give them both a hug. "Hey! I didn't know you were coming."

"What? I texted you," Rhea said as she pulled out her phone. The message she'd sent flashed across the screen.

He shrugged his shoulders. "Oh, I guess my phone died."

"Well, don't look so happy to see us," Emery teased, punching him in the arm.

The corners of his mouth curled into a sheepish grin. "No, it's not that. Trust me, I'm happy to see you. Over the moon, actually. I guess I'm just a little surprised."

"Surprised? Why would you be surprised?" Emery asked.

Mason looked from Rhea to Emery, then back at Rhea. Just as he was about to answer, Rhea changed the subject. "Where's the beer? My lovely roommate and I just walked a long way."

Mason flashed a toothy grin. "Be right back." He turned on his heel and started walking toward the common area.

Emery tugged on her roommate's arm. "I don't want a drink. I think I'm okay—"

Rhea ignored her. She called out to Mason as an idea occurred to her. "Bring back twenty-two cups, two ping pong balls, a table, and your friend . . ." She drifted off as her eyes focused on an attractive guy from across the courtyard. Mason followed her gaze, realizing that the "friend" she was referring to was none other than Warren Bradley.

"You mean Warren?"

Rhea grinned. "Uh huh. You two are going down."

Unable to help himself, Mason smiled back. "Don't toot your own horn just yet."

Rhea watched as he walked inside the common room, then turned her attention to Emery. "Have you ever played beer pong before?"

Emery pursed her lips. "Is that a rhetorical question? Obviously I haven't."

Rhea explained the rules in detail, despite the short amount of time it took for Mason to return with supplies. Rhea had Emery repeat a few of the rules back to her, just to make sure she understood.

Mason and Warren appeared at the doorway, carrying a worn, wooden table. They set it down with a grunt, tossing the cups and ping pong balls on top.

"You girls set up. We'll get the beer," Mason said, making his way back toward the common area.

Rhea skipped after him and, when she got close enough, motioned for him to lean in. "Emery doesn't have much experience with this sort of thing," she whispered. "So is it alright if we divide up the teams? Maybe I can be your partner, and she can play with Warren?"

Mason smiled. "I don't see why that would be a problem."

"Great, I'll let them know." Rhea strutted back across the courtyard, noticing that Warren was already busy chatting with Emery.

The game started off rather uneventful for both teams. Rhea figured Mason and Warren had already been drinking prior to their arrival and, judging from their poor aim, her assessment was correct. In the middle of Mason's turn, Rhea scampered over to the opposite side of the table, stumbling over empty cans along the way.

"Hey," she giggled, poking her roommate in the side. "How are you feeling?"

"You girls need a moment?" Mason teased.

"Yeah, this game doesn't seem to be going anywhere fast," Rhea joked. She watched as Warren made his way over to Mason's side of the table, then pulled Emery around so their backs were to them. "So, how are you feeling?" she asked again.

"Well, I feel like I'm terrible at this game," Emery responded.

"Maybe you'd be better if you actually drank. Here," Rhea offered as she pulled out a beer, snapping the top back. "Drink this. Fast."

Emery eyed the foaming can. "No, I'm okay. Really. But thanks anyway."

Rhea was about to pressure her some more when she

felt something vibrate near her feet. She set the can down and knelt toward the ground, searching for the source of the buzzing, then picked Emery's bag up off the pavement. "Your phone's ringing."

Emery pulled out her phone, a look of pure disgust crossing her face. "It's Anthony," she scoffed.

"Aren't you going to answer it?" Rhea couldn't help but feel confused by her roommate's reaction. She knew things weren't going well between them, but she didn't understand how things could have plummeted so quickly in such a short amount of time.

"Nah, I don't feel like talking to him. I'm just going to let it go to voicemail. He never leaves voicemails." As soon as she said the words, her phone chimed. Emery let out a long sigh. "He left a voicemail." She shot Rhea an apologetic glance, then turned her back to listen to it.

Rhea waited anxiously for Emery to turn back around. She'd sensed from the beginning that Emery wasn't happy with Anthony, and while she'd done her best to be supportive, there was only so much she could say without feeling like she was overstepping.

Emery clicked her phone off, then whirled around to face Rhea. "No, no, no," she muttered, shaking her head angrily. She slammed her fists onto the table, the impact shaking the partially full cups.

"What? What is it?" She'd never seen Emery so angry—so hostile—before. To be honest, it was slightly alarming and was definitely new territory on the roommate front.

A soft groan escaped Emery's lips. "Anthony's here."

Before Rhea could get a word in, Emery was halfway across the lawn, marching toward the front of the building.

"This is not good," Rhea muttered as she jogged to catch up. She followed Emery to the front door, her curiosity peaking as they shuffled through a crowd of people.

Emery swung the door open dramatically, her gaze landing on a scene in the middle of the street, where a shouting match seemed to be escalating. In the middle of it all was Anthony, who appeared to be throwing an immature temper tantrum.

Rhea couldn't help but roll her eyes. *How did he know we were even here?*

Out of nowhere, Emery's voice echoed throughout the parking lot. "Anthony!" She crossed her arms as she waited for him to turn around.

Anthony paused with his mouth agape, then sullenly walked toward his girlfriend. Emery yanked his arm, giving him no choice but to follow her to the side of the house, away from the budding crowd of people.

Rhea tiptoed behind her, wanting to keep a safe distance, yet remain close enough to hear their conversation.

"What are you doing here?" Emery scolded, her voice barely above a whisper.

"I wanted to see you. We've hardly hung out since you started school and you don't exactly answer my texts or my calls. I didn't have a choice."

Emery glared at him. "How did you even know I was here?"

"Well, I . . . I checked your status online." A flush of embarrassment spread across his cheeks.

Emery clenched her jaw, her hands curling into fists. "Get out," she hissed.

"Excuse me?" Anthony asked in disbelief as Emery turned to walk away.

She ignored him and stomped back toward the building without a hint of remorse, her head held high as she pushed her way through the masses.

"Emery, don't you dare walk away from me!"

But she kept walking.

After a minute of pointless shouting and pleading for her to come back, Anthony retreated to his car and roared his engine, the tires screeching as he sped off.

Rhea expected her roommate to be in a frenzy of tears, but Emery seemed perfectly fine. She was back at the table, casually chatting with Warren as if nothing had happened. Rhea decided it was best to let it go so they could try to enjoy what remained of their evening.

As the night carried on, she noticed Emery becoming

more and more flirtatious with Warren. Her attraction to him was so obvious that at one point, she even considered pulling her roommate aside, but decided against it.

"I thought she had a boyfriend," Mason thought aloud.

Rhea glared at the back of Mason's head. "She does. But after that fiasco a couple of hours ago, who really knows?"

Mason realigned the cups, whistling at Emery and Warren to get their attention. As soon as Emery looked up, Rhea slid her arm through Mason's and rested her head against his shoulder. She could have sworn she saw a tinge of jealousy flicker across Emery's face, but it was probably just her imagination. *Why should Emery get to have all the fun? I'm the one who's single.*

Rhea tugged playfully at Mason's hair, grabbing a ping pong ball with her free hand. "Ready to win?"

"You bet," Mason affirmed, unfazed by her sudden shift in behavior.

Every time she and Mason scored, Rhea made sure to squeeze his arm or give him a hug. It was when they won the game that she decided to make a bold move. Without the slightest hesitation, she turned toward Mason, pulled his body against hers, and kissed him. His lips moved in sync with hers, the short breaths in between fogging up the small space between them. When Rhea pulled back, she looked into his eyes, searching his face for a reaction. She wanted his approval. She *needed* it.

Mason took a deep breath, interlocking his fingers with hers. He squeezed her hand and smiled, his eyes focused solely on her. Breaking eye contact was the last thing she wanted to do, but eventually, Rhea shifted her attention to the stillness at the other end of table.

Emery and Warren were nowhere in sight.

Rhea knelt to the ground, rifling through her bag for her phone.

No missed calls. No unread texts.

Feeling uneasy, she punched in Emery's number, waiting impatiently for her to pick up.

No answer.

"Looks like they left," Mason observed as he leaned against the table.

Rhea finished keying in a text message, then looked up at him. "Yeah, I'm not sure where they went." She looked around the courtyard one last time. It was unlike Emery to just leave without saying anything.

"Do you want another drink?" Mason offered.

She weighed her options and, for once in her life, decided to be semi-responsible. "Actually, it's getting pretty late. I think I'm just going to head home."

Disappointment clouded his face. "Okay, no problem. I'll walk with you."

"That's okay. I'm actually pretty wiped. Some peace and quiet is just what I need," she assured as she headed toward the door.

Mason insisted, but finally gave up after Rhea declined his third offer. She could feel his eyes on her as she walked away from Sychem and down the street. Not too far from her, two figures, hand in hand, could be made out in the distance. She tried to discern whether Emery was one of them. Although she couldn't be sure, there was one thing Rhea would soon find out.

Emery never returned home that night.

17

A patch of sunlight peeked through a gap in the curtains, the light hovering over the left side of Emery's face. She blinked a few times to try and rid the feeling of dryness from her eyes, realizing she'd left her contacts in overnight. Glancing up at the curtains, she waited for her eyes to shift into focus. It only took her a few seconds to realize that she wasn't in her dorm room.

Concerned, she lifted her body up off the bed, her eyes drifting to the shirtless figure sleeping peacefully on the couch a few feet away. Emery dropped her head into her hands, a quiet sigh escaping from her mouth.

She had stayed the night. At Warren's.

For a moment she considered waking him, then thought better of it. A wave of guilt washed over her as she recalled the dramatic ordeal with Anthony. *Worst girlfriend ever. Are we even still dating?*

Emery recalled the same vivid dream that haunted her as of late. She'd crept down the hallway in uniform, gun in hand, but this time, she'd worn the ring her mother had given her. In the distance, a reflection of some sort caught her attention. She drew closer to the shimmering sight and pulled an item that was lodged in the wall: a horseshoe-shaped pendant. She'd tucked the pendant into her pocket when a scream filled the hallway, followed by a gunshot.

And then she woke up.

The rate of occurrence in which she had these dreams was starting to worry her. Each dream contained new information, a new piece of a puzzle. The only problem was she had no idea what puzzle these pieces belonged to.

Emery inched closer to the edge of the bed and swung her legs gently toward the floor. Her purse sat on the other side of the room. She tiptoed as feline-like as she could, hoping that the hardwood floors would keep their creaking to themselves.

Her shoes sat next to the couch, so she put them on first, then gathered the rest of the items that had spilled from her bag, taking extra caution as she picked up her jangling keys. Slinking over toward the door, she put her hand on the knob, glancing back at Warren who was snoring in a deep slumber. It was rude to leave without saying goodbye, but her priority at that moment was getting back to her dorm room before Rhea woke up.

Unfortunately, she had no such luck. Emery tried to

sneak in as quietly as she could, but much to her dismay, Rhea was wide awake in her bed. As soon as the door opened, her roommate sat straight up and gave her a wicked smile.

Emery put her hand up, even though she knew it wouldn't keep Rhea from asking questions.

"Good morning, sunshine," Rhea teased, her eyes twinkling. "I assume you slept well?"

"Don't patronize me. And yes, I did sleep well."

Rhea rolled her eyes. "Not that I should even have to ask, but where exactly did you sleep last night?" She fidgeted with her hair, unable to sit still.

Emery hesitated. Lying crossed her mind, but any excuse she came up with would be met with doubt and suspicion. She couldn't say that she'd stayed at Anthony's because of the massive blowout Rhea had witnessed, and she wouldn't have stayed anywhere else because Rhea was basically her only friend at Darden. "I slept at Warren's," she answered as politically as she could, "but nothing happened."

Rhea cocked her head. "You're telling me that you slept in a bed with a gorgeous guy and nothing happened? I don't believe that for a second."

"First of all, I didn't sleep *in bed* with him. I was in the bed and he was on the couch," Emery responded, trying not to let her agitation get the best of her. "Nothing happened."

"Well, sleeping over at a guy's place who isn't your boyfriend while you still *technically* have a boyfriend isn't exactly innocent," Rhea pointed out as she hopped down from her bed. "Some people might even consider that cheating." She raised an eyebrow. "Are you going to tell Anthony?"

"And add fuel to the fire? Of course not."

"No need to get defensive," Rhea muttered.

Emery glared at her roommate, wishing that she'd just let it go and stop talking.

An awkward silence filled the room.

"Alright, then. Enough about that. Do you want to go shopping this afternoon?" Rhea asked in an effort to lighten the mood.

"No," Emery said, her voice flat. "I have some homework and studying I need to catch up on. I think I'm just going to head to the library."

Okay, so that wasn't entirely true. Spending her Saturday studying and doing homework was what she *should* have been doing, but Emery's next round of training was in a couple of hours.

"Oh," Rhea said with a hint of disappointment. "I guess I'll see you later then."

Emery grabbed a change of clothes from her closet and headed toward the bathroom, locking the door behind her. She turned on the faucet and stepped into the shower, trying to clear her mind as the water trickled onto her skin.

If only it could wash all of my lies away. It was becoming harder and harder to recognize herself. The real Emery wouldn't betray her boyfriend. And the real Emery certainly wouldn't lie to her friends and family. *Who am I becoming?*

After washing the conditioner out of her hair, Emery turned off the faucet and reached around the curtain for her towel. Little droplets of water dripped steadily from her elbows as she stepped onto the bathroom mat. She pressed her ear against the door, trying to make out any noise that would signal whether or not Rhea was still in the room. After a few seconds of silence on the other side, Emery opened the door, cautiously poking her head around the edge. Rhea was nowhere in sight.

One less confrontation to deal with.

Emery trekked toward the library, realizing it had been a couple of months since she'd spoken to her best friend. She pulled up Riley's contact information, a picture of a blonde girl with stunning, sapphire eyes staring back at her. *If only Riley would transfer to Darden.*

Her call was answered in two rings.

"Em, there you are! I was wondering when you were going to call. It's been way too long. How are you?"

Emery smiled. Her best friend's voice immediately reminded her of home. "It's so good to hear your voice. I've been meaning to call you, but—" she paused, shaking her head. "Well, there is no excuse. I should have called a while ago."

"Pumpkin, don't worry about it. We're all busy," Riley reassured.

Emery laughed. "Okay, good. How have you been?"

"I've been great, but really, enough with the pleasantries! I want details. So," she paused for dramatic effect, "tell me about this dreadful roommate of yours."

Emery laughed. That was Riley—always blunt and straight to the point. It was just one of the many things she loved about her best friend.

"Dreadful? I'm not sure what you're talking about."

"Oh, please. I've seen the photos of you two online. She seems . . . well, not like us. I'm actually surprised you two hang out so much. You seem like polar opposites."

Emery could have sworn she heard a dash of envy in Riley's voice. "Actually, Rhea's not that bad," she said, preparing to eat her words. "I think you might like her."

"Uh huh . . . right. Just be careful," Riley warned. "I wouldn't trust her as far as I could throw her."

It was typical of Riley to be forthcoming, but it wasn't like her to attack someone she'd never met. Emery knew that her best friend wasn't the jealous type, but maybe their infrequent communication over the past couple of months had hit a soft spot. She couldn't risk having her best friend freak out on her, especially during a time like this. Riley was her support system, her rock.

They talked for ten more minutes. Emery was even able to mention her "new lifestyle" without worrying that Riley would take it literally. Indeed, she had a new lifestyle as a participant in The Alpha Drive, but adjusting to a new school also conveniently fell under that category.

Near the end of the conversation, Riley offered two pieces of advice. The first was to end things with Anthony. Emery knew this was coming since Riley had witnessed their downhill spiral over the past year. The second was to make more friends and slowly push Rhea out of her social circle. While Emery didn't necessarily agree with these ideas, she pretended to, just to appease Riley.

As she hung up the phone before her best friend could interject any additional thoughts, Emery realized she'd been walking aimlessly in front of the library. It wasn't like she'd planned on doing any homework or studying—she'd just wanted to get away from Rhea's judgements. Her boyfriend constantly judged her and now her roommate and only friend at Darden judged her.

Great.

Her thoughts were interrupted as her phone pinged with a reminder. *I'm supposed to be somewhere.*

Emery looked down at her watch, realizing that her next round of training started in exactly five minutes. She dashed back toward Rosemary Hall—almost running into fellow students along the way—through the deserted lobby and over to the elevator doors.

Once inside the FCW's common room, Emery threw on her training clothes, which were, not surprisingly, folded into a neat, orderly pile, and double-checked the holoschedule for room details. It read ignis.

As if I haven't played with fire enough the past couple of days.

Emery followed Theo down the corridor, palms sweating. She entered the ignis room with caution, half expecting the room to be on fire the minute she set foot inside, but it was pitch black. Giving her eyes a second to adjust, she walked further into the room. A couple of minutes passed as she stood in the stillness, her loud gulps the only thing audible in the eerie silence.

After five more minutes of waiting, she figured that her training must have been cancelled or rescheduled. Maybe Theo had brought her to the wrong room. She turned toward the door to leave, but there was one small problem.

The door was gone.

Suddenly the floor beneath her began to tremble, as if a volcano were about to erupt. Her knees buckled as the floor began to split, creating a deep crevice in the landscape. Emery stumbled backwards as fiery red and orange flames exploded from the crack, a piece of ash landing next to her shoe. She looked around for something to climb, her eyes locking on a large piece of concrete that jutted up from the ground.

Emery darted toward the formation, hopping over the cracks and molten ashes along the way. She pulled herself up onto the concrete, her hands burning from the intense heat. A cough tickled her throat as a heavy cloud of smoke formed in her chest. Just as she was about to pass out from the fumes, she heard a familiar voice screaming in distress.

Riley's voice.

Panicked, Emery peered over the edge, watching as her best friend was eaten alive by flames. The pit was deep, a never-ending black abyss.

"Put her out of her misery," a voice boomed from overhead.

Without thinking, Emery dove headfirst toward Riley. She watched as the flames danced on her clothes, expecting third-degree burns to sear through the fabric on her arms and legs. It was then she remembered that her clothes were flame retardant. Newfound adrenaline coursed through her veins. "Climb onto my back!"

Riley reached out, her consciousness wavering, and Emery grabbed her hand, pulling her best friend's body onto her back. Riley cried out in pain as the fire burned through her flesh, her fingers melting into one other. Emery scaled the formation, her fingers latching onto the crevices in the rock. She clenched her teeth through the heat until she finally reached the top. Lugging herself and Riley up over the edge, she gently placed what was left of her burnt, decrepit friend on the ground. Smoke lifted from Riley's body, her skinless face frozen in terror.

Riley was dead. Her best friend was dead.

Unable to control herself, Emery wept hysterically. First her mother, now her best friend. What was the point of this training? How was killing off her mother and best friend training her to defeat 7S?

Between coughs and sobs, Emery noticed something odd. Riley's right hand was clenched into a fist, just like her mother's had been. There was hardly any skin left on Riley's hands, so she gently pushed her deformed fingers back to reveal another capsule.

Except this one wasn't orange. It was green.

Before she could analyze any further, her ears began to ring and her vision grew fuzzy. Emery fought to keep her eyes open, but finally succumbed, the image of her dead friend vivid against her eyelids.

18

An unfamiliar room surrounded her. Emery lifted her head and gazed groggily at her surroundings, the sound of Theo's voice echoing in the distance. She laid her head back down and blinked rapidly, trying to restore her vision. Footsteps approached the table, and a large head appeared above her.

"You're awake," Theo observed, looking her up and down. "And your wounds have healed nicely. In record time, I might add."

Emery lifted her arms in the air, trying to recall exactly what had happened. It had been hot. There had been fire. And . . .

"Riley!" she shrieked, her body shooting straight up from the table. She began to shake, jolted by the sudden memory.

"Riley is fine," Theo soothed as he helped her lay back down. "It wasn't real. Your chip was programmed to make you see her."

"Wait . . . what?"

"It wasn't real."

Emery stared at him with unforgiving eyes. "Your whole organization . . . they're monsters. What kind of cruel training is this?"

Theo turned away from her and began pacing back and forth across the room. "Training has to be physical, mental, and emotional. We have to test your limits. Push you to see how far you can go. Like I said, we don't know what 7S will have in store for us once we deploy our forces."

"But someone told me to kill her . . . to . . . to put her out of her misery," Emery stammered as the gut-wrenching image of Riley's burnt body resurfaced.

"It was a simulation. We wanted to see what you would choose."

Emery gulped. "Did I fail?"

"On the contrary, you passed with flying colors." Theo tipped his fedora at her. "Well done."

Emery slowly brought herself up to a sitting position, gently placing her feet over the edge of the table. "My hair and my face . . . they were burnt to a crisp," she recalled. "Any part of my body that wasn't covered by the flame retardant fabric was completely deformed."

"Sanaré fixed all of that." Theo pointed to the empty syringe sitting on the counter, checking his watch at the same time. "Well, it's getting late and I'm sure you're exhausted. I'll let you get your rest." He grinned. "I'll see you at your next training. Good job today."

"Wait. That's it?"

"You're not the only participant, Emery. I have others who require my assistance."

Before she could say another word, Theo was halfway out the door.

After thirty more minutes of much needed recovery, Emery regained her strength. She stormed back to the common room, wanting nothing more than to rip off her training clothes and destroy them. She tossed her overshirt onto the table, covering the holodevice that had revealed her training schedule just hours earlier.

"Hello?" a voice echoed from under her shirt. "Is anyone there?"

Confused, she quickly swiped her shirt from the table and bent down so she was eye-level with the device. There was no image, just sound. She paused before answering. "Who is this?"

"Who are you?" the voice countered.

"This is Emery. Emery Parker."

"Really? *The* Emery Parker?"

Emery pushed the device with her index finger, wondering if maybe the sanaré was causing her to hallucinate. "Yeah, that's me."

"It really is my lucky day. Hold on just a second."

There was a brief pause followed by a bunch of short beeps, as if a madman were furiously punching numbers on a phone. A green light on the holodevice blinked and Emery watched incredulously as a hologram of a young guy, about her age, appeared.

"Emery Parker, I have waited for what seems like years to meet you." He grinned, shaking his wavy, brown hair out of his eyes. "I'm Torin Porter."

The name didn't ring a bell. "I'm sorry. Do I know you?"

"No, but you're about to." He cleared his throat. "I was messing around, hacking into things like I normally do, when one day, I finally cracked the code to access your world's mainframe. I've watched everything that's been going on ever since."

Emery brought her face closer to the hologram, lowering her voice to a whisper. "What do you mean *my* world?"

Torin nodded. "Your world. Dormance."

Okay, so he knows about Dormance. "What exactly have you been watching?" she questioned, her heart racing. "Are you a member of the Seventh Sanctum?"

"It's not what you think, Emery," he responded, seeing the fear in her eyes. "I need to show you something. Do you trust me?"

She hesitated before answering. She could run and tell Theo, but what good would that do? He'd just put her through hell, forcing her to save her best friend from a scalding, fiery death in a training simulation.

Screw him.

Emery met Torin's gaze. Even through the hologram, she could tell his eyes were pleading, and although she couldn't quite put her finger on it, she trusted him. Sort of. She grazed the back of her neck, remembering the microchip. "I want to, but I can't. They'll know."

"Don't worry about that," he coaxed. "I manipulated the status of your chip before we started talking. The FCW will think you're asleep in your dorm room. They don't monitor you while you're sleeping," he assured, grinning mischievously.

"How could you possibly know that?"

"I've been watching, remember?" Torin glanced to his left, his patience wearing thin. "I need you to come with me. Now."

Before she could respond, a second hologram appeared, two dime-sized, crystal objects floating in mid-air. Emery reached out to touch them, quickly withdrawing her hand as the objects materialized and descended toward the table. They clinked as they hit the surface.

"Whoa," Emery breathed as she reached out to touch them.

"I need you to take the crystal dials and place one on the inside of each wrist," he instructed.

Emery did as she was told and, just as she was about to ask what they were for, the crystal dials spun clockwise, making one full, 360° rotation before merging with her skin. Amazed, she flipped her forearms upside down and shook them, expecting the dials to fall out, but they remained one with her skin.

A gust of wind swept through the room, forcing her to close her eyes. Her feet began to tingle as an odd sensation moved slowly up her body, all the way to the top of her head. It was like being poked over and over again with dull pins and needles.

Suddenly, the tingling stopped. Emery looked down at her arms. Her eyes widened as thousands of particles danced in the open space. *I'm a hologram.* She wiggled her fingers, amazed at the technology. Even as a hologram, she could smell, feel, and hear like a normal human being.

When she looked up, she was no longer staring at a holographic image of Torin. There they stood, face to face, his piercing, aquamarine eyes staring into hers.

Emery shifted her feet back and forth, testing the legitimacy of the ground beneath her. She surveyed the overly tidy room she was standing in, trying to make sense of her surroundings. "What just happened? Where am I?"

"In my apartment. In the real world. The 7S world." He stepped back, preparing for her reaction. "You're the holoversion of yourself."

Surprisingly, Emery didn't react. Not even a flinch. She was too preoccupied by the sights outside the double paned window. From what Theo had described, she'd expected to see a dismal world, covered in ash and dust, not a soul in sight.

This was exactly the opposite of that.

"Is this what your world looks like?" he asked, watching her changing expressions.

Emery shook her head. "No," she breathed. "This world . . . it's *alive*. Bustling. It's beautiful." She walked closer to the window, looking for the latches to unlock it.

"Open window," Torin instructed.

Emery watched incredulously as the glass turned translucent, then disappeared altogether. A cool breeze drifted through the room. She poked her head out, scrunching her face at the view before her. "Where are all the cars?"

"That's the first thing you notice?" He laughed. "Why would we need cars when we can teleport?"

She looked at him, her eyes wide with astonishment. "Teleportation is real?" Her gaze shifted to the crystal dials in her wrists, noticing that he had some as well.

"Yeah. How else—?"

"Hold on. You're telling me that teleportation, like

wormholes and portals and stuff, is real?" Emery laughed, hardly able to believe her own words.

"That's exactly what I'm saying. How else do you think you got here?"

"I don't know." She shrugged. "Magic?"

"You're a funny girl." A smile touched his lips. "In a way, I guess it is kind of like magic."

"How does it work?"

Torin shrugged. "You just have to find a station, walk into a T-Port, state your destination, and the crystal dials do the rest."

"A T-Port?"

He nodded. "It's essentially a platform. We call it a T-Port."

Emery shook her head, amazed at how normal he made it sound.

"Anyway, I brought you here because I knew you wouldn't believe me unless you saw this with your own two eyes." He walked toward a glistening, silver platform in the far corner of the room, waiting for her to follow. "So, instead of telling you, I'm going to show you."

Emery tilted her head to the side. "Show me what?"

He stepped into the T-Port and extended his hand. "That everything Theo told you . . . is a lie."

Emery hesitated. *Theo, a liar?* Maybe she should just go back and forget this ever happened. It was probably all a hallucination anyway. Or was it?

She pushed her doubt aside and reached for his hand.

His fingers closed around hers as he pulled her onto the platform. "7S Headquarters" he instructed.

Another gust of wind and a few tingly seconds later, Emery found herself standing underneath looming skyscrapers in the middle of what looked like downtown Chicago— an overly, technologically-*advanced* Chicago.

People were milling about, looking busy and important, like they had somewhere to be, all dressed in white and grey pantsuits. Holograms of other people's faces floated in front of many of them, mouths opening and closing in rapid conversation, as they hurried to their next destination. Emery immediately felt out of place in her assassin-style training clothes.

Torin strode toward a giant, titanium tower, the words *Seventh Sanctum* embossed in gold above the sleek entryway. Her eyes traveled up the building until they reached the very top, where a circular logo was mounted, the number "7" and the letter "S" conjoined within a sphere.

"Welcome to 7S headquarters," Torin announced gleefully. "I know you've heard a lot of things about the Seventh Sanctum—"

"Mostly bad," Emery interrupted, her eyes trained on the logo.

"Well, I'm here to set the record straight," he went on, ignoring her cynicism. "I need you to forget everything you think you know." He raised his eyebrows.

"Can you do that?"

She sighed. "After the day I've had, I'm not making any promises."

"Okay, here goes," Torin said as he cleared his throat. "7S is actually the good guy, Emery. *We're* the ones trying to break everyone out of Dormance, *not* the other way around. The FCW is the one who wants to destroy the world and start anew."

Emery knew he could see the skepticism building in her eyes. Even so, he continued. "That's why they've taken out half of the population and placed them in a simulated reality—it's their way of building an army to eventually wipe out the rest of the world."

She looked at him in disbelief. "Wait. So, you're telling me that the Federal Commonwealth is the one responsible for creating Dormance?"

He nodded.

"How do I know you're telling the truth?"

"Does this look like the world Theo described? Does it look corrupted, oppressed, and degraded to you?" he challenged.

Emery considered this for a minute. "No. It actually looks quite lucrative, which brings me to my next question. Why would the Federal Commonwealth want to destroy this world? I mean, look at it." She gestured to the clear, pollution-free sky.

"Because they're the ones who despise the thought

of free will. The microchip—the one that they embedded into your neck—its end purpose is to *control* you. To rid you of your free will." He stepped directly in front of her so that she had no choice but to look directly at him. "Once they deploy their army and take over this world, they'll embed the microchips into every single person on the planet, giving them the power to control, well . . . everything. Freedom will be a thing of the past." He shook his head. "Please tell me you believe me."

Emery stared at him as she skimmed her tongue against the roof of her mouth. A long sigh escaped from her lips. "I just don't understand why Theo would lie to me."

"Emery, I've been trying to hack into the FCW's mainframe for months. To reach out to you. To help you. If I were the bad guy, why would I waste my time doing that?"

She considered this for a minute. "I don't know," she said as she let out a frustrated groan. "I feel like I don't know anything anymore."

Torin bowed his head. "You're going to make me pull out the big guns, aren't you?"

Emery raised an eyebrow. "What do you mean?"

"Here," he said as he typed a complex code into his phone. "Watch this."

A hologram appeared above the screen. A blonde girl

with a pixie haircut was busily pulling up files on a computer. Emery recognized her immediately.

Naia.

"How did you—?"

"Shhh," Torin hushed. "Just watch."

Emery watched as her own file appeared on the screen. A few seconds later, Naia's phone rang.

"Where are we at?"

Emery froze. She'd recognize that refined drawl anywhere. Theo.

"Still on track, sir," Naia responded. "Once testing is complete, we can use the device to render the rest of the world comatose."

No. Emery stepped away from the hologram, feeling unsteady on her own two feet. *It can't be.* Theo's voice sounded again.

"Good work. Please keep me informed of any setbacks."

"Roger that, sir."

Torin shut the hologram down, his eyes searching her face for a reaction. "So? Do you believe me now?"

Emery closed her eyes as she nodded her head. "I trusted them. I can't believe I—"

Torin stepped closer to her. "Don't beat yourself up. I'm sorry, I never wanted to show you that. I just didn't know how to make someone as stubborn as you believe me."

Emery couldn't help but smile. "Well, you did it. I believe you."

"Okay, good." He paused. "So now I have something really important to ask you."

Emery maintained eye contact, already knowing what he was about to ask.

"Will you help us? Will you help 7S shut down The Alpha Drive?"

She took a deep breath before answering. Did she really have a choice? She'd heard it from the horse's mouth: the Federal Commonwealth was responsible for creating Dormance.

"I guess I have to," she sighed. "What do you need me to do?"

Torin punched his arms in the air, like he'd just crossed the finish line of a close race. "You can be our eyes and ears inside Dormance," he explained. "I'm only able to hack into the holodevice in that room you were in—"

"The common room?"

"That's the one. So the conversations I've heard are limited to the location of that device."

Emery pondered this, another question springing to mind. "If you have the ability to teleport me into the 7S world, why haven't you sent someone from 7S into Dormance?"

"Because no one in my world has a microchip. If I tried to teleport there myself, I wouldn't have a way out.

I'd be stuck there. Your chip is your ticket in . . . and your ticket out."

Emery narrowed her eyes. "You have an answer for everything, don't you?"

"I try." He winked. "So, you're sure about this? You'll be our inside-woman?"

She heaved one final sigh. "Yes, I'm sure."

Torin flashed a toothy grin as he pulled his phone from his pocket. "Can I see your phone?"

She handed it to him, watching as he typed in a long combination of numbers and letters.

"There," he said as he handed the phone back to her. "Now your phone is programmed so I can reach you via hologram. No more going through that device in the common room."

"You're a man of many talents," she admired, slipping the phone back into her pocket. "So how should we do this?"

"I want you to let me know once you find out anything regarding the Federal Commonwealth's strategy. Our best bet is to talk at night when you're about to fall asleep since that seems to be the only time they don't monitor. If we need to talk during the day, we can make that work too. I'm able to manipulate your chip in emergency situations, but doing that too often could arouse suspicion."

She nodded. "Better to be safe than sorry."

"Agreed. So, I'll connect to your phone once a week. Thursdays at 11 P.M. The more we know, the more we can prepare for whatever they have planned. Got it?"

"Got it," she affirmed.

"Time's almost up. I need to get you back before they realize something's up."

They walked back to the platform in sync. She flushed as Torin's fingers brushed against hers.

"I'll talk to you soon," he smiled, waving his hand.

Emery nodded and just like that, she found herself back in the common room, her crumpled shirt sitting exactly where she'd left it.

19

Torin stood in front of the platform Emery had just disappeared from. "Whoa," he breathed as he looked down at his hands. His fingers were trembling. His mouth was dry.

What did she do to me?

He collapsed onto a bench right outside of 7S Headquarters and buried his face deep in his hands. Counting backwards from ten always seemed to clear his head and steady his breathing. From within his pocket, his phone chimed, a female voice breaking the silence. "Will images of crashing waves satisfy your current needs?"

Torin rolled his eyes. The Seventh Sanctum had launched its new stress-relief program for all employees and, of course, he'd been chosen as a beta tester. The program had some kinks, but for the most part, it got the job done.

"Sure, why not?" he responded as a visual of a beach

appeared before him. The sounds of the city drifted away as the rumbling of the ocean took over. He gazed at the virtual crashing waves, then closed his eyes and listened as they rolled onto the shore.

Still, his thoughts shifted back to Emery. Her mesmerizing grey eyes. The way her lips pursed before she spoke. The barely discernible dimples at the corners of her mouth. He hadn't expected to be so attracted to someone he'd just met.

Initially, his goal was to finally meet *the* Emery Parker that the FCW couldn't shut up about and tell her to run for her life. To get out as fast as she could.

Butterflies fluttered in his stomach. As much as he didn't want to admit it, he cared for her. Fear seized his entire body. *What if she changes her mind? What if she likes her life in Dormance?*

Torin exited the stress relief program and stood up from the bench. The peaceful visual of the beach and ocean waves under a crisp blue sky disappeared and was quickly replaced with the bustling humdrum of the city. He walked over to the nearest T-Port and recited his home address.

His apartment wasn't much to look at. Sure, it was neat and tidy, but in the way of furniture, there wasn't much. A couch. A coffee table. A bed. A desk. Just the bare essentials. He made a decent living working for 7S, but he didn't know what to spend his money on. It's not like he had anyone to impress.

Torin plopped down on the couch and kicked his feet up on the coffee table. He couldn't help but wonder what Emery was doing at that exact moment.

"I need to distract myself," he muttered as he left the couch and walked over to his desk. He waved his hand across the virtual screen to start up the computer and typed in his credentials. What could he do to pass the time? Watch holovideos of people doing stupid things? Nah. That was pointless. Funny, but pointless.

Perhaps he could start a side project? Now, *that* seemed like a more productive use of his time. Just as he was about to pull up a recent holoprint, he remembered something.

He'd coded Emery's phone.

Giddy like a child on the first day of school, he typed in the code, tapping his feet impatiently as he waited for it to connect. An image of what appeared to be Emery's dorm room surfaced. It appeared she'd set her phone on the desk because she was standing at a distance, crouched over the sink, brushing her teeth.

Feeling a little like a stalker, Torin keyed in more code to activate the program's stealth mode. In this mode, he could see her, but she couldn't see him—a side project he'd completed months ago and considered useless . . . until now.

Torin sighed as he watched her spit the last of her toothpaste into the sink, then pull her crimson hair into a low ponytail. Holy smokes, was she beautiful. Not in that stunning, supermodel kind of way. But in that real, naturally flawed kind of way.

Torin sat back in his chair, suddenly averting his eyes from the screen. This was creepy. He was being a total creep. There was no doubt about it. If he was going to do this without feeling like a total stalker, he needed to think of it in a different way. It wasn't stalking. It was . . . research.

Yeah. Research.

In order to help her, he needed to understand her world. He needed to learn more about her so that he could keep her safe. In a way, he was acting as her guardian, protecting her from all that was bad and evil in the world. Like a superhero.

A superhero? Really? He shook his head, laughing at himself. *I need to get out more.*

Emery unknowingly took Torin on a tour of the Darden campus, spending the majority of her time in the library. He was surprised at just how dedicated she was to her studies, even though she knew Dormance was all a simulation. At one point, he could have sworn Emery looked right through the camera, her grey eyes piercing straight through him. He'd held his breath, panicking at the thought of being caught. But when she turned away, he'd actually found himself wishing that she *had* caught him, if only to hear her voice again.

After a few hours at the library, they traveled back to her dorm room. Emery ventured over to her closet, and he averted his eyes as she slipped into her pajamas. When he looked back at the screen, she was still standing by the closet, but she was staring into space, clearly caught in a daydream. A hint of a smile touched her lips.

What was she thinking about? Was there even the slightest chance that she could be thinking about him?

Emery snapped out of her daze and walked over to her desk, grabbing her phone along the way. The room went dark as she clambered into bed.

Torin leaned back in his chair, fighting to keep his eyes awake. Emery's smile floated across his mind. It was the last thing he saw before falling into a deep peaceful sleep.

20

It had been two weeks since Emery's massive blowout with Anthony. She figured their relationship was over, and was surprised when she received a call from him late in the week. He'd asked her to come over to his place to talk and have dinner, even offering to cook. But all Emery could think about was her visit to the 7S world. As if things weren't confusing enough already, now she had to live her life as a Darden student, an Alpha Drive participant, and an inside-woman for the Seventh Sanctum.

Oh, goody.

First things first. She had to keep her life in Dormance in check. And seeing as things hadn't exactly improved with Rhea, having dinner with Anthony seemed like the least tormenting option. Anything would be better than sitting in awkward silence in a tiny dorm room, even dinner with her maybe-maybe-not boyfriend.

Emery arrived at Anthony's house at about seven o'clock in the evening. He greeted her at the door with a dozen red roses in hand. She smiled appreciatively at him, expecting to feel a flurry of butterflies in her stomach. Sadly, the caterpillars stayed in their cocoons.

Anthony had already cooked dinner and set the table, transforming his family's home into the ideal romantic couple's getaway. His parents weren't home—they were probably on a cruise somewhere in the Caribbean.

She watched as he pulled a vase out from under the sink and set it delicately on the dining room table, plopping the flowers in one by one.

"I just want to let you know," she hesitated, knowing that this would be the start of their fight, "I'm not staying."

He gave her a baffled look. "Why not?"

"I'm not staying," she said again, more firmly this time. "I need to get back to Darden tonight."

"Fine," Anthony muttered as he carried the steaming platter of shrimp risotto to the table. His kitchen skills had always been impressive, but Emery wouldn't allow that to persuade her to stay. She was free to make her own decisions, and she was dead-set on leaving at the end of the evening. *Let's get this over with.*

"So, how have you been?" she asked in an attempt to start the conversation. "We haven't spoken in a while."

"And whose fault is that?" The hurt in his eyes was clear as day.

Emery slammed her glass of water onto the table. "Seriously? Are you trying to set me off?"

"I'm sorry. I shouldn't have said that," he apologized, scooping some shrimp risotto onto his plate.

A weary sigh escaped her lips, and she could only hope that he'd sense her frustration. "I don't want to fight, Anthony. It's exhausting."

They agreed it was best to take turns and share their feelings on an individual basis. Emery went first, expressing the need for space since she was adjusting to life at a new school. Anthony listened carefully, and when it was his turn, explained that he felt like he'd been replaced, seeing as the only person she seemed to hang out with anymore was her roommate. He even had the nerve to mention that she'd hardly spoken with Riley over the past few months.

At this accusation, Emery moved to the edge of her chair, her knuckles turning white from gripping the underside. "You called Riley, didn't you?"

Anthony paused, unsure whether or not he should admit his wrongdoing. "Okay, yeah, I talked to Riley," he confessed. "She also mentioned that you've been hanging out with Mason and his friends. Why are you suddenly keeping all of these secrets from me?"

The harsh tone in his voice ignited her anger even more. "You had no right to call Riley behind my back. If I wanted to talk to you, then I would have picked up the phone and called you."

"That doesn't answer my question about Mason," he pressed.

She scowled at him, eyes narrowing. "Yes, I've hung out with Mason, like, twice. Big freaking whoop."

His face turned beet red. "Don't you remember the conversation we had last summer about Mason? How I mentioned I was uncomfortable with you hanging out with him?"

She did, in fact, remember this conversation like it had happened yesterday. They'd run into Mason at a deli last summer. She'd introduced the two, immediately sensing the clash in their personalities. Apparently, Anthony picked up on it too because five minutes after their encounter, he'd asked her to keep her distance from Mason. She hadn't thought much of his request, so she'd obliged simply to appease him and end the conversation. The possibility that it could come around full circle never even crossed her mind.

The rattling of dishes interrupted her train of thought, and she watched as Anthony trudged away from the table. Emery looked down at her own plate, her food completely untouched. She scooted her chair back and meandered over to the living room, the plopped down on the plush, leather couch.

"Are you finished with your plate?" he called out, sounding disappointed.

"Yeah. I wasn't as hungry as I thought I was. Thank you for cooking though," she said, fidgeting with the necklace he'd given her last Christmas.

He sighed as he brought the dish to the sink. Padded footsteps made their way toward the living room. Anthony sat in the recliner next to her and kicked his feet up, setting a pillow on his lap. They sat in uncomfortable silence for a few minutes. Eventually, he turned to face her. "You know you're going to end up with him, right?"

"Huh? I'm going to end up with whom?"

"Mason. You're going to end up with Mason," he clarified as he set his drink down on the coffee table.

"Where is this coming from?" Emery questioned. "Why would you say that?"

"You know when you just have a feeling? Well, I have a feeling—and I've had it for a while now—that you're going to end up with Mason. It's so obvious." He shot her a sideways glance.

"That's the most ridiculous thing I've ever heard," she argued. "I hardly even know him. Clearly, he's interested in Rhea since their tongues were down each other's throats the last time I saw them." Emery knew she sounded defensive, but she didn't care. If she were being completely honest with herself, the sight of Rhea and Mason kissing had bothered her more than she'd expected. The image of

Mason's hands in Rhea's hair, their lips locked, floated across her mind. That night, she hadn't wanted to leave but the sight had repulsed her, so she'd grabbed Warren's hand and ran for it. She could guess how that night would play out, and she hadn't wanted to stick around to see the end of it.

Anthony eyed her incredulously, his hands gripping the armrests tightly. "If you're so jealous of Mason and Rhea, maybe you should just tell him how you feel."

"Maybe I will," she shot back, rising to her feet. Normally, Emery avoided confrontation at all costs. But tonight was different. She was beyond agitated at these accusations and she wasn't going to let Anthony walk all over her like he always did. "Maybe that's exactly what I need," she continued. "Maybe the problem isn't me. Maybe it's the fact that I'm dating you and you're *always* judging me. Always wishing I were someone else." Much to her surprise, she didn't feel ashamed after the words left her mouth. They left her feeling . . . empowered.

Anthony looked at her with a pained expression.

Even though Emery could tell her last words had struck a chord, she kept going. "You know what's funny? You invite me to a nice dinner to 'talk' and here I thought you were actually going to apologize for showing up the other night, unannounced, like an attention-deprived, insecure jerk." She crossed her arms over her chest to hide her heavy breathing, hoping he wouldn't notice how exhilarated she felt.

Anthony looked down at his feet as he collected his thoughts. "I'm sorry I made you feel that way. I just want us to go back to the way we were, before you left for boarding school." His voice cracked. "I just don't know how to get back there. I don't know where we made a wrong turn." He sighed. "You're so different now."

"Did you ever stop to think that maybe I don't want to go back to the way we were? I didn't even know who I *was* back then," she admitted. "You're right. I *am* different now. And, in my opinion, I'm better off for it." With one swift move, she seized her purse from the couch and started toward the door. "And take this stupid necklace back," she yelled as she unclasped the silver heart from around her neck. "I don't want it anymore."

He followed close behind her and grabbed her by the wrist as the necklace fell to the floor. "This isn't over," he stated firmly.

Emery escaped from his grip, just missing the side of his face. "You're not the only one who has a say in that." Her eyes were empty and barren, her face expressionless. She swung the door open with impressive force, making sure to slam it behind her so that her now ex-boyfriend wouldn't dare follow her outside.

21

Rhea rifled through her binders, looking for any semblance of note-taking over the last semester. She couldn't believe that final exams for the fall semester were upon them. It felt like just yesterday that she'd started at Darden—meeting Emery for the first time, enrolling in classes, making the usual stroll down Alpha Drive to see what kind of trouble they could get into. It was unreal how quickly time had passed.

She banged her head against the desk, seconds away from giving up all hope of passing her finals. In that moment, Rhea wished she'd spent a little more time on school and a little less time on her social life. Of course, that thought was fleeting, as were most thoughts that involved self-pity. She lifted her head up off the desk, the door handle jiggling noisily.

Emery walked in and sat down at her desk, pulling her laptop and books out of her bag. Although things between them had improved, their relationship hadn't exactly returned to normal. Rhea knew that Emery was still stressed about Anthony, and the pressure of acing her final exams wasn't helping. Rhea had tried to empathize with her roommate, but it was clear that Emery didn't want to talk about things any more than she had to. So Rhea had waited. Patiently. But her patience was running out.

"Okay, can we discuss the elephant in the room?" she asked hopefully, trying not to sound too desperate.

Emery glanced up from her laptop. A sigh escaped her lips. "What elephant?"

Rhea's body tensed with frustration. "Ever since your fight with Anthony, you've been . . ." she paused, unsure how to finish the sentence.

Emery crossed her arms. "I've been what?"

Great, her guard's up. Rhea looked her square in the eye as she searched for the right word. She didn't want to offend her roommate or make things even worse. "You've been . . . distant."

Emery opened her mouth to defend herself, then closed it again after a few seconds. "I know," she admitted. "I'm sorry."

Rhea placed her hand on her roommate's shoulder, kneeling down so that they were eye-level. "You know that you can talk to me about anything. I'm here for you."

Emery smiled at her appreciatively. "I know that. It's just that with everything going on lately, I feel like . . . I haven't had any time to talk."

Rhea could tell that there was more to the story than she was letting on. What was she hiding?

"Is it because you haven't had time or because you haven't wanted to?"

Emery bit a hangnail from her thumb. "I guess it's a little of both," she confessed. "I promise we'll talk later though. Right now, I have a lot of studying to do."

But they didn't talk later. The days went by as they studied, taking their final exams for each class until, finally, they packed up and parted ways for a full month.

Winter break.

+ + +

Emery approached the doors of Rosemary Hall, suitcase in hand. December had gone by without as much as a text from Rhea, making the return to campus that much more dreadful. The only person she'd consistently talked to over the break was Torin.

When she and Torin first met, Emery was so distracted by the fact that Theo had lied to her that she forgot to fill Torin in on what little she knew about The Alpha Drive and the Federal Commonwealth's plan of attack. Over the break, Emery told him about her training with the elements as well as the mysterious orange serum that had the ability to heal all wounds, and even reverse death. But even with this information, they weren't any closer to uncovering the strategy to take down 7S.

Emery sighed. Nothing was going as planned. Things with both Rhea and Anthony were bad. Really bad. So much of her attention had been focused on her relationships in Dormance that she hadn't given much thought when it came to uncovering 7S's strategy.

How did things get so turned around?

A sense of peace upon her return to campus would have been nice, especially since things at home had been a little out of the ordinary during winter break. Her mother had scheduled a last-minute getaway to their family cabin in Northern Arizona. Emery and Alexis had piled into the car without so much as a complaint, knowing that the cabin also happened to be their mother's favorite vacation spot. They spent many nights outside by the firepit, snuggled up in blankets, watching as the flames crackled and popped.

On the way back, her mother noticed that Emery wasn't wearing the ring she'd given her. Emery promptly replied that she'd been in a hurry to pack and that it was safely tucked away in a drawer in her dorm room. As soon as the words left her mouth, a familiar expression clouded her mother's face.

Fear.

Again, Emery tried not to read too much into it. But later that night, Alexis discreetly mentioned that their mother had been out of sorts ever since Emery had left for boarding school. She seemed to be in a trance that no one—not even Alexis—could break her out of. And so, Emery decided to chock it up to the "empty nest syndrome", or half-empty in this case. Her mother missed her. That's all there was to it.

Emery dropped her suitcase by her side, fumbling through her purse for her access card. Her fingers brushed by her phone as it buzzed with a message. She pulled the phone from her bag, surprised to see that the text was from Rhea. "Are you back?" was all it said. She couldn't put her finger on why, but the message infuriated her. After a month of hardly speaking to one another, that was all she got? Emery decided not to respond.

She swiped her access card across the sensor, waiting for the green light to indicate permission to enter. The wheels of her suitcase clanged loudly against the tile steps as she hauled it up the stairs. The hall was extremely quiet, considering it was the first day the dorms had reopened for residency since winter break. Emery paused for a moment, gazing at the long hallway ahead of her.

As if on cue, Rhea stepped out of the doorway to their room, turning the key behind her. She walked briskly in Emery's direction, eyes glued to her phone. After a few steps, she finally lifted her head. "Oh, hey. You're back."

Emery gave a weak smile, hoping that Rhea wouldn't see right through it. "Yep. I'm back."

Rhea tapped the screen on her phone. "Sorry, I'll catch up with you later. I'm running late."

Emery scrunched her forehead. "For what?"

"For class," Rhea replied as she started down the hallway, her stride picking up pace.

"But class doesn't start . . ." Emery's voice trailed off as she watched her roommate push through the wooden door to the stairwell.

There were still a few days before Darden opened for the spring semester—some of their teachers weren't even assigned yet. She racked her brain, trying to recall if Rhea had signed up for any clubs or activities. Honestly, how would she know? Communication wasn't exactly their strong suit as of late.

Emery rolled her suitcase into the chilly dorm room, realizing that Rhea hadn't turned the heat on yet. She hurried over to her closet and pulled out some fuzzy boots and a sweatshirt. It was a common myth that Arizona didn't have cold winters, but forty-two degrees sure felt cold. That was all she needed to justify dressing like an eskimo for a solid month and a half.

Two hours went by without a word from Rhea. Emery switched her phone on and off a couple of times, just in case the network was down. She finished unpacking the rest of her suitcase, her eyes glued to her phone the entire time. Finally, after what seemed like a lifetime, it pinged. She darted over to her desk as a reminder popped up on the screen. *Next round of training begins in ten minutes.*

Emery shoved her phone in her pocket and rushed down the hallway, almost tripping over a few stairs on the way to the lobby. Once inside the common room, she checked the holoschedule to confirm which training she was scheduled for: aeris.

Naia appeared with her usual tray of sparkling water, then led Emery down the long corridor to the aeris training room, winking at her before turning to leave. "Good luck," she whispered as she closed the door behind her.

Emery stepped cautiously to the center of the room, noticing that the floor was covered in a mesh material—like a flexible, chain-link fence—but she couldn't see any farther than five feet below the surface. She bent down, her fingers grazing the metal when suddenly, a giant whoosh shot her straight into the air. Her body snapped into a u-shape as she traveled about thirty feet upwards until her back smashed into what she assumed was the ceiling, her arms and legs flailing against the wind. The sheer force was enough to pin her to the wall, her hair billowing wildly around her head. Within her boots and gloves, her fingers started to go numb as the icy air blasted from the giant fan below.

Just when she felt like she was about to pass out, the pressure changed and her body slowly floated down from the ceiling. Instinct told her to lay flat on her stomach and extend her arms and legs outward while bending slightly at the elbows and knees. And just like that, she was in control.

She was flying.

The realization took hold as Emery floated around the vast space. She felt like an eagle, gliding gracefully through a cool winter's breeze. Below her the fan blades whirred round and round, the sound a soft melody to her ears. It was so peaceful. So relaxing.

That feeling didn't last for long. Her body tensed as something whizzed by her head. She looked up in confusion from the fan blades as tiny objects soared toward her from every angle. Squinting, she did her best to make out the inbound shapes.

They appeared to be tiny missiles. And bullets.

Panicked, she began to dodge them, one by one, using her hands and feet to control her body's position. Up, down, left, right. There were so many bullets.

Too many.

A tiny bullet grazed her right cheek as another tore through her opposite shoulder. Searing pain ripped through her icy skin. She cried out in agony as another bullet blasted through her kneecap, her entire leg immediately going numb. *My clothes are supposed to be bullet proof. What's happening?*

She howled again, not sure how much more pain she could take. Suddenly, the bullets stopped. A green mist filled the air and the whir of the fan blades slowed. Emery drifted back down to the surface, waning in and out of consciousness. The green mist filled her nose and lungs until it consumed her, her world fading into black.

When she awoke, Theo leaned over her, empty syringe in hand. "Welcome back."

Emery opened her mouth to speak, but no sound came out. It seemed that the torrential winds had irritated her larynx and made her hoarse. She swallowed. Surprisingly, nothing hurt, which meant that the sanaré had done its job. To signal that she was okay, she gave a thumbs-up.

After spending an hour in recovery, Emery was released for the day. Her legs felt like they were made of cement, and every time her foot made contact with the ground, it took all of her strength to lift it again. She'd just made it to her dorm room when someone banged on the door. *What now?* With slight hesitation, she opened it.

There stood Anthony, a bag of burgers and fries in hand.

Why had she answered the door? She was exhausted. Drained. All she wanted to do was collapse onto her bed and sleep. "What are you doing here?"

Anthony shuffled his feet as he cleared his throat. "We've hardly talked since our fight and I didn't even get to spend Christmas with you this year." His voice broke. "I tried to give you space, but I can't do it anymore. You're my girlfriend and I want to be with you."

Even in her drained state, she felt a pang of guilt. "Burger and fries, huh? You sure know the way to a girl's heart," she joked, her eyes softening.

The last thing she wanted was for Rhea to intrude on their conversation, so she led Anthony to Rosemary Hall's common room. As per usual, the room was empty, the drab furniture exuding a less-than-pleasant, musty odor. Emery patted the seat of one of the couches, watching as dust particles bounced off the fabric and floated into the air. She crossed her legs carefully, half expecting her knee to start bleeding profusely from her nonexistent bullet wound.

Anthony laid the burgers and fries out on the table in front of them. He placed a straw in Emery's drink and handed it to her, his eyes flitting back and forth between the food and the door.

Emery yawned as she looked at the food. She should have been famished, but her mind was consumed with the training and what Torin would make of it. If bullets were their strategy, it was a pretty lame one.

She turned her attention back to Anthony as he leaned into the cushions and stretched his arm across the back of the couch. As they made eye contact, it hit her.

I don't want to be with him anymore.

Anthony spilled his heart out, expressing how he'd been so lonely the past couple of months with nowhere to turn and no one to talk to. He'd always been good at placing blame on others and she was feeling the effects of this more than ever. Emery ate her burger in silence, offering only a nod of her head or blink of her eyes to signify she was paying attention.

When they finished eating, she walked him downstairs to his car, fabricating an elaborate excuse as to why they couldn't talk longer.

Anthony trudged behind her down the stairwell. "I just poured my heart out to you and you're not even going to let me stay?"

Emery pushed open the door that led to the parking garage. Right before they reached his car, he stepped in front of her, stopping her in her tracks. He grabbed both of her hands, his eyes desperately searching hers for answers. "I'm not sure what's going on, but we're going to work through it," he whispered as he squeezed her delicate skin.

Emery looked down at their entwined fingers and sighed. "No," she said as she pulled away, "we're not."

Anthony let go, watching as her arms dropped to her sides. "I don't understand."

"I know this isn't what you want to hear, but I've done some thinking. A lot of thinking, actually. And I don't think we should be together anymore." Emery waited for him to respond, but the deafening silence only grew louder.

"I just need to be on my own for a while. I've grown so much over the past couple of months and I need some time to figure everything out. I'm sorry, Anthony." She inhaled deeply, stuffing her trembling hands into her pockets.

"I don't know what to say," he choked, "but I guess if that's what you want, then there's nothing I can say to change how you feel."

As he turned toward his car, she reached for his arm, grasping his sleeve tightly. "I'm really sorry."

Anthony pulled something from his pocket. It was the necklace he'd given her last Christmas. The same necklace she'd thrown at him during their last fight.

"This belongs to you."

Emery shook her head. "It's beautiful, but I can't keep it."

"Em, it was a gift. I want you to have it."

Emery knew better than to start another fight. She turned around and moved her hair out of the way as his rough, calloused hands draped the necklace around her neck. As he hooked the clasp, his index finger brushed against the nape of her neck.

Emery froze. *No.*

"There's like a bump or something . . ."

She whirled around to face him, the necklace falling onto the cement at her feet.

Anthony was eerily still for a minute, as if he'd been turned into a statue. Emery snapped her fingers in front of his face, trying to get him to blink or make some sort of movement.

"This can't be happening," she said out loud as Theo's warning hurtled to the front of her mind.

Emery frantically waved both hands in front of his face, but he didn't flinch. *No, no, no.*

She bent down to pick the necklace up off the pavement, but when she stood back up, Anthony's head was turned. He looked around the parking garage with a bewildered expression on his face.

"Are you okay?" she asked, hoping that, by some miracle, he hadn't seen the chip.

He took a step back, eyes shifting nervously. "I'm fine," he said as he made his way to his truck.

"Anthony!" she called after him, feeling puzzled by his reaction.

He turned to look at her. "I'm sorry. Do I know you?"

There it was. Emery felt her heart drop as all of the color drained from her face. *This can't be happening.*

"Anthony," she said as calmly as she could, "I'm Emery. Your girlfriend of over a year."

He scoffed, shaking his head in disbelief. "Listen, sweetheart. I don't know what kind of day you've had, but I am not, nor was I ever, your boyfriend."

Emery watched with her mouth agape as her nonexistent ex-boyfriend climbed into his truck and sped off. She stood there, frozen in time, the necklace dangling limply from her index finger.

22

Theo groaned as he watched the scene unfold, the holoscreen zooming in on Emery's face. He slammed his fists onto the metallic control station, the buttons shaking angrily from the impact. Of all the participants, he never wanted Emery to experience such a heart-wrenching experience. And neither did his superior.

Pacing the perimeter of the room, Theo geared himself up for what he knew would be the most uncomfortable conversation of his life. "Call Victor Novak," he commanded into the open space, his voice echoing throughout the control room. He waited for the holoimage of the President's face to appear, but as always, it was just a shadow.

"President Novak speaking."

"Sir, it's Theo. Do you have a moment?"

A chuckle resonated from the other end. "For you, Mr. Barker, I have not one."

Theo paused, irked by his response. His lips pressed into a firm line, his mood turning sour. "I assure you, this will only take a moment. It's about Emery Parker."

Silence.

"Sir?"

"It better be good news, Mr. Barker."

Theo bit his tongue. "Unfortunately, it's not. About fifteen minutes ago, Emery ended her relationship with her boyfriend. He saw the chip, sir, and per Alpha Drive protocol, his memory has been erased."

An incoherent string of words sounded from the other line.

"I'm sorry, sir. Can you repeat that?"

"This is indeed problematic, seeing as we're close to finalizing our strategy. We need her. She can't lose focus because of a petty mishap with her boyfriend." Another unpleasant gargle escaped from his throat.

"Sir? Are you asking me to bring Anthony's memory back?" Theo clamped his mouth shut, realizing his question sounded more like an accusation.

"Of course not." Condescension dripped from the President's voice. "We need both the ring and the pendant—the two things that only she has access to—otherwise everything falls apart. We just need to make sure she's still on our side. "

Theo turned his back and rolled his eyes. He'd heard this story a million times before. "How do we do that?"

There was a pause as the President hummed. "Before we get to that, are you sure there's nothing you want to tell me?"

Theo froze. His thoughts whirled back to when Emery's vitals were low; when her microchip looked like it had been tampered with. "No, sir."

The President sighed. "You know that I hate liars more than anything, Mr. Barker."

Theo gulped. Should he come clean? It was highly unlikely that the President knew about the incident.

"A little birdy told me that, a while back, someone may have tampered with Ms. Parker's chip. Is this true?"

Theo turned around in his chair. "Who told—?"

"It doesn't matter *who* told me," President Novak interrupted. "What matters is that I'm in charge of The Alpha Drive and I'm not being informed of critical details when I should be."

Theo lowered his head in defeat. "My apologies, sir. It won't happen again."

"See to it that it doesn't." He coughed. "Now, seeing as Ms. Parker's chip may have been tampered with, we need to understand how such an event could occur. I'll need you to put Emery through a simulation. We need to see if she's going to crack and reveal The Alpha Drive to the public. If she does, we'll know where her loyalty stands."

Theo's mind began to whirl with the possibilities. Simulations were one of his favorite past times.

"And the next time you receive any sort of intel," Victor paused, clearing his throat angrily, "I want a full report. I will not be left in the dark again."

But before Theo could say another word, the line went dead.

23

Torin knew he wouldn't be able to keep it a secret for long. But this . . . this had happened too soon.

He sat in front of the 7S board of directors with his eyes lowered, his thoughts shifting back to just a few hours prior. He'd been right in the middle of hacking into the Federal Commonwealth's mainframe to check up on things when a low-level employee had caught him red-handed. So much for flying under the radar.

The Commander was alerted right away and Torin was apprehended from his office and dragged into the conference room on the seventh floor . . . the same conference room he'd eavesdropped on when he'd found out half of the world was comatose.

"Mr. Porter," the Commander began, "you've been brought here for your failure of disclosure with regard to Project Viper."

Torin raised his eyebrows. "Project Viper?"

The Commander approached the table with a stern expression. "Did you or did you not fail to disclose that you successfully hacked into the Federal Commonwealth's mainframe?"

Torin sighed, drumming his fingers on the desk. It was no use pretending to act innocent. They knew. Time to confess.

"I failed to disclose that I'd hacked into the mainframe."

The Commander's mouth pressed into a harsh line. "And can you tell the board, for the record, what your directive was?"

Torin sighed as murmurs filled the room. "My directive was to report to the Commander once I successfully hacked into the Federal Commonwealth's mainframe."

The room fell silent as the board documented his statement.

Torin lowered his head, then muttered, "But can you really blame me?"

"Excuse me? Would you care to repeat that?"

Torin looked up at the Commander with wide eyes. *Oh, now you've done it.*

The Commander didn't wait for him to answer. "Yes, we *can* blame you. You are at fault here."

Torin wasn't sure what had gotten into him, but he felt the need to defend himself. "Look, I was never told *why* I was hacking in the first place. Everything around Project Viper has been so secretive that no one knows what we're even working toward or what the end goal is." He hesitated, wondering if he should speak the words he wanted to say next. "Project Viper? This is the first time I've heard the name. I didn't even know what this project was called, and I've been working on it for months! So, forgive me for wanting more information." He bit his tongue, knowing that his last statement would get him into more trouble than it was worth.

The Commander slammed his fists on the desk. "You are a Corporal. Nothing more. Corporals do not ask questions, they simply do as they are told. *Why* we do what we do doesn't matter. You just do it. We made that abundantly clear when we brought you onboard."

You are a Corporal. Nothing more. The words rang in Torin's head like an underwater scream. He slowly raised himself up off the chair and placed his hands on the desk, his fingertips an inch away from the Commander's. "Why we do the things we do *does* matter. Yeah, I withheld the status of the project from you for a little while. Of that, I'm guilty. But only because you didn't provide me with the information I needed to do my *job*."

"Your *job* was completed the minute you hacked into the Federal Commonwealth's mainframe."

"But—"

"But nothing. You leave me no choice," the Commander barked. "Torin Porter, you are hereby suspended from your duties as Head of Project Viper." He waved his hand in the air to dismiss him.

Suspended? They couldn't suspend him. They *needed* him.

"You can't be serious!" Torin yelled as the guards grabbed his arms. "I'm the only one even working on that project!"

Darkness rolled over the Commander's eyes. "I changed my mind. Effective immediately, you are wholly suspended—from your position as Corporal, as Head of Project Viper, as well as any other duties at the Seventh Sanctum."

Torin felt his heart drop into his stomach. *This isn't happening.*

"Get him out of here," the Commander ordered, turning his back as he walked away.

The guards escorted Torin to the front of the building, stripping him of all badges and devices that belonged to the organization. Torin kept his head lowered as the guards shoved him outside. The double doors slammed shut behind him. And that was it. In seconds, he'd gone from Corporal Porter to jobless loudmouth.

Torin ran his fingers through his hair as he looked around at the bustling city before him. A girl with dark red hair walked by him, busily talking on her holophone, as a visual of a guy's face floated in front of her. And that's when he remembered. Emery.

How was he going to reach out to Emery? He'd connected to her phone through *his* phone—a 7S device—which, of course, he no longer had in his possession.

Torin eyed the nearest T-Port and sulked over to it, directing the machine to teleport him to his apartment. His body materialized at his apartment complex, and he trudged up the stairs, head hanging low. As he unlocked his apartment, he gazed around at his neat and orderly home. Why couldn't his life be like his apartment, where everything was perfect and in its place?

Torin fell into the couch and heaved a loud sigh before putting his face in his hands. There had to be another way to get through to Emery. After throwing himself a two minute pity party, he pulled himself up off the couch and strode over to his desk. He cracked his knuckles as the computer screen illuminated before him, then set his fingers on the virtual keyboard and opened his latest coding template.

He had a lot of work to do.

24

It had been three weeks since Emery's brutal break-up with Anthony. No matter how hard she tried, the scene wouldn't seem to flee her mind. The burger and fries. The walk down the stairs. The unclasping of the necklace. Anthony's blank stare. It played over and over again in her head, like a bad record on repeat.

To fill the void, Emery found herself spending more and more time talking to Mason. Things with Mason were easy—comfortable—and hanging out with him kept her mind from wandering down the deep dark hole that was her life. Their friendship had grown tremendously over the past few weeks, but unfortunately, they weren't the only ones taking notice. Rhea's teasing knew no bounds, and she was constantly saying that Emery was "on to the next one".

Latin class started in an hour, and Emery was busily typing away to finish her essay. As close as she was, the finish line seemed so far away, especially with Rhea impeding on her progress.

"So, you never actually told me what happened between you and Anthony," Rhea pried. "I mean, I never got any details or anything."

Emery stopped typing. She very well knew she couldn't explain the break-up without tipping off The Alpha Drive. "That's not true. I gave you details," she responded, eyes still focused on her laptop.

"Emery," she demanded with a snap of her fingers. "The least you can do is look at me when you speak."

Emery glanced up from her laptop. *Sheesh, someone woke up on the wrong side of the bed.*

"Like I already told you, Anthony brought over burgers and fries. We talked for a little and then we broke up. I walked him out to his car and he left." She shuddered at that last part. Thinking about what had actually happened made her cringe every time the memory drifted across her mind.

"What about Mason?"

"I already told you, Mason's just a friend." *At least that part is truthful.*

"Whatever happened to Warren?"

"I don't know, we still talk sometimes." Emery sighed, her agitation growing. "Are we done playing 20 Questions?"

Rhea snorted, even though Emery couldn't find the slightest bit of humor in their conversation. "Alright, alright, calm down," Rhea muttered. Sensing the tension, she changed the subject. "Hey, let's do something tonight. It's been a while."

Truthfully, Emery wasn't in the mood. Her focus as of late had been solely on The Alpha Drive. Much to her surprise, she was actually exceeding her own expectations. She gazed back up at her roommate. "Aren't you forgetting something?"

"What's that?" Rhea asked as she tossed a bowl of soup into the microwave.

"We have a chemistry test tomorrow."

Rhea rolled her eyes as she hit the start button. "Let me ask you something. Do you plan on being a chemist?"

Emery considered this, her thoughts shifting to her mother. Even though she didn't talk much about her time at Darden, her mom had revealed that her favorite class was Intermediate Chemistry with Professor Kemp, the same professor Emery had this year. She couldn't quite figure out why her mother liked Professor Kemp so much—he always seemed to be watching her, scrutinizing her every move. It was unnerving, to say the least.

Her thoughts whirred back to Rhea's question.

"Well, I was a member of the chemistry club at my old school," she recalled, sinking back into her desk chair.

"Okay, really? That was a rhetorical question." Rhea

slid the bowl out of the microwave, blowing on the rapidly rising steam.

Emery could tell that Rhea was a little on edge, but she wasn't sure why. It's not like she had any reason to be. Emery was the one training for a crazy initiative, living a double life, and dealing with the after effects of memory purge. But none of that mattered. Or at least, that's how it felt since no one knew.

No one *could* know.

Not being able to talk about what had happened with Anthony was driving her to the brink of insanity. Lugging that secret around was almost more than she could handle. *I could crack at any second.*

"You and I both know that you don't need to study," Rhea pleaded. "You're literally the poster child for the perfect student. Come on, it'll be fun."

Emery picked at her cuticles. "Fine, we'll do something. But you're going to study with me until then."

"Oh, I would," Rhea paused, "except I've actually got a study group in fifteen minutes for a different class."

Emery could immediately sense that she was being lied to, but she didn't have the energy to start yet another squabble. "Suit yourself," she muttered as she turned back to her laptop.

Rhea threw her bag over her shoulder and walked out the door, her uneaten bowl of soup sitting dejectedly on her desk. As soon as the door closed, Emery got up and opened her roommate's bottom desk drawer. Underneath a pile of plastic-wrapped notebooks were all of Rhea's textbooks for her spring classes.

Good luck studying without your textbooks, she thought bitterly as she slammed the drawer shut. Enough was enough. It was time to find out where Rhea was always running off to.

Emery grabbed her things and quickly locked the door behind her. She hurried down the hall, making sure to keep Rhea within view. Following too closely was dangerous; if she wanted this to work, she had to keep a safe distance. Emery stood at the top of the stairwell, waiting for Rhea's footsteps to cease. As soon as she heard the door to the lobby creak open, she darted down the stairs, her shoes pounding against the tile. Her rhythm faltered as she pushed through the door to the lobby.

What stood before her rendered her immobile.

A tall, cloaked figure in black robes blocked her path. Before Emery could discern what was happening, she felt her body go slack, eyes shutting as she fell into the hooded figure's arms.

+ + +

A ceiling fan came into view, the shadows on the walls dancing with each rotation of the blades. Emery blinked a few times as her surroundings came into focus. It was familiar, this place. The worn, wooden desk. The palisade-blue walls. The indented mattress that fit her body's shape perfectly.

She was back in her room. She was home.

A wave of dizziness washed over her as she slowly brought herself to a sitting position. After a deep inhale, she steadied her feet on the ground below her, then pushed herself up from the bed. The last thing she remembered was . . .

Fear seized her entire body.

She couldn't remember.

Her hand met the bedframe for support. Had her memory been erased? She grazed the back of her neck with her free hand, the surface still just as lumpy as the last time she'd touched it. *I still have my microchip.* Before she could analyze any further, a loud clatter sounded from downstairs.

Emery tiptoed out of her bedroom into the hallway, noticing that the door to her sister's room was slightly ajar. She poked her head inside, but it was empty.

Unease settled over her.

Instead of following the noise, she crept along the upstairs hallway to the game room that overlooked the kitchen. With her body pressed against the wall, she leaned just far enough to see around it.

Her mouth dropped open.

Without thinking, Emery stepped out from behind the wall, revealing herself to the audience below.

"Em, there you are," her mother fussed from the kitchen. "Come downstairs. Dinner is almost ready."

Emery's eyes shifted from her mother to Alexis to the back of a man's head—a head adorned with a black fedora. A chill ran down her spine.

Theo.

She froze as he slowly turned around in his chair. "Yes, why don't you join us?"

Emery turned away from her family's prying eyes. *Don't let them see your reaction.* She walked down the hallway, her hands shaking the entire way. *What is Theo doing here? Did I do something wrong? Why is he having dinner with my family?*

Emery took a deep breath as she descended the staircase, her fingers sliding along the cool railing. She needed to quiet her thoughts and appear calm and collected, but it felt as though she wore the very expression she so desperately needed to hide.

"Something smells good," she complimented as she entered the kitchen. She gave her mom a quick hug, her eyes landing on the table where Theo and her sister sat. Emery walked cautiously toward them as Theo turned in his chair, his eyes glinting mischievously. Although Emery had no idea what was going on, if there was one thing that had been drilled into her head, it was that no one could know anything about The Alpha Drive.

It was her only play.

"I don't believe we've met," Emery stated firmly as she stuck her hand out to Theo. "I'm Emery."

Theo chuckled as he raised himself from his chair. He met her grip. "I know who you are. And we actually have met before."

Emery gulped. *Crap. What do I say?*

Without another word, she took the open seat across from Theo, her eyes cast down as she unfolded her napkin and placed it across her lap.

Alexis piped up, breaking the uncomfortable silence. "So, Em, we've heard all about your experiences at Darden so far. Care to share more?"

Emery didn't shift her gaze as she fiddled with the edges of her napkin. *Theo told them about my experiences at Darden? Meaning The Alpha Drive?* A million thoughts swirled through her head—most of them involving dashing out the door and never looking back. Somehow, she managed to maintain her composure.

"Emery?" her mother pressed. "Your sister asked you a question. Don't be rude. Especially when we have company. I raised you better than that."

"That's okay," Theo interrupted. "Although, I am quite curious as to why Ms. Parker is being so quiet. She's normally quite outspoken."

At this, Emery raised her head, her eyes meeting Theo's. *What is he doing? Why is he here?* His head was tilted to the side, a smirk curling at the corners of his lips.

Emery had to think fast. *Questions. Keep asking questions.*

"I'm sorry, Mr. . . . Barker, was it?"

Theo nodded.

"You'll have to jog my memory. You look familiar, but I can't put my finger on where we've met before."

Theo smirked. "I was just telling Sandra about your many accomplishments," he drawled, gesturing toward her mother. "Especially your last assignment."

Emery racked her brain for a response. *My last assignment? Does he mean my last training?*

"My last assignment?" Emery scratched her head. "I'm not sure I recall . . . I have quite a few classes at Darden." She flashed a fake smile, surprised at how steady her voice was. Her confidence rose. *Two can play this game.*

"I'm sure you'd remember this one." His eyes twinkled. "Your Latin was practically flawless."

Emery sat still. It took her a minute, but she finally realized what he was doing. A hint of a smile touched her lips, so she quickly bowed her head, hoping it would remain hidden. *He's testing me.*

"It's not every day that we get an esteemed Darden faculty member over for dinner," Sandra said as she brought the meal over to the table. "I hope you like pot roast." She smiled at Theo as she sliced into the tender, juicy meat.

"If you'll excuse me for just a minute," Emery said as she pushed her chair away from the table. "I need to use the ladies' room."

She made her way down the hall, a smile spreading across her face as she shut the door behind her, then collapsed against the wall. Her hands flew up to her temples, massaging them gently.

That was close.

Emery pushed herself from the wall, her eyes landing on the mirror in front of her. As she stared at her reflection, her thoughts turned grim. Sure, it was a test, but why was Theo testing her? Did he know something? The possibility knocked her down a few notches. Her mind flitted to Torin. It *had* been a while since she'd spoken to him.

Was he in trouble?

Emery pulled out her phone, checking for the last communication they'd had. Over three weeks ago. A knot twisted in her stomach. She slid her phone back into her pocket, her mind reeling with all of the possible scenarios. *He's fine. Everything is fine.* But as much as she wanted to believe those words, she knew something wasn't right.

She could feel it.

25

How did I wind up back here?

Torin sat in front of the multiple holoscreens that floated over his desk. Remembering the code he'd written for 7S was difficult enough, but trying to remember a code that he'd revised hundreds of times? That was nearly impossible.

He banged his head on the metal desk as numbers and letters swirled through his brain. He looked back up at the screen, scrolling through the last few lines of code. It was the same spot he'd gotten hung up on last time. *Come on. Think.*

Torin took a swig of water, then closed his eyes, willing the combination to magically appear. Instead, an image of Emery's olive-colored face and deep red hair entered his view. The pool of grey staring back at him was enough to pull him under. He stayed still for a minute, captivated by her image, not wanting to open his eyes. With a smile, he watched as she was whisked away into the depths of his subconscious. When he opened his eyes, it came to him.

The code.

Before he forgot or became distracted, Torin punched the last line of code into the system, watching as the text appeared on the screen. He rubbed his hands together with glee. This wouldn't connect him directly to Emery's microchip, but it would break him into the Federal Commonwealth's mainframe. Even though it wasn't exactly what he'd hoped for, it was a start.

The FCW's underground common room came into focus as Theo entered the room. His mouth was moving, so clearly he was talking to someone—but the recipient was out of frame. Torin tapped his fingers against the desk, his impatience growing with each passing minute. He observed Theo's body language: shoulders back, fists clenched, eyebrows raised. Whoever he was talking to sure was making him tense.

Torin moved to the edge of his seat as Theo walked to the center of the room. A quaint figure came into view. "Come on, turn around," Torin muttered to the back of the girl's head. She was short, no taller than five feet, five inches, and her brown hair swayed delicately across her back. He had no idea who she was.

Torin stared at the back of the girl's head, wishing that she would turn around, but she remained firm in her stance, not moving an inch. Just as he was about to give up hope, she let out a high-pitched laugh, one that made Torin nearly fall from his seat. He'd heard that laugh before, many times over. He'd heard it while he'd been "researching" Emery. Torin gaped at the screen as recognition took hold.

The girl was Emery's roommate, Rhea.

26

For the past month, Emery had brainstormed every possible way to get in touch with Theo. She'd tried responding to the messages he'd sent, only to find that there was an error with the delivery. She'd even snuck out of her dorm room at odd hours, hoping that the elevator might magically "appear" downstairs. But no such luck.

He was unreachable.

There were so many questions that needed answering. Didn't she deserve to know *why* he'd scheduled a dinner party at her family's home? Why he'd felt the need to test her in the first place?

Emery's phone buzzed, a pile of coins and paperclips shifting noisily against the wood. She snatched it from her desk, her eyes lighting up as a message from Theo appeared on the screen.

Finally.

Emery rushed downstairs to the silver-paned elevator and, once she was confirmed for entry, sat in the same gold-trimmed chair she always did. She closed her eyes and tapped her heel against the leg of the chair, hoping that Theo would arrive shortly. Her eyes shot open as the door creaked on its hinges.

Theo strode toward her, his hands in his pockets. He looked especially dapper today in a deep charcoal-tinted blazer and black dress pants, the same suede fedora adorning the top of his head. His lips curled into a half smile as he took a seat, his hands clasped tightly over his knee. "Emery, nice to see you again."

She uncrossed her legs as she leaned forward, her elbows resting on her knees. "I've been trying to reach you. You must be the most popular man in Dormance."

Theo beamed, flattered by her last statement. "Well, that's not entirely true, but thank you. Now, what is it that you would like to discuss? Clearly, from the number of missed messages I received, there's something on your mind."

His brash tone irked her. "I guess you could say that." She took a deep breath. "Four weeks ago. At my house. *You* were there. We had dinner with my family and I need you to tell me why."

Theo raised his eyebrows, amused at her authoritative tone. "Ah, yes. I could tell by your reaction that you were shocked to see me at your house, with your mother and

sister no less." He cleared his throat. "I would apologize for not warning you ahead of time, but
as you know, that's not exactly in my nature."

Emery bit her tongue to keep her retort at bay. Her lips pressed firmly together.

"It was a test," he admitted, shifting his weight in the chair. "An emotional simulation, if you will. You see, we've noticed that lately you've seemed a little . . . out of sorts. Your focus seems to be elsewhere."

Yeah, because I know you're a liar. She swallowed, hoping that he couldn't see the guilt written all over her face. *Focus on the simulation.* "Why did you feel the need to test me?"

"Simple." He cocked his head to the side. "To confirm that we can trust you."

Emery shifted uneasily in her seat, flashing back to every conversation she'd had with Torin. Had they caught on to her? To them?

After a moment of silence, her mind was put at ease. "I saw your break-up with Anthony," Theo confessed. "I know that must have been heart-wrenching for you."

A wave of relief washed over her. They didn't know. This was about Anthony, not Torin.

"Oh, well, I hope you can understand that I don't really feel like talking about it," she said, as the memory resurfaced. "I just want to move forward." Her voice cracked.

"But you're okay?"

Emery nodded her head. "Yes. I'm okay."

"It pleases me to hear that." As he opened his mouth to continue, Naia came through the door.

"Ms. Parker," her voice was sweet, like honey, "are you ready for your next training session?"

Emery couldn't help but cringe at the thought of her last training: bullets grazing her cheek, tearing through her flesh. She cupped her shoulder, remembering the pain from the bullet as it ripped through her skin.

"Before I go to my next training, I have a question about something that happened in my aeris training."

Theo stood from his chair, then motioned for her to continue.

"My uniform," she recalled, "it wasn't bulletproof. The bullets tore right through my skin."

Theo nodded. "I remember. You came out of that training with a nasty shoulder wound." His eyes darkened as he shifted his attention to Naia. "Naia is actually the one in charge of your trainings."

Naia's smile fell. "Please accept my sincerest apologies. A full-scale investigation will be launched to ensure our systems are up to code."

Emery could have sworn she saw a twinkle in Naia's eye. Before she could respond, Theo ushered his assistant out of the room.

"Well, you should be off," he said with a tip of his hat. "I assume you know your way around by now. Good luck." He waved as the door shut quietly behind him.

Emery eyed the hologram from across the room and walked over to it, grabbing her clothes from the coffee table on the way. *Well, that was weird.* She didn't know whether to feel relieved or concerned. Emery gazed at the last line of the schedule. Last but not least, terrae training. What glorious landscape had they conjured up for her this time?

The terrae training room was situated at the far end of the hall. Emery pushed the door open and walked to the center of the room, her padded footsteps the only audible sound in the empty space. Curling and uncurling her fists, she braced herself for whatever simulation was in store. Everything was still as the dark room illuminated, rays of sunshine poking through a vast thicket of trees. It didn't take her long to figure out that she was in a forest.

Emery closed her eyes and breathed in the soothing scent of pine. Nothing happened for a few minutes and it appeared that this training would be more peaceful than her other sessions. But that thought was quickly dispelled from her mind as a dark storm cloud appeared above her, covering the warm rays from the sun. A cool breeze wafted over her, chilling her to the bone. Behind her, a low snarl sounded from the bushes. Emery turned, eyes wide with fear, as the snarling grew louder. Whatever was making the sound wasn't alone. Multiple glowing yellow eyes stared at her from behind the brush.

Run.

She dashed away from the creatures, searching the forest floor for a path that didn't exist. Her arms pumped at her sides as she glanced over her shoulder, trying to catch a glimpse of the beasts. They slithered on the ground behind her, part human, part lion, part . . . snake?

Her legs picked up speed as she faced forward again, her eyes darting back and forth for some sort of safe haven. Caves weren't safe—the creatures would most likely just crawl in there with her. Same with water—snakes could easily slither through a stream. But up high—up high, she might actually stand a chance.

Emery spotted a tree about ten feet away, a thick branch that was low enough for her to hop onto jutting from the side. Rasps of hot breath stung the backs of her legs as she continued to run, her calves on fire from the sensation.

Just a few more steps.

With a giant leap, Emery catapulted herself onto the protruding branch. She grunted as her stomach rammed into the bark, her body dangling over it in a u-shape. The creatures nipped at her shoes, barely missing her big toe. Emery pulled herself up to a standing position, wiping the debris from her shirt as she began to scale the tree, only stopping when she was far enough away from the beasts. When she reached a steady platform of branches, she gazed down at the creatures, faintly recognizing them from a mythology lesson during one of her Latin classes. They looked like manticores—their bodies half lion, half snake with underdeveloped dragon's wings and scorpion's tails. But the most frightening part of all were their heads.

Human heads. With row after row of sharp, dagger-like teeth.

The largest manticore of the pack glared at her from the ground, hissing and snarling at her. Emery pressed her back against the tree, fighting to steady her nerves and catch her breath. *It's not real*, she reminded herself.

She racked her brain for more information on manticores. The words leapt across her mind as if the textbook were right there in front of her. *Like its cousin the Sphinx, manticores often challenge their prey with riddles before killing.*

Emery took a deep breath before looking back down at the swarm of beasts, then whistled, hoping to catch their attention.

It worked.

"Riddle me this," the lead manticore sang, its voice a melody of pipes and trumpets. "The one who makes it sells it. The one who buys it doesn't use it. The one who's using it doesn't know he's using it. What is it?"

I've heard that riddle before.

Emery smiled as she flashed back to when she was a little girl, sitting on her father's lap. Every night her father would read her stories, ending each one with a riddle.

Although she'd been young, she could remember every riddle he'd ever told her. This had been one of them.

"It's a coffin," she called out, her voice raspy from all the running.

The manticores shrieked as her answer hit their ears.

Emery's hands shot up as she tried to block out the shrill noises from below. She squeezed her eyes shut, wishing more than anything that this training would end, when, to her delight, the noises suddenly stopped.

Her eyes shot open. There was nothing but the tops of city buildings for miles. Skyscrapers surrounded her, and she quickly realized that she was at the top of a tree rooted in the middle of a park.

Emery slowly began her descent, her shoes scraping the bark from the tree, calves tingling as they regained feeling. The last branch was only a few feet from the ground, so she hopped down with ease, landing with a soft thud on the grass. There was no sign of life anywhere; the city was completely deserted.

She was alone.

As she dusted her hands off, a small spherical device rolled toward her feet. Unsure what to make of it, Emery knelt down to get a closer look. The device clicked open, showcasing a green capsule situated in between four prongs. Just as she reached out to touch it, the device closed, the green capsule disappearing from sight. A small button on the side of the device caught her eye. Seeing no other option, she pressed it, taking a few steps backward as a precaution.

The sphere shot high up into the air, out of eyesight. Emery waited for a moment, expecting to hear some sort of explosion. There was no sound—but there was a blinding white light and a slight tremor in the ground.

Emery shielded her eyes, falling to her knees as the world around her went white. She blinked a few times, doing everything she could to regain her vision. When she opened them for a third time, a green haze surrounded her.

A figure appeared in the distance.

Emery squinted, trying to make out who it was. The mist wafted over her, through her nostrils and into her lungs, the feeling reminiscent of what had happened during her aeris training. A delicate figure with crimson hair walked toward her.

"Mom?" Emery whispered, barely able to keep her eyes open.

Her mother nodded. "Exarmet," she whispered.

"What?"

"Exarmet."

Emery knew she should try to fight it, to stay awake, but she also knew that there was no coming back from this one. The mist was too enticing. She succumbed and closed her eyes, allowing the green haze to take her away into a heavy sleep.

27

"Tell me one more time."

Theo tapped his fingers against the phone, calculating his answer before responding. "Something's not right. With Emery's trainings."

After her last training in terrae, Theo had debriefed her like he always did. Emery had mentioned again that she'd seen her mother during the simulation, although when he'd asked for more information, Emery had frozen up, then stated she couldn't remember.

Something was off.

"Naia's in charge of her trainings, correct?" President Novak grumbled.

"That is correct. I'm going to have a word with her, sir."

"No," the President interrupted, "you won't. The incompetence in your office is truly baffling. I'll speak to Naia myself."

Theo felt a pang of embarrassment at the President's insult. The last time he'd felt that offended was the first time he and Victor had met which, coincidentally, happened to be during the FCW's election.

The election process was overly competitive, and even though they'd only just met, Victor had attacked Theo's character over and over again, saying that he didn't have what it took to be a successful President. Theo fought tooth and nail, knowing that, in the end, he'd be the one to wave the white flag. The votes were close, but Victor still came out on top, leaving Theo no choice but to run for a position with less power. Fortunately, the votes were in his favor, and he'd been appointed Head Chairman.

So far, his time as Head Chairman had been rewarding. But like everyone else, he was looking to move up. Dormance was becoming more and more disjointed under President Novak's reign. Their strategy for deployment needed to be finalized and fast.

Over the years, Theo had learned that the best way to diffuse a tense situation with the President was to extinguish it—to put fire out with water. Unfortunately, President Novak held the opposing view—to fight fire with fire.

"Just continue to keep an eye on Emery," Victor commanded. "It'd be a shame to see our plans go to waste. You wouldn't want to be the one responsible for that, now would you?"

He rolled his eyes. "No, sir. You have my word."

"Good. Now, while we're on the subject, I'd like to talk about candidate 083. Rhea Alexander."

This statement caught Theo by surprise, seeing as it was the first time Victor had mentioned Rhea since she'd agreed to participate in The Alpha Drive. "What about her, sir?"

"I need you to take Rhea out."

Theo felt his jaw drop. "I'm sorry?"

"Remove her. Disqualify her. Kill her. I don't care how you do it, just make sure it gets done."

Theo hesitated for a moment. "Why?"

"It doesn't matter *why*," Novak snarled. "Just see to it that it gets done."

If there was ever a time to stand up to the President, this was it. Sadly, Theo couldn't bring himself to do it. "Understood, sir."

"Whatever it takes?" Victor pressed, his breath growing louder.

"Whatever it takes."

Before the President could terminate the call, Theo tapped the end button, listening to the sweet silence as the other line went dead.

28

Finally. Spring Break, Emery thought. It was hard to believe that she'd managed to keep on with her daily routine and train for The Alpha Drive with little to no hiccups. From an emotional standpoint, her terrae and aeris trainings had been far less damaging than her ignis and aquam sessions. Even so, Emery couldn't help but feel like she was carrying the weight of the world on her shoulders.

She'd completed each of the landscapes to the best of her abilities and, although Theo hadn't confirmed when the training would end, she figured she had to be close. It was only a matter of time before she found out whether she'd passed or failed. Unfortunately, uncovering even one piece of the Federal Commonwealth's strategy seemed like a farfetched dream that would never come to fruition.

Emery snapped out of her daze and looked over at her roommate, who was busy packing a suitcase for her trip back home.

"Have you seen my straightener?" Rhea asked.

"The last time I saw it, it was in the cupboard underneath the sink."

Rhea opened the compact door, rifling through the disorderly bins of cleaning items and hair supplies. "Aha," she announced, pulling the metallic straightener from the jumbled pile. She threw it into her suitcase and zipped her overstuffed luggage closed.

"Are you sure you don't want me to take you to the airport?" Emery offered for the third time that evening. She wished Rhea would just say yes so that they could move on with their lives.

"It's okay. Really," she insisted.

"Well, how are you getting there? Are you going to call a cab?"

Rhea hesitated. "Actually . . . Mason offered to take me."

Emery stopped what she was doing. This was the first she was hearing of this arrangement and, to be honest, she wasn't too happy about it.

Rhea propped up her suitcase and wheeled it over toward the door.

"Oh," Emery said as she stood up from her chair, "you're leaving now?"

"Yeah, Mason just texted me and told me he was here. We're going to grab a bite to eat first and then he's going to drop me off." Rhea pulled up the handle from the suitcase. "Have a great break," she said hurriedly, blowing a kiss as she opened the door.

Emery waved halfheartedly as Rhea closed the door behind her, the lock turning securely in place.

For the rest of the day, Emery couldn't help but wonder how the interaction between Rhea and Mason had gone. Were their feelings simply platonic, or did they have a deeper connection? Were they secretly dating? She felt her cheeks warm as they blushed a bright shade of pink. *Why do I even care?*

Emery brushed her thoughts aside as she opened her laptop. She needed to busy herself to keep her thoughts from venturing back to Mason and Rhea. Icons on her computer appeared, and she clicked on the one to open her email. As the messages loaded, her thoughts drifted to Torin. Where was he? Why hadn't he reached out to her? There was so much new information he needed to know. *I can't wait any longer.*

Now was as good a time as any. She had to find a way to connect to his phone. The only problem was she had zero knowledge about hacking and coding. That was Torin's territory. He'd always been consistent when it came to reaching out to her, so what had changed?

It was then that fear struck her. Thoughts of Torin being captured, questioned, and tortured entered her mind. Had something terrible happened to him? *Stop thinking like that. He's fine.*

Emery focused on her phone, opening the same screen Torin had when he'd first coded the device. She scrolled through paragraphs of text until she reached the bottom, where it read: Sender Device Disconnected.

A lump formed in her throat. Someone had found them out. But who?

Sighing, Emery dropped the phone into her lap. *There's nothing you can do until he reaches out to you. Focus on something else.*

By ten o'clock that evening, Emery had written down every single conversation with Theo and Torin, and every last detail from her many training sessions. A giant brainstorming plot lay before her, with circle after circle connecting to line after line. There were so many connections, but not enough to make sense of a larger, more complex scheme. Emery tossed her pen down on the paper and threw her head back into her chair. She closed her eyes. *I need a break.*

As if her mind had been read, her phone pinged. Much to her surprise, the message was from Mason. She slid her finger eagerly across the screen, the words, *Plans tonight?* illuminating from her phone like miniature rays of sunshine. She texted him back fervently, asking what he had in mind. He mentioned that he was having a small get-together at his dorm—just a few close friends hanging out.

His timing couldn't have been more perfect.

After she'd changed clothes, Emery decided to take a detour and stroll down Alpha Drive on the way to Mason's dorm. Her eyes landed on the Sychem building. The door was wide open and, while she couldn't make sense of it, something told her to go inside. Unable to shake the feeling, she decided to follow her gut.

Emery made her way inside, passing through the deserted courtyard and into the Sychem common room. Her eyes scanned the area for some kind of sign—something to signal that she was *supposed* to be there, that it wasn't all in her head—but there was nothing.

Feeling foolish, Emery walked around the perimeter of the room, slowly making her way to the center. Her foot caught on a rug as it brushed over a slight bulge. She flipped the rug over to find a trap door staring back at her. With wide eyes, she pulled it open as dust particles swarmed the air around her. Below, propped against the wall, was an iron ladder that was at least twenty feet long.

Without a second thought, Emery cautiously climbed down the ladder until she was close enough to the ground. Her feet landed with a soft thud as her eyes attempted to focus in the dim lighting. The hallway before her was frighteningly familiar. Her breath caught
as the realization hit her.

It was the same hallway from her dreams.

Emery crept down the corridor, pinching herself to make sure she was awake. A reflection caught her eye, just like in her dream. *It can't be.* But there it was.

The horseshoe-shaped pendant.

She hesitated before plucking the pendant from the wall. If things went according to her dream . . . there'd be a scream and then a gunshot. Emery froze, paralyzed with fear. Then waited. And waited. But there was nothing.

No scream. No gunshot.

Emery hurried back to the ladder, climbing it as fast as her arms would allow. She ran through the courtyard, looking behind her shoulder every few steps. After what felt like forever, she finally made it outside. She stood in front of Sychem, the pendant dangling from her fingertips.

Emery had no idea what it was or why she'd dreamt about it, but for some reason, it felt like she'd been meant to find it. With the pendant secured around her neck and tucked underneath the front of her shirt, Emery picked up her pace and jogged the rest of the way to Mason's dorm, wanting to get as far away from Sychem as possible.

Scribner Hall appeared to be much newer than Rosemary Hall. The exterior was painted grey and rose to as high as six floors. Four small turrets stood atop each corner and, best of all, there were elevators. Emery couldn't help but smile to herself as she thought about the secret elevators at Rosemary Hall. Her hand rose to her neck as she checked one more time to make sure the pendant was out of sight, then stepped inside the metal box and rode it to the fifth floor.

As Emery inched closer to the door, a gold **5B** staring her in the face, her nerves heightened. She raised her hand to knock on the door then lowered it, noticing it was slightly ajar. Her hand rested on the knob as she pushed her way through the door.

A few people in the living room looked up at her from their bean bag chairs, video game controllers in hand. She smiled and gave an awkward wave before introducing herself, then made her way into the bedroom, where most of the noise was coming from. More bean bags sat on the floor in front of a giant, flat screen television. Two guys sat in the chairs, pounding on their controllers, while two more stood in the back, cheering them on.

Emery glanced to her right, noticing another guy who had his back to her. He was sitting at a desk, messing with the sound system, his shaggy, blonde hair peeking out from underneath his baseball cap. The guys were so focused on their game that they didn't even notice as Emery walked right in front of the television.

Mason turned to face her as she patted his shoulder, a big grin spreading across his face. "You made it," he said as he opened his arms for a hug. "I wasn't sure you were going to come."

"Of course I came," Emery replied, wishing that their hug had lasted a little while longer.

"Let me introduce you to everyone." He grabbed her hand and led her out of the room, giving brief introductions as they made their way to the kitchen. Mason opened a refrigerator chock full of root beer and orange soda. "Pick your poison."

"Orange soda," she said as he tossed her a can. She caught it with ease, then followed him back into the bedroom.

"Emery and I call next game," Mason asserted.

"What are you guys playing?" Emery asked through an eruption of cheers.

Mason laughed. "It's a combat simulation game. We can be on a team. We just need to shoot the players on the other team to win."

Emery nodded as she watched the remainder of the battle. She'd played video games as a kid, but it'd been years since she'd picked up a controller.

"Your turn," a lanky guy said as he handed her a controller.

As soon as the landscape loaded, it was complete chaos. It took her a minute to get used to the bulky controller and numerous buttons, but eventually she found herself moving around the horizon with ease. Their audience cheered as they shot members on the enemy team, their scores rising with each kill. They finished the first game, undefeated, then moved on to the next one. It felt like the entire room was on an endless sugar-high and, as nerdy as she felt playing video games, Emery couldn't deny that she was actually having fun.

A few hours and couple of orange sodas later, Emery felt a familiar sensation. The screen grew fuzzy as black dots clouded her vision and her hands grew shaky. She quickly excused herself and made her way toward the restroom. Closing the door behind her, she sat down on the lid of the toilet, her head swaying lightly in her hands. It only took a moment for her to ascertain that sitting didn't make her feel any better—it actually made things worse.

Her mouth went dry as her microchip began to buzz, causing the hairs on her neck to rise. This was all too familiar. She'd had this exact same feeling when she'd gone out with Rhea on Alpha Drive, right before . . .

Right before she'd met Torin.

It's him, she thought through her haze. *Torin's trying to reach out to me*. Her chip continued to buzz as she lay there on the floor. "I'm here," she croaked, her vision fading in and out. "Torin, I'm here."

Another excruciating five minutes went by until the buzzing started to subside. Emery opened her eyes, her vision restoring itself back to normal. Feeling stable enough to stand, she grasped the edge of the sink and pulled herself up, then rinsed her mouth with water. *I need to eat something.*

Emery pulled open the door to the bathroom, then headed to the kitchen to scrounge for food. Mason's dorm was much quieter than it had been twenty minutes prior. Emery stumbled through the deserted living room into the kitchen, pulling a bag of chips from the pantry. They crunched as she popped them into her month. Sensing that someone was watching her, she whirled around.

Mason stood directly in front of her. "Hungry?"

Emery swallowed the remnants before answering. "Yeah, I sort of . . . raided your pantry."

He grinned. "My bad. I should have ordered a pizza or at least put out some chips." He shook his head. "I'm a terrible host."

She smiled, feeling innately comfortable in his presence. "So, where did everyone go?"

He tilted his head. "They left," he answered as he made his way into the living room and plopped down onto the couch, kicking his feet up on the coffee table. He patted the seat next to him, so Emery followed, leaning her head back into the cushy, leather seat.

"Are you okay?" Mason asked.

Emery turned to look at him. "Yeah, why do you ask?"

Mason blushed. "I noticed that you disappeared for a little there. I hope we didn't bore you too much."

"Oh, that's not it at all," she laughed. "I actually had a lot of fun. Thanks for inviting me." She paused, not sure whether to tell him about what had just happened. "Hey, do you remember that first night when . . . well, when you helped get me back to my dorm?"

Mason nodded. "I remember it well. Why?"

"Well, I just had something similar happen, so if I seem a little out of it, that's why."

"Are you sure you're okay?" he asked again, his forehead wrinkling with concern. "You were basically unconscious that night, so I need you to tell me if you start to feel like that again."

Emery waved her hand dismissively. "No, I'm okay. I'm pretty sure it's passed."

"Well, only if you're sure," he said with a smile. "Hey, I'm going to clean up a little."

"I'll help," she offered.

Mason tossed her a trash bag as Emery cleared the coffee table of remaining debris in one fell swoop, the cans and cups sliding into the oversized bag. She bent down to pick up some more cans from the floor, but as she stood up, the room began to spin around her. *Not again.*

Small black dots reappeared, her ears ringing with an unpleasant tone. She frantically searched for Mason, but he'd left the room, so she stumbled into the nearest bedroom and collapsed onto a bed. Floating in and out of consciousness, she laid there, hoping that he would stumble in on her sooner rather than later.

29

Mason heard a thunk as he tossed the last of the trash into the overflowing garbage bag. Gently setting the bag against the couch, he strolled over to the source of the noise, finding himself standing in the doorway to his bedroom. There was Emery, lying face up in what appeared to be a very uncomfortable position, knees bent over the bedframe, her head turned to the side as if she'd hit it against the wall on the way down. He rushed to her side and kneeled onto the carpet, grabbing her wrist to check for a pulse.

"She's still breathing," he muttered to himself. Trying to ignore the feeling of déjà vu on Alpha Drive earlier that year, he did the first thing that came to his mind and darted to the bathroom, pulling a washcloth from the overhead cabinet. He ran the washcloth under cool water, folding it into a rectangular shape on the way back to the bedroom.

Mason moved her hair to the side and laid the washcloth on her forehead, checking to make sure she was still breathing. He watched her chest move slowly up and down, her mouth exhaling small wisps of air.

Ten minutes later, her eyes fluttered open, a pool of grey staring up at him. He could tell she was trying to focus, so he sat back a little to allow her eyes to adjust.

"Whoa," she breathed as she slowly brought herself upright. "How long was I out for?"

"Not too long, I don't think. I came as soon as I heard the noise. It sounded like you fell."

Emery looked over her shoulder, observing her surroundings as if she'd never been there before. "At least I fell on the bed," she cracked, trying to make light of the situation.

"Do you want water or food or anything? Do you feel nauseous?" He bit his tongue. *'Atta boy, bombard her with questions.*

Emery smiled gratefully. "I actually feel fine. I just think I need to rest."

Mason took a moment to really look at her. Her hair was disheveled and tangled. Drops of sweat lingered along her hairline. And her mascara was smudged underneath her eyes. Even so, she was still beautiful.

As he drew closer to her, he could feel her warm breath on his face, her eyelashes fluttering against his cheek. Before he could process what was happening, he found himself in a passionate embrace, her lips locked tightly with his.

Mason slid his fingers through her hair, not once breaking contact with her soft, supple lips. As if their bodies were one, they laid down on the bed, heads resting gently against the pillow. She broke away for a moment, looked at him, and smiled. He smiled back and lightly kissed her on the forehead.

A soft exhale escaped her lips as she moved closer to him, her legs intertwined with his, head resting in the nook between his chest and shoulder. They laid there in silence for a few minutes. Mason watched as her chest rose and fell ever so calmly. He fought to stay awake, the sweet smell of lavender consuming his senses, until his eyelids felt so heavy that they closed, where he could finally surrender to this perfect moment.

30

The sound of birds chirping outside wasn't the worst way to wake up. A strip of sunlight shone brightly against Emery's eyelids. She rustled the covers over her face and pressed her ear against the pillow in order to block the incessant piping from outside. As she reached to put her hand under the pillow, she realized that the sheets felt unfamiliar.

Emery shot up immediately, the pendant bouncing on her chest. Feeling alarmed, she wrapped the sheet around herself, even though she was fully dressed. She blinked rapidly, hoping that her contacts would shift back into place. Her nerves calmed as she browsed her surroundings, the events from last night flooding back to her. *I'm at Mason's.*

She walked into the dark kitchen, noticing that the door to the bathroom was open, but Mason was nowhere in sight. A bout of nausea hit her as she opened the refrigerator. One last water bottle was tucked into a small crevice in the very back. She grabbed it and took a giant gulp, her hand resting on a wrinkled piece of paper on the counter. The handwriting was barely legible, but she could manage to make out what it said: *Come to 6E when you wake up.*

After brushing her teeth with her finger, Emery grabbed one of Mason's jackets from his closet and trekked upstairs to room 6E. The door was ajar, a dank, musty smell coming from inside. Before entering, she paused to get her thoughts in order.

I kissed Mason.

While Emery was familiar with *friend* Mason, *more-than-friend* Mason was completely new territory.

A sensory overload of moldy pizza hit her as she entered the apartment. Her hand flew over her nose immediately as she made her way through the living room. There was Mason, sitting on a bean bag, grumbling at the TV and beating his video game controller to death. *More video games?* There were two other guys in the room, although she couldn't distinguish whether or not she'd met them the night before.

Well, this is awkward.

She waved. "Good morning."

Mason diverted his attention from the car crash on the screen. "Morning," he chirped, gesturing to the empty seat beside him. "I see you found my jacket."

Emery blushed and made her way over to the empty seat next to him. Mason leaned back into the bean bag, a yawn escaping from his mouth. She knew she shouldn't feel uncomfortable, but for some reason, she did. Didn't he want to talk about last night? She gave him a weak smile, then asked, "Do you want to get breakfast?"

Mason's eyes lit up as he dropped the controller. "You read my mind. I'm starving."

+ + +

It was the last day of Spring Break and Emery couldn't believe everything that had happened. Her friendship with Mason was blossoming into something more, and at a frightening speed. They'd spent almost every day together—going out to dinner, seeing movies, and even attending their first concert together. Each rendezvous had been better than the last. As much as she tried to suppress her feelings for him, she couldn't deny that they were growing with each passing day.

But she knew that this was dangerous territory.

Emery couldn't help but feel like she was betraying Rhea. Even though Rhea had made it abundantly clear that she wasn't looking for anything serious, Mason still felt somewhat off-limits. Yet here she was, hanging out with him, wanting to spending time with him, *falling* for him.

Rhea appeared as the door creaked open, her purse

overflowing with magazines, water bottles, and partially opened pretzel bags. Emery rushed from her desk to help her, propping her foot against the door. Rhea scuffled inside and dropped her enormous bag on the floor, her suitcase waddling crookedly behind her. She grunted as she fell into her desk chair and pulled out her phone without even so much as a glance at Emery.

Emery cleared her throat. "Hey, you're back. How was your break?"

"It was fine," Rhea responded, eyes still glued to her phone.

Emery shifted her weight from one foot to the other. "Oh, that's good. I thought you wouldn't be back until later tonight. I would have picked you up."

"It's fine."

Why is she being so short with me? "If you don't mind me asking, who picked you up from the airport?"

Rhea looked up at her with an annoyed expression. "I took a cab."

She sounds bitter. "You should have called me."

Silence.

It was clear that Rhea wanted to be left alone, but that was nearly impossible to do when they lived together in such a small space.

After a few minutes, Rhea finally broke the silence. "Actually, Mason was supposed to come get me, but he told me he was busy." Her eyes hardened as she scowled.

"With you."

Emery froze in position, speechless.

"So," Rhea said as she crossed her arms, "is there something you'd like to tell me?"

31

Emery and Mason sat in silence across from each other at the Dorsey Hall café. After spilling to Rhea, Emery immediately called Mason.

"So, Rhea's mad. I mean, really mad," Emery sighed. "She says that I *took* you from her."

Mason shook his head, his finger tracing the crooked lines on the wooden tabletop. "No one took anything from anybody," he reassured, even though his own voice was lined with guilt.

"Rhea said that I betrayed her and that friends don't betray each other." She shrugged. "So, in her mind, I guess that means we're not friends anymore."

"I've known Rhea for years. She'll come around. It's just the sting of a new relation—err—whatever this is," he stuttered, looking down at his hands.

Emery hesitated, not sure what to say. *What are we? Friends? More than friends?*

Mason reached out, taking both of Emery's hands into his. They were warm and inviting, his skin smooth and uncalloused. "Listen, I like you and I don't care what anyone else thinks. I want to make this work." He took a deep breath. "Emery Parker, will you do me the honor of being my girlfriend?"

Images of Anthony and her failed relationship immediately flooded Emery's mind, whirling her into a state of panic. She flashed back to when Anthony had first asked her to be his girlfriend. Every year at her public school, the dance department held a fall concert. After practice one day, when they were both in the trainer's room, she'd invited him. "I'll be there," he'd said. But Emery hadn't taken his promise to heart. She'd learned a long time ago that having high expectations meant constantly being disappointed. But Anthony had shown up. At the end of the evening, he'd walked her outside and told her to close her eyes. When she opened them, two dozen vibrant, red roses stared her in the face.

"Will you be my girlfriend?" he'd asked.

The memory faded as Emery looked at Mason. All she could envision was the look on Anthony's face—the look when he'd stared her square in the eye and hadn't recognized her. A one-year relationship wiped from the mind of the one person who'd known her on an intimate level. It was almost as if she had a clean slate.

The only problem is I didn't ask for one.

Emery knew that the time for grieving was over. In order to move forward, she had to move past Anthony. But it terrified her knowing that Mason could, at any moment, see the chip and fail to remember her. Or that she could be deployed at any second without warning. Was it worth the risk?

Emery pulled her hands to her lap and shook her head. "I'm sorry, Mason. I really like you, but I'm just not ready. After everything that happened with Anthony . . . it's still so fresh—"

"Of course," Mason interrupted. "I'm sorry. It was a stupid question."

Emery grimaced. "It wasn't a stupid question at all. I'm flattered. Really, I am."

Mason let out a nervous laugh. "Let's just forget about it. Still friends?"

"Yes," Emery nodded. "Still friends."

Mason gave a half smile, then glanced down at his watch to check the time. "So, do friends still go to the movies together?"

Emery's heart fluttered. She'd just shot him down, yet here he was, being a complete gentleman. It made her like him even more. "They certainly do."

Mason scooted back his chair and picked up their coffee cups. As he walked to the trashcan, Emery couldn't help but notice how his shoulders slumped. She felt terrible, but throwing herself into a new relationship at a time like this wasn't the answer. *It's for the best*, she told herself as she followed him out the door.

But try as she might, her heart just wouldn't agree.

32

There was no denying it. Rhea was a wildcard. *How do I take out a wildcard?* Theo thought as he slid his chair over to the control station.

A few options sprang to mind. He could go the vindictive route and have an Alpha Drive participant turn on Rhea. Or he could go the easy route and inject something into her bloodstream via her microchip. Or both.

Decisions, decisions.

Theo rummaged through the drawers of the main station, searching for any remaining syringes of lethargum. While its main use was to render subjects unconscious, at a high enough dose rate, lethargum was lethal. As much as he didn't want to kill Rhea, Theo didn't dare disobey the President's orders, or else his head would be next on the chopping block.

To his delight, he found a syringe filled with the bright green liquid tucked in the very back of the cabinet. He readied the syringe as he pulled up Rhea's file, injecting the serum into the machine.

An unexpected reflection appeared on the holoscreen. Naia stood behind him with crossed arms, a disappointed look on her face. "What do you think you're doing?" she questioned as she took a step closer.

"That's really none of your concern," Theo responded, hiding the syringe from sight.

Naia tilted her head as she surveyed the file on screen. "I see you're interested in participant 083, Ms. Rhea Alexander." She gave a wry smile. "And seeing as I run the training simulations around here, yes, I do think it is of my concern."

Theo gritted his teeth. "I will only say this one time. You need to leave."

Naia shook her head with a soft chuckle. "I'm not leaving until you tell me what's going on."

Theo stood from his chair. "You can't get involved. President's orders," he lied.

Naia narrowed her eyes as her mouth pressed into a firm line. "We'll see about that." She turned on her heel to leave, then stopped to face him again. "Oh, and Theo? Don't do anything stupid."

Theo watched Naia as she stormed out of the room, the empty syringe sitting idly on the seat of his chair.

Too late.

33

I've had enough, Emery thought as she looked over at her roommate. Rhea sat at her desk with her head thrown back, music blaring from her headphones. They'd hardly spoken in days and the tension between them was only getting worse.

It was time to put her foot down.

Emery waved her hand across Rhea's line of vision, watching as her roommate popped the neon-pink buds from her ears.

"What?" she barked.

"I know you're still upset with me, and you have every right to be," Emery paused, "but enough is enough."

Rhea scoffed and inserted the buds back into her ears.

Emery grabbed the cord and threw it onto the floor. "Listen, we only have one month of school left. One. I don't want to end on a bad note," she implored. *I've already lost Anthony—I can't lose Rhea too.*

Rhea stood up, looking her square in the eye. "You know, I would have expected betrayal from anyone else, but not you."

If it weren't for her blurry contact lenses, Emery could have sworn she saw a small tear form at the corner of Rhea's eye. A pang of guilt hit her as she looked at her roommate. Deep down, all either of them wanted was to forget the lies and the betrayals and go back to being friends. Unfortunately, it was starting to feel like they'd never get back to that point.

"Rhea, he asked me to be his girlfriend, but I said no," Emery repeated for what felt like the thousandth time. "Mason and I aren't dating. Seriously, what more do you want me to do?"

Rhea seemed to consider this. "I don't know. It just feels like I can't really trust you. And that's hard for me."

"I know," Emery whispered. "I'm sorry. Just tell me how to fix it."

"Even though you guys aren't dating, it seems like you still hang out a lot."

There was no denying this because it was the truth. Emery and Mason *did* still hang out, but just as friends. Why couldn't Rhea see that?

"Let me guess," Rhea chided. "You two are hanging out tonight?"

Emery felt her cheeks burn with embarrassment. *Guilty.* "We're just going to the Darden mixer to check out which clubs we want to sign up for next year." *If there even is a next year.* "You should come."

"And hang out with you and Mason?" Rhea sneered. "No thanks, I think I'll pass."

That was it. Emery had reached her breaking point. If Rhea wanted to be stubborn, then so be it. It was no use getting hung up on it. It's not like Dormance was real anyway.

That evening, Rhea left a few minutes before Emery did. She didn't mention where she was going, and Emery didn't even bother to ask. At a time like this, it was best to just give Rhea space and hope for the best. Things had a funny way of working themselves out. Eventually.

Emery met up with Mason across campus, just outside the Student Union. Darden's end-of-year-mixer was a chance for current students and prospective students to visit different club booths and converse with the various members. While the Darden administration saw it as a networking opportunity, most students saw it as an advantage to skip out on homework.

Bus after bus was lined up outside the building. Emery recognized a few of the school names, feeling disheartened when she didn't spot her old school. A part of her hoped that Riley would be there, but it looked like her old school wasn't participating this year.

Mason and Emery walked into the Student Union, the halls already buzzing with chatter. At least thirty booths were scattered along the hall, their brightly colored banners hanging behind the tables. Emery wasn't paying attention and accidentally bumped into Mason's back, who had stopped dead in his tracks. He whirled around with an alarmed look on his face. "Oh, this isn't good."

Emery tried to look over his shoulder to see what had gotten him so riled up, but he straightened his posture to block her view. "What's going on?" she asked, trying to keep the gnawing feelings of worry at bay.

"Do you really need to know?"

Emery rolled her eyes. "Yes, I do. How bad can it be?"

"Well, for starters, my ex-girlfriend is here," he muttered, trying not to make a scene.

Emery knew this shouldn't bother her, but it did. "Where?"

Mason cocked his head toward a tall girl with strawberry blonde hair and freckled cheeks. She watched as the girl tossed her head back in a fit of laughter. As if she could sense that someone was watching her, the girl made eye contact with Emery, her glowing smile fading into a grim line. The girl called out to Mason, beckoning him to come to her.

Emery was aware of some of the history between Cadence and Mason. Cadence was completely self-absorbed and spoiled—anything she wanted she got—

including one of Mason's closest friends. Mason had caught her one summer, red-handed in a cheating scandal, but even so, Cadence found the nerve to dump him right then and there.

Out of respect for Mason, Emery stepped in front of him and marched over to where Cadence was standing. When she was no more than a foot away, she extended her hand assertively. "I'm Emery."

The girl glared at her under flawlessly full, arched eyebrows. "Cadence," she drawled, her voice dripping with arrogance.

"I know how you treated Mason," Emery said, her voice lowering, "and I want you to stay away from him."

Cadence's lips curled into a demonic smile. "How cute. Mason has you fighting his battles for him." She snarled. "I wouldn't get too comfortable if I were you. He always comes back."

Emery gave her a look of disgust before turning on her heel. She grabbed Mason by the arm, then led him down another hallway, trying to get as far away from Cadence as humanly possible. But even after two hours, Mason still wouldn't let go of the encounter. Emery drowned him out for what felt like the hundredth time, scanning the hallway for an exit strategy.

"I guess I just don't understand why—"

"I'm ready to leave," Emery interrupted. "I'm exhausted and all we seem to be focusing on is Cadence.

We haven't even stopped by any of the booths. This whole thing is pointless."

Mason shut his mouth mid-sentence. "Fine. Let's go then," he said as he stormed toward the door.

They walked in silence the rest of the way, arriving at Scribner Hall fifteen minutes later. The silence had been unbearable, but what happened next was ten times worse.

"I can't believe you just approached my ex like that," he muttered.

Emery look at him with wide eyes. "Really? What was I supposed to do? She looked straight at us."

"You should have just ignored her."

"No," Emery shook her head. "I shouldn't have. She deserves to know that what she did was wrong." She could feel her anger rising. "Why does it even matter? Do you still have feelings for her?"

"Of course not," Mason scoffed. "And even if I did, why would you care? It's not like you want to be with me either."

The words cut into her like a knife. "It's not like that. I already told you," she sighed, "I'm just not ready yet."

When he didn't answer, Emery sighed. His silence made the decision for her. "Look, I'm just gonna go."

"No, don't go," he begged, the bold, brash man she'd just witnessed fading from sight. "I'm sorry. Just stay. Please."

Emery hesitated, her hand on the doorknob. "Fine. But I'm still mad." She followed him into the living room, taking a seat on the opposite end of the couch. Her eyelids fluttered as she yawned and, just as she was about to doze off, an unfamiliar ping sounded throughout the room.

Mason leaned forward to pick up his phone from the coffee table.

"Who is it?"

Mason scooted closer to her and squeezed her arm, as if to apologize in advance for what he was about to say. "It's Cadence."

Emery clenched her jaw and squeezed her eyes shut. "What did she say?"

"It's not important," Mason assured. "Let's just forget about it."

Emery was surprised at how smoothly her response left her mouth. "Mason, we're friends. And as friends, we're not going to hide anything from each other anymore. Tell me what she said."

Mason groaned, but gave in, knowing there wasn't any way out of it. "She said . . . she said that she's still in love with me."

"Of course she did," Emery murmured, feeling too emotionally drained to express a higher level of anger.

"I'm blocking her number right now," he said, his fingers striking the screen rapidly.

"You don't have to do that."

"I know. But I want to." He finished updating the settings on his phone, then set it down on the coffee table.

More buzzing sounded, this time from the inside of her purse. Emery pulled out her phone with a confused expression. Even though it was a restricted number, she decided to answer.

"Hello?"

"Yes, is this Emery Parker?" a morose voice asked.

"This is she. May I ask whose calling?"

"This is Judy, calling from the Phoenix Hospital."

Emery's heart dropped.

"We have Rhea Alexander here in what appears to be a concussion. We need you to get here immediately to—"

But Emery was already halfway out the door.

Twenty minutes later, Emery arrived at the hospital. She whipped her car into the closest available parking space and hurried inside. As expected for afterhours on a Friday, the waiting room was swamped. She bolted toward the front desk, hands shaking, trying to get a nurse's attention without seeming too irrational.

"Can I help you?" a slender woman in blue scrubs asked.

"I just received a phone call from a woman at this hospital," Emery said through hurried breaths. "Her name was Judy. She said my friend, Rhea Alexander, suffering from a concussion."

The woman punched the keys on her computer, clicking the mouse incessantly before responding. "Ah, yes. Emery Parker, I presume?"

She nodded.

"You're her emergency contact. One moment please."

Emery looked at her as if she'd just been hit by a freight train. *I'm* *Rhea's emergency contact?* As if she couldn't feel any lower, she sank a few more feet, like someone had tied her to an anchor and thrown her overboard to drown.

The nurse returned with another woman who had a shiny, plastic name tag on her left breast pocket, the name **JUDY** printed in neat block letters.

"I need you to fill out some paperwork," Judy said, as she handed Emery a clipboard. "Once you're finished, I'll take you back to see her."

A glimmer of hope passed through her thoughts. "She's awake?"

"No," the nurse managed as nicely as she could, "but we need you to verify that it's her."

Emery gasped. "She's not dead, is she?"

"No, Ms. Parker. She's still breathing." She motioned toward the nearest chair. "Please. Have a seat and fill out the forms. I'll be back momentarily."

Emery clutched the clipboard, her knuckles turning white as she sat down. Her phone began to ping nonstop with messages from Mason. She shut it off to keep the only sane part of her brain from exploding.

She scribbled Rhea's information as quickly as she could, doing her best to ensure her writing was legible. When she finished, Emery shot up from her seat and bolted back over to the receptionist's desk. She spotted Judy and waved the clipboard, summoning the nurse to come her way.

"The doctor has one more test to run," Judy explained. "I'll come get you when it's okay to head back there."

Emery returned to her seat, not sure what to do in a situation like this. She didn't have Rhea's parents' phone numbers and, even if she did, she wasn't sure it was a smart idea to call them just yet. Of course, any parent would want to know if their child was in the hospital, but Emery couldn't bear to deliver bad news. She knew that now wasn't the time to be selfish, but it seemed wise to wait until she had more information at her disposal.

Thirty minutes went by with no news. Emery sat on the edge of her seat, drumming her fingertips against the cold, metal armrests. She peered around the hospital for any sign of Judy. The gold plated clock above her read one o'clock in the morning.

Footsteps sounded from the opposite end of the hall. Emery jumped up when she realized it was Judy.

"We're ready for you," Judy stated, placing her hand gently on Emery's shoulder.

She followed the nurse back to one of the rooms, stopping just outside number 103. She took a deep breath and forced herself to look through the window. There lay Rhea, lifeless, in a crisp, freshly laundered hospital gown. An oxygen mask covered her nose and mouth, and her arms were dotted with IV needles. An empty bag was hooked to one of the stands by her bed, and Emery realized it must be for a catheter. She quickly wiped a tear from her eye as she turned to face the nurse.

"The doctor is unable to determine the cause of Rhea's episode. We'll need to run more tests. She's stable, for now, but still unconscious."

"Episode? What episode?"

Judy cleared her throat. "Rhea appears to have had some sort of seizure."

Oh my god. "When will she wake up?"

"We can't know for sure," Judy coaxed. "Whenever you're ready to go in, feel free. I'll be just down the hall."

Emery smiled bleakly as Judy gave her a reassuring pat on the shoulder. She watched as the nurse walked down the brightly lit corridor, then turned her attention back to Rhea, her eyes clouding with tears. She opened the door to the room and grabbed a tissue from the nearest counter. A low beeping noise was the only thing signaling that Rhea was still alive. It was barely audible, but without it, it'd be easy to mistake her for dead.

Emery shut the door behind her and slid down against it, her bottom lip quivering uncontrollably. She squeezed her eyes shut as she sobbed into a tissue.

This was all her fault.

She should have asked Rhea where she'd planned on going earlier that day. Even a partially decent friend would have done that.

Emery continued to cry as she scooted closer to the bed. Rhea's hand was cold and clammy, but she didn't care. She laced her roommate's fingers with her own and laid her head on the blanket, her eyes stinging from the salty tears.

"Rhea," she whispered, "I know you can't hear me, but I want to tell you that I'm so, so sorry." She sniffled before continuing. "I promise to be a better friend and I'll never let something like this happen to you again." She placed her hand on Rhea's cheek, gently caressing her pale skin with her index finger. She could have sworn she felt Rhea's body shudder, but it was just a figment of her imagination—her hopeful, delusional imagination.

Rhea was in a coma within a comatose world. And she didn't even know it. *Well, isn't that something.*

Emery moved her hand delicately from Rhea's cheek to her disheveled hair. She brushed a stray strand from her roommate's face. Even though she was unconscious, the expression on her face was eerily peaceful.

Just as Emery was about to grab another tissue, she noticed an odd glow on the pillow. She touched the striped fabric near Rhea's neck, determined to figure out where it was coming from. Her curiosity loomed as she caressed the back of Rhea's head, her fingers outlining a small square above the nape of her neck. Emery moved her fingers over the lumpy skin once more, just to be sure.

No, it can't be.

Yet there it was, tucked behind piles of dark auburn hair, in the same place Emery had hers.

The microchip.

34

Two weeks of coding, and a whole lot of nothing. *I'm screwed,* Torin thought to himself. His suspension period was locked in at sixty days, and it was horrifying to think that by the time he'd be reinstated, the Federal Commonwealth could have already attacked. Time was of the essence and, for that reason, waiting around, twiddling his thumbs, just wouldn't do.

Even though he'd recreated the code as best he could from memory, it always seemed to be a line or two off. Each time he tried to connect to Emery's phone, crickets greeted him on the other end. He hadn't slept in days—this last stint had him at seventy-two hours—but he was determined to crack it. He didn't have a choice.

He'd tried connecting to her microchip and, just when he thought he may have gotten through, the power went out. He'd cursed the spring thunderstorm, knowing that if he'd been at his office at 7S Headquarters, the back-up generators would have kicked on to save the day.

But he had no such luck. Because he was *suspended*.

With a yawn, Torin adjusted the final line of code, his fifty-ninth try that evening. It was getting harder and harder to keep his eyes open. "Let's give it a go," he muttered to himself. He squeezed his eyes shut as the connection started up.

Four beeps. He had to make it through four beeps to connect with her. Torin opened his eyes, tapping his foot against the ground.

One beep.

He glanced at the virtual monitor, waiting impatiently for the next one.

Second beep.

Torin drew himself closer to the screen.

Third beep.

This was it. Just one more beep.

He rolled his neck, the joints cracking loudly from the motion.

Come on, come on.

Another moment of silence, and then it came.

BEEP.

Torin tugged on his earlobe, not sure if he'd actually heard a beep, or if his half-dream state was playing tricks on him. But, clear as day, an image of Emery's dorm room filled the screen.

"Yes, yes, yes," he muttered as her face popped up in front of him. She was even more beautiful than he remembered. Her eyes were wet, as if she'd been crying, and it was then he remembered Rhea. *I'm too late.*

"Emery, oh no. Are you okay?"

She shook her head as another tear slid down her cheek.

Torin noticed that the other side of her dorm room was completely cleared out. Empty. It confirmed his thoughts. *Rhea's gone.* "Tell me what happened."

"Something happened to Rhea. She was rushed to the hospital. When I went there, I accidentally saw her chip." Her bottom lip quivered. "And now she's gone."

Torin sat back in his chair, wishing more than anything that he could comfort her in person.

"I didn't even get to say goodbye." A loud sob escaped from her throat.

"Oh, Emery, I'm so sorry. What can I do?"

She sniffled into a tissue as she blew her nose. "Just take my mind off of Rhea. Please. I need to think about anything but her and what a terrible friend I am."

"Okay. Um, well, for starters," Torin stuttered, "I was suspended from 7S. So that's been great."

Emery's eyes widened. "You're suspended? For how long?"

"Six more weeks," Torin sighed. "But, the good news is while I've been trying to reach you, I've also been working on hacking into the 7S system to regain access. Once I figure that out, I can enter the building again and the system will recognize me as an active employee."

Emery wiped her eyes. "About that . . . I'm starting to think that I'm not cut out for this."

Torin shifted in his seat as he brought the hologram closer to his face. "Don't say that. We can do this. We've already come so far."

"I don't know, Torin," she sighed. "Look at everything that's happened. Anthony's memory has been erased and now Rhea's gone." She sniffled. "I can't lose anyone else."

He nodded as her words sunk in. "But isn't that more of a reason to fight?"

Emery raised her head. "I'm not sure I follow."

"Maybe, if we defeat the FCW and deactivate Dormance, we can bring their memories back. Maybe it's not a lost cause," Torin suggested.

A glimmer of hope crossed Emery's face. "Do you really think so?"

Torin nodded. "I do. So, what do you say? Are you in?"

Emery nodded as she took a deep breath. "You're right. I won't let them win."

"You're right about that," he said with a smile. "Okay, we have a lot to catch up on. How about you take me through what's happened since the last time we talked?"

He pulled up a schematic of the Federal Commonwealth's underground quarters, a document he'd sent to his personal computer before he was apprehended. He figured it would come in handy.

Emery eyed the schematic, recognizing the common room, and pointed out where the rest of the training rooms were. He switched the schematic to edit mode, then drew them in.

Emery's eyes followed the movement of the stylus. "I haven't had the opportunity to walk through the corridors yet, so I have no idea what else is down there."

"That's okay," Torin said as he finished his edits. "Tell me again about your training."

"Well, my first training was aquam, where I almost drowned to death. My mother was floating at the bottom of the sea and was holding an orange capsule." She shuddered, thinking back to her mother's lifeless body. "My second training was ignis, where I had to save my best friend from burning to death even though some voice told me not to. Come to think of it, she was also holding a capsule."

"An orange one?"

Emery shook her head. "No, it was green."

"Hmm." Torin tapped his stylus against the table, waiting for her to continue.

"In aeris, I could fly. I dodged bullets that came at me from every direction. A green mist filled the room—at least, I think it did. I can't remember because I ended up blacking out. And in terrae . . ." her voice drifted off, her concentration fading.

"Go on," he urged. "What happened in terrae?"

Emery sighed as her head fell into her hands. "I was in shifting landscapes. First, I was in a forest, running from some genetically mutated animals I'd never seen before." She paused. "Well, that's not entirely true—they were manticores. I learned about them in my Latin class. To escape, I had to answer a riddle."

"Then what?"

"After that, I was in a city where a bomb went off. The same green mist filled the air and I passed out."

"The Seventh Sanctum Headquarters are in a city," Torin thought out loud, looking for any plausible connection he could find. "Did the city look like Chicago?"

Emery crinkled her nose. "Honestly, I don't know. All cities kind of look the same."

"Did you see the Chicago Bean?"

She shrugged. "I wasn't looking."

"Well, do you know what kind of bomb it was?"

"I don't know. The kind that kills you?" she retorted.

He pressed his mouth into a firm line. "Emery, I know you're upset, but this is important."

"I don't know," she grunted as she threw her head back in frustration.

"Come on, Emery, I need you to think. We need details if we're ever going to figure this out."

She sighed. "Like I said, there was a green haze after the bomb went off. That's all I remember."

Torin scribbled a few things on his virtual notepad, his eyes scrutinizing the words.

"Is anything connecting?"

He hurled the stylus across the table. "I've got nothing. Zip, zero, nada. A big, fat goose egg," he said as he massaged his temples. "I need some time to process all of this. I haven't slept in days."

"Well, you should probably get some sleep then. Let's call it a night. I can't think straight anyways," Emery sighed.

"You're right. We both need some sleep. Don't stay up all night thinking about this," Torin ordered as he shut down the virtual blueprint. "We'll reconvene in a couple of days."

"Okay," Emery agreed. "Oh, and Torin?"

His eyes locked on hers as he waited for her to continue.

"Thank you." She smiled. "For listening to me. You're a good friend."

Before he could respond, the line clicked. He watched as the holographic image of her faded away, much like their lives would if they didn't figure this out.

And soon.

35

Theo tapped his fingers impatiently as he waited for the other line to pick up. He'd found his numerous attempts to contact President Novak rather annoying as of late. About a year ago, he'd suggested that the President move his office into Dormance so that the members of the Federal Commonwealth could have easier access to him, but Victor had refused. "There needs to remain an air of mystery around the President," he'd said. "I can't be at everyone's beck and call—it'll look like I have nothing better to do."

Theo rolled his eyes at the thought. He hung up, then dialed the number again, this time pacing back and forth across the room, his recently polished shoes clacking against the marble floor. The pacing stopped when he heard heavy breathing on the other end.

"What is it?" Novak's voice was harsh.

"I'm calling to confirm that Rhea Alexander is no longer a participant in The Alpha Drive," Theo responded.

"Marvelous," Victor drawled. "I'm hoping this was completed with as little impact as possible to Emery?"

"For the most part," Theo lied, praying that Victor wouldn't ask any further questions.

The President cleared his throat. "You've always been a terrible liar, Theo. Lucky for you, I don't care to know the details. Just keep an eye on Ms. Parker."

Theo wiped his brow, letting out a faint sigh of relief. "Yes, sir."

"On another note, is the lethargum ready?"

"The final batch will be ready tomorrow, sir."

"And has our strategy been finalized?"

"It's in the final stages, sir. It should be ready within the next week."

"Now that just won't do," Victor chided. "Finalize it. Tonight."

"But sir . . ." Theo warned.

"We deploy tomorrow. No excuses."

36

Emery looked over to the left side of the room, where Rhea's things had sat just a week prior. The bed was stripped of its colorful sheets, the desk bare except for the dust accumulating in the corners. Not even a trace of a fingerprint remained.

She walked over to Rhea's old desk, running her hand along the dilapidated wood. As if she didn't have enough running through her mind, today was the day she'd find out whether she'd passed or failed her training. *It's about time.*

Emery pulled out a pair of black jeans and a black tank-top from her closet. After many months of training, it was easier to show up downstairs wearing the basics, since she'd just have to change her clothes anyway. As she searched for a pair of socks, her hand brushed over a silk pouch at the back of the drawer. A smile spread across her face as she grabbed the strings of the pouch, noticing that it felt lighter than last time. She drew open the strings, only to discover that the ring her mother had given her wasn't there.

Emery lowered her head into the closet drawer, searching frantically for any sign of the ring. Five frustrating minutes later, she sat on the floor with the drawer sitting beside her, socks and underwear strewn everywhere. She racked her brain as she toyed with the pendant around her neck. Had she moved it elsewhere? Not that she could recall.

Her focus was interrupted as her phone buzzed with a reminder to head to the FCW's underground quarters. Emery gathered the heap of socks and underwear as quickly as she could, threw them into the drawer, and placed it back on its hinges. Still feeling puzzled by her ring's disappearance, she grabbed her bag and headed out the door.

She made it downstairs in record time, her heart beating rapidly from within her chest. Her nerves heightened as hundreds of questions filled her thoughts. *Did I pass? Will I finally get to meet the other participants?*

The common room looked the same as it always did. Emery slowly walked through the door, her heartbeat audible in the eerily quiet room. As per usual, her clothes were folded in a neat, orderly pile, but, at second glance, she noticed that something was different. The long-sleeved shirt she'd worn for every training session now had a zipper with a tiny charm dangling off the end.

It bore the same symbol as her now-missing ring.

How peculiar.

Emery pulled the shirt over her head, eyeing the next piece of her ensemble. Long gone were the black nylon pants she'd come to know and love—they'd been replaced with a pair of leather pants, the color suggestive of freshly spilt crimson blood. She slipped the leather pants on, relieved to find that they had some elasticity to them.

The crystal dials Torin had given her glimmered in her bag and Emery dropped them into her back pocket for safekeeping. The footwear was the same, but there was one other item sitting on the table that was completely unfamiliar to her. She picked up the foreign object, examining its odd shape.

It looked like an earpiece of some sort.

Emery stuck the contraption into her ear, her finger grazing a raised button. Just as she was about to push it, a door creaked open behind her. Theo slithered in, his hands wrapped around a miniature tablet. "We're ready for you."

Her pulse quickened as she followed him out of the common room and down the hallway to a chamber labeled **Arbitrium**. Emery recalled the word from her Latin class; it meant *decision*. That class had already paid off in ways she never could have imagined. It was a good thing she'd paid attention.

Theo turned around, pulling a blindfold from his front left pocket, and made a spinning motion with his fingers. Emery obliged, relaxing as the cool silk was draped across her eyes. He led her into the chamber, positioning her in what felt like the center of the room. She stood there, heart pounding, ears alert for any sounds that might hint at what was going on. All she could hear was the rustling of shoes and the clearing of throats.

She wasn't alone.

"Welcome candidates," an unfamiliar voice announced. "We know you've all waited for quite some time and are anxious to get your results." There was a pause. "So, without further delay, let's get started."

Emery gulped, her palms covered in sweat, mind racing. *What if I didn't pass?*

"Because there are so many of you," the voice continued, "we'll announce the results all at once. We'll start with those that have failed since we won't be needing your services."

Suddenly, all Emery could focus on were the deafening thuds of numerous bodies as they dropped like sacks of potatoes onto the marble floor. She tried to count the number of thuds, but there were so many that it was nearly impossible. A whoosh of air hit her as the person to her right collapsed to the ground, one of their extremities landing on top of her right shoe.

Oh god. This is it.

Emery panicked for a moment, her body rigid, waiting for her bout of unconsciousness to swoop in. She squeezed her eyes shut. *Any minute now.*

But it never came. She relaxed her muscles and let out a small breath of air.

"Congratulations to those that are still standing," the voice resumed. "You have passed."

Emery tried not to smile, but couldn't help the slight upward movement at the corners of her mouth.

"Welcome to The Alpha Drive," the voice rumbled.

Almost immediately, she felt her body jolt, her arms and legs tingling like crazy. An ice cold wind surrounded her as her hair whipped viciously back and forth. It was the same feeling as teleporting to the 7S world. Emery reached her hands up against the current to pull off the blindfold as she hurtled through time and space. Right as she pulled it off, her body fell hard against the ground.

In the blink of an eye, she found herself lying face down on an asphalt street, her legs shaking from the bumpy ride she'd just taken. Her eyes widened as people began to materialize next to her out of nowhere. Her attention shifted to her fingers. No moving particles. She lifted her hand to touch her face, then her arms. *I'm not a hologram. This is my real body.*

Emery pulled herself up off the ground, her smile fading as her eyes focused on the unmistakable landmark in front of her.

It glimmered in the remaining sunshine, rays of light bouncing off its edges.

The Chicago Bean.

They'd been deployed. To Chicago. To the 7S world.

Trying not to panic, Emery reached for her phone. She had to find Torin—he needed to know that they were here. "It's too dangerous," she whispered to herself, watching as Theo's body materialized on the ground in front of her.

She observed her surroundings, realizing that she was in an alleyway of some sort. Tattered, brick buildings lined the street, begging to be restored. The clouded sun lowered overhead, the rays of light ceasing to reflect off the silver structure.

Emery turned around, noticing two familiar heads of hair lying face down in the street. She watched as they raised themselves up slowly, like the walking dead.

Mason and Warren?

Emery sprinted over to them, disbelief radiating from her face. Mason looked up, his expression one of pure bewilderment. She stopped a few feet from him, eyes wide, her expression matching his. Just as she opened her mouth to speak, Theo came up behind her and pressed the button on her earpiece. A bulbous force-field emerged, much like the one in her aquam training, and wrapped itself around her head. She waved her hands in front of her face, bringing them close to the energy barrier buzzing around her. Before she could say anything, Theo grabbed her arm and pulled her to the side of the alley, his expression stern.

"Reach into your left boot," he commanded.

Too stunned to ask why, Emery bent down, her fingers grazing a small pocket on the inside of her boot. She pulled out a black, spherical device the size of a golf ball.

I've seen this before.

Turning the ball over in her hands, she noticed it had a similar button to the one on her earpiece. Before she could gather her thoughts, Theo grabbed the device from her and opened it. He inserted a small green capsule, just like the one from her terrae training, into the four center prongs.

"Our strategy," he beamed as he closed the device, cupping it securely in his hands.

Torin was right. Emery tried to maintain a neutral expression. Her last landscape in terrae had been a city— she looked around her, realizing that the training landscape and this landscape matched.

I have to find Torin.

Theo turned and walked down the alleyway, gathering people along the way. Emery tiptoed away from the group and snuck around the corner, peeking her head around to make sure she couldn't be seen before pulling out her phone. Oddly enough, a familiar voice echoing from a few buildings down as her phone began to ring. As if he'd read her mind, Torin's head popped out of a window just a block down the street.

"Oh, thank god," she muttered, eyeing the entrance to the apartment's stairwell. Emery jogged over to his building and grasped onto the side rails, pulling herself up until she made it to the top floor. She tumbled gracelessly into the window, yelping as her head hit the corner of the wall.

Torin rushed over to lift her to her feet. He dragged her away from the window where they couldn't be spotted. "Holy smokes," he breathed. "So, you're here. And you brought friends." He crossed his arms solemnly as if he didn't trust her anymore.

"We don't have time for hurt feelings," she grunted, pacing in the small space.

"What on earth is on your head?" he asked, reaching out toward the moving particles.

Oh, that. She'd almost forgotten about it. "Don't touch it," she scolded as she slapped his hand away. "It's a force field or something."

He stared at her miraculously. "For what?"

"I don't know yet, that's why I'm here."

"Why didn't you tell me you were coming?"

"How could I, Torin? I literally just found out that I passed my training and in an instant," she snapped her fingers, "I was here. In Chicago."

"You're telling me that they brought all of you here, force field helmets and all, without going over the strategy first?"

Emery looked at him, realizing how crazy that sounded. "I know it doesn't make sense, but yes. That's exactly what happened." She peered out the window, hoping that no one was looking for her.

"I have to go back out there before they get suspicious," she said hurriedly, "but I need to tell you something."

Torin uncrossed his arms and moved closer to her.

"I didn't give you as much detail as I should have after I finished my terrae training," she said, taking a deep breath. "The same spherical device and green capsule I saw in the training . . . Theo has them. It's a bomb. Their strategy is a bomb."

"A bomb?" Torin looked at her with an intense expression, the lines in his forehead creasing. His eyes grew wide as he recalled something. "Lethargum," he whispered, "Theo mentioned lethargum capsules multiple times in his conversations."

"What are lethargum capsules?" Emery asked impatiently. "And why is this the first time I'm hearing about this?"

"I didn't pay much attention to it because it sounded like gibberish. Don't you agree?"

"Wait," she paused, recognizing the language almost

immediately. "It's Latin. It means lethargy." She looked at him with wide eyes as the realization sunk in. "I know what their strategy is," she whispered.

37

Torin took a deep breath. "Go on," he urged. "Tell me what you're thinking."

Emery nodded as she gathered her thoughts. "Lethargum means lethargy, which is another word for inactivity. Fatigue. Lifelessness." The last word lingered in the air like an unwanted guest who refused to leave.

"Lifelessness," Torin repeated.

"That green capsule is comatose gas," she whispered. "How did I not see this before?" She smacked her palm against her forehead. "In my terrae training, when you put that capsule in the spherical device, and then press the button on the side . . ."

"It explodes and releases the gas," he finished, his fingers tapping against his thigh. "That helmet you're wearing must protect you from it or something." He reached out again to touch the moving particles, then slowly drew his hand back.

"That's it. That's their strategy," Emery confirmed, feeling lightheaded. "They're going to put the rest of the world in a coma. In Dormance."

Just as Torin opened his mouth to respond, the sound of gunshots filled the streets outside. They both jumped, startled by the sudden noise.

"I have to go," she said as she rushed toward the window. "Stay here and do whatever you need to do to warn 7S!"

"We can stop them!" he called behind her. "Let me help you!"

"It's too dangerous!" she yelled over her shoulder as she climbed back down the stairwell. "Stay here, Torin. I mean it!"

Emery let go of the railing and dropped to the street, gravel crunching under her boots as she landed. She dashed down the alleyway, hoping that they hadn't left her behind. As she rounded the corner, she collided headfirst with Mason, their bodies jolting in opposite directions from the impact. Two rifles spilled from his hands and scattered across the pavement.

"Ouch," Mason groaned, his hand caressing his forehead. "Where did you wander off to? We've been looking everywhere for you." He walked over to where the rifles had landed and picked them up, then tossed one over to her, pulling the strap of his gun securely around his neck.

Emery looked down at the rifle. "What's this for?"

"For defense, what else?" Mason cocked his head to the side, his eyes blazing. "Come on, the others have already left."

Before she could open her mouth to tell him what was really going on, Mason took off. Emery secured her gun over her shoulder and followed him through the alleyway, her pace quickening with each stride. "Where did everyone go?"

"Where do you think?" he responded, his eyes focused straight ahead. "Obviously, Seventh Sanctum Headquarters."

It took everything in her not to seize a handful of his hair and drag him back to Torin's apartment, back to safety. She had to find a way to tell him the truth, or at least get him away from the chaos.

In the distance, people screamed as shots were fired left and right. Emery crouched behind a trashcan near the end of the alleyway, pulling Mason down with her. She peered around the edge, just far enough to catch a glimpse of what was going on. Either Torin had warned 7S or they'd figured it out on their own because the bloodshed in the streets was no coincidence.

7S soldiers stood armed at the ready, equipped to impale anyone who came near them. Floating hovercrafts and deadly machines she'd never seen before lined the streets, making The Alpha Drive look ill-equipped. She recognized a few of the fallen ones as students from her

Latin class. *So much death.* Emery looked over at Mason, who was watching the same atrocious scene with wide eyes. *I can't do this by myself. I need his help.*

Just as she was about to reveal the truth, Mason burst upwards, his arms pumping at his sides as he raced to the middle of the skirmish. Emery popped up, her reflexes like a cat, and raced after him. A 7S soldier charged at Mason headstrong with a dagger, but it wasn't an ordinary dagger—electrified currents pulsed around the blade.

Emery stopped mid-run, watching in horror as the scene unfolded. The soldier attempted to stab Mason, but he blocked the attack, flinging his rifle around to strike his opponent brutally in the jaw. His assailant buckled to the ground as blood sprayed from his mouth, red specks dotting the pavement like warped polka dots.

Emery darted over to the 7S building, jumping over slain bodies along the way, doing her best to keep her eyes focused on what was in front of her instead of what lie beneath her. She'd almost reached the door to headquarters when, all of a sudden, she was rammed into the side of the building. The icy, titanium walls smashed against her cheek. Her left hand reached for her rifle, as her right arm was twisted behind her back. A moan escaped from deep within her throat.

"Shhh," a familiar voice hushed.

It was Torin.

Emery wriggled free and elbowed him in the side. Hard. She spun around, a drop of blood dripping from her lip, and seized the throat of his shirt, knocking him against the same wall he'd just shoved her into.

"Don't sneak up on me like that again," she growled through clenched teeth.

His eyes wide with terror, Torin lifted his hands up in surrender. Emery let go of his shirt with balled fists. "What are you doing here?" She looked him up and down, noticing that he was wearing the exact same outfit she was, earpiece and all. Her eyes widened in disgust. "Where did you get those clothes?"

"It's not what you think," he pleaded. "A 7S soldier broke into my apartment right after you left, so I knocked him out—"

"And you took his *clothes*?" she interjected.

"I can't let you do this by yourself," he huffed. "Whether you like it or not, I'm a part of this too."

"I told you to stay put," she scolded in the same tone she used with her younger sister.

Torin puffed his chest out. "I'm not going to apologize because whether you like it or not, you need my help."

Emery scrutinized him for a moment, then bowed her head. As much as she hated to admit it, he was right. She needed him. "Fine. Come on then, *partner.*"

They crept to the front of the building and surveyed the perimeter for Mason. Torin slinked in front of her, scanning his fingerprints and retina for entry into 7S Headquarters. With no sign of Mason, Emery followed him inside the building, the automatic doors locking securely behind them.

The inside of the building was eerily quiet for the deadly combat that was occurring just outside the walls. As they reached the elevator doors, Torin scanned his fingerprints and retina a second time.

"Wait, the 7S world still has elevators?" She raised an eyebrow. "Aren't we just supposed to teleport wherever we need to go?"

Torin shrugged. "Maximum security. This is the service elevator. Just trust me, okay?"

Emery sighed as she stepped into the metal box.

Torin pressed the button for the top floor, floor 164. "You know, the Burj Khalifa used to be *the* tallest building in the world. It stands at 2,723 feet and has 163 floors," he thought aloud. "Except now, it's the *second* tallest building in the world." He grinned goofily.

"We're about to prevent the rest of the world from being forced into a coma and *that's* what you're thinking about? The tallest building in the world?"

"Snapple cap," he winked. "I've got more where that came from."

Emery looked at him incredulously, wishing she could slap him on the side of the head and knock some sense into him. "Focus. Now," she reprimanded.

After what felt like centuries, the elevator finally dinged, indicating that they had reached the 164th floor. The doors opened, the light from within illuminating a hallway that led to a staircase. Emery rushed forward, her fingers making contact with the slick rails. As she began to climb, she turned around to face Torin. "I need you to stay here."

"I'm not letting you go out there alone," he insisted, trying to push his way past her.

Emery grabbed his wrist. "You're wasting time. I need you to stay here. Hide over there," she ordered, gesturing toward the staircase. "If I need you, you'll know."

Emery waited for Torin to position himself under the staircase before walking up the steps. When she reached the last one, she took a deep breath and reached for the doorknob. With tremendous force, she pushed through the metallic frame, a cool gust of air whizzing past her. Nothing could have prepared her for what she saw next.

She was on the rooftop with a dozen other people, none of whom she recognized. Sitting in the center, was a circular, metal cage, the top open like a firepit. Within it was the black spherical device that contained the green capsule.

The lethargum.

Emery stepped forward, unsure of what her next move should be, when a figure rose from behind the cage.

"How nice of you to join us," Theo hissed. "We just finished setting up." He slithered toward her like a snake stalking its prey. "Care to do the honors?"

She gulped, watching as his finger hovered over a singular button on a remote control.

"When I press this button, it'll activate the timer on the bomb. The bomb will be launched into the air and we'll have a spectacular show of green haze as it travels with the wind currents and fills the lungs of everyone in the 7S world." He spun around to look at the contraption, his eyes gleaming with pure evil.

I can't let him win.

Without thinking, Emery lunged toward him, arms outstretched, fingers reaching desperately for the remote. She knocked it from his grip, watching as it flung from his fingers, landing just out of reach.

"Don't just stand there, you imbeciles!" he bellowed as he grappled with her on the ground. "Do something!"

Theo leaned his body backward, violently elbowing the inside of her knee. Emery grimaced, crying out at the jolt of pain running through her leg. Quickly regaining focus, she realized that his weight was unevenly distributed. Bucking him forward with a swift movement of her hips, she kneed him in the groin, watching victoriously as he toppled off of her in extreme pain. His body crumpled into the fetal position, his head between his knees.

Her leg throbbing, Emery crawled toward the remote as quickly as she could, adrenaline coursing through her veins. It was only a foot away. She extended her arm, fingers spread as far as they could reach. Just as she was about to grab it, a hand swiped the remote from the ground. Emery looked up, her eyes landing on none other than Warren Bradley.

"Warren, please." She tried to lift herself from the ground, but she was too weak.

His index finger hovered over the button.

"Warren, no!"

The bomb was released from the cage. It shot straight up into the air until all that remained was a small speck of dust that could barely be seen with the human eye. A bright flash illuminated the sky like fireworks on the fourth of July, sparks flying in every direction. Immediately after the flash appeared a green ball of fiery gas. It hovered for a moment over the city and then ruptured with great force, stirring everything in its wake. Emery could feel the building sway from left to right, and see the waves rippling through the air. She watched through her helmet as the lethargum whirled around her, the gas combining successfully with the particles in the air.

An idea hit her like a bolt of lightning.

Hoisting herself up from the roof, she sprinted back toward the metallic framed door, her feet pounding down the steps. Emery swiveled around the edge of the staircase, her hands digging in her pockets for the crystal dials. She dropped one onto each wrist and scanned the area for Torin, who was in the far corner of the room, standing in front of a T-Port.

"Brilliant!" she called out as she rushed over to him.

He turned around at the sound of her voice. "All the years I've worked here and I never knew we had a T-Port on the top floor." He shook his head bleakly. "This would have saved me so much time getting to and from work."

Emery flicked him in the head with her thumb and middle finger. "I need to teleport back to Dormance—to the FCW common room," she demanded.

"Wait, what? Why?" Torin asked with wide eyes.

"No time for questions. Just trust me."

Torin sighed. "Please tell me you have a plan."

Emery smiled. "I most certainly do."

"Well that makes one of us," he said as he readied the T-Port.

"Connect to my phone," she instructed as she stepped onto the platform, feet planted firmly on the metal surface. "I'll walk you through it once I get there."

Before he could respond, the familiar gust of air whirred around her, transporting her body back to where it had all begun.

38

Emery opened her eyes, grateful to be standing in the middle of the FCW common room. Her vision adjusted in the dim overhead lighting as she marched out the door to the hallway. The ignis and aquam training rooms whirred past her as she jogged along the corridor. At the end of the hallway was a door.

Emery looked for a posted label with the name of the room, unable to find one. Pushing the door open with the butt of her rifle, she poked her head inside. The door didn't lead to another room at all, but instead, to another hallway.

Emery entered the hallway cautiously, her heart beating so loud she could hear the pounding in her ears. She crept along the brick walls, noticing that there were no doors to the left or right of her. After a few minutes of walking, she stopped dead in her tracks. She'd been here before. It was the same hallway from her dream—the same place she'd found the pendant.

I'm underneath the Sychem building.

From a distance, the sound of footsteps paced back and forth. Emery glued herself to the wall, inching forward slightly until she was close to the edge. A long-haired, brunette girl paced back and forth and was guarding a massive, steel door. Emery inhaled deeply, squinting her eyes just to be sure. *Oh my god.*

It was Rhea.

She whirled back around the wall, her heart pounding out of her chest. *What in the world is Rhea doing here? Is she one of them?* Emery hadn't seen her since the incident at the hospital and, according to The Alpha Drive rules, Rhea wouldn't have a clue who she was. It'd be like Emery never existed. Like they'd never even met.

I don't have much time. I have to do something.

Emery stepped out from the hallway into the open space, standing about ten feet from her old roommate. Rhea locked eyes with her, a gigantic rifle in her right hand and an electrified dagger in her left holster. The blue currents sparked violently.

"Rhea," she said as she moved closer, "do you remember me?"

Rhea raised her rifle, her face showing no sign of recognition. "Unauthorized personnel. You can't be down here. Leave. Now."

"It's me, Emery," she coaxed as she took her hand off of her weapon. "We used to be roommates at Darden.

Do you remember?" Emery thought she saw a flicker of recognition in Rhea's face, so she inched a few steps closer.

"Stay back!" Rhea boomed, her finger on the trigger. "I said leave!"

Emery jumped back, startled. "Rhea, I can't leave. I need to get behind that door." Her eyes flitted between her old roommate and the steel frame. "Please."

As Emery took another step closer, Rhea lowered her gun and drew the electrified dagger from the holster, then flung it directly at her head. Emery swiftly moved to the right, the dagger just missing her ear. At the same time, Emery lifted her rifle and, without thinking, pulled the trigger, a single shot bursting through Rhea's chest.

It was the gunshot from her dream.

"No!" Emery shrieked. She fell to her knees at the same time Rhea's lifeless body crumpled to the ground. "Oh my god, oh my god," she sobbed as she crawled over to her fallen roommate. Blood oozed into a deep pool of crimson around her. "I didn't mean to, I didn't mean to," she wept, rocking back and forth as she held Rhea's head to her chest. "I'm so sorry, Rhea. I'm so, so sorry."

She squeezed her roommate's hand, watching as her head lolled to the side. Emery stayed there for a few moments, unable to break her eyes away from Rhea's pale, lifeless face. This was exactly how she'd felt at the hospital, except worse. Because this time, it was all her fault.

This time, she'd killed Rhea.

After what felt like a century, Emery finally gathered the strength to stand. She wiped the tears from her eyes, her body still trembling from shock. She looked down at her deceased roommate, then glared at the door she'd been guarding just moments before.

Her death . . . it has to mean something.

Emery searched for the room name, her eyes landing on a familiar word. **Imperium.**

"Control," she said aloud, her Latin skills coming in handy once again. Realizing that a key card was needed to enter, she began searching Rhea's clothes, resisting the urge to gag. She checked Rhea's pant pockets and boots with no luck, but eventually found what she was looking for tucked deep inside the pocket of her vest.

Tears formed in Emery's eyes again as she swiped the card in front of the reader, listening as the latches within the door unlocked. The door swung open and she found herself inside an enormous control room. Desks, screens, buttons, and knobs covered the entire surface area. Sitting in the middle of the room were a dozen seven-foot-long pods, each covered with dome-shaped, glass cases.

Emery ambled closer to the pods, gaping at the incredible amount of technology surrounding her. She peered into the glass, lowering her head closer to the case to get a better look. What she saw rendered her immobile.

Lying deep below the glass case was Theo's body.

Emery leapt backwards, her hands flying over her mouth. She counted the pods again.

Twelve.

How many people were with me on the roof before the bomb exploded?

Twelve.

"This is where the FCW keeps their bodies," she whispered to herself. "This is where they control Dormance." Emery looked around anxiously, wondering where they kept the rest of the dormants' bodies. The pod holding her own body could be hidden somewhere in this underground fortress.

Her eyes wandered around the room until they landed on a vault, the word **SANARÉ** plastered overhead.

The serum.

She rushed over to the surprisingly old-fashioned vault, the dial reminiscent of the locker she'd used in gym class at her public high school, except this one had letters instead of numbers. She spun the dial multiple times, trying every five-letter combination she could think of. After eight tries, she slunk down next to the vault and hit her head against the wall.

Think, Emery. Think.

She closed her eyes to clear her thoughts from her mind. *Five letters.* She sat still, imploring the answer to come to her. As Emery opened her eyes, she looked down at the charm dangling from her blood-spattered uniform. That was it.

A-L-P-H-A.

After five spins, she tugged at the door of the vault, grinning as the locks released and the door swung open. Her smile quickly faded as rows and rows of empty shelves lay in front of her.

No, she thought frantically, wiping her hands along the shelves. She knelt down so she was eye level with the bottom shelf. A solitary orange capsule sat, abandoned, in the very back.

Emery reached for it and brought the capsule close to her face, examining it closely. After shaking it, she realized it was sanaré—not in liquid form, but in gas form. For a split second, she felt victorious; but then it dawned on her that there was only one capsule. There wasn't enough.

I can't save Rhea and save everyone else, she thought glumly, feeling defeated all over again.

Emery dashed over to the main control unit and started typing on the virtual keyboard. Her hand swiped over a sunken area on the unit, feeling a familiar shape underneath the tips of her fingers. She glanced down as her index finger traced the silhouette of a fish, the image practically identical to the ring her mother had given her. Below the fish was another sunken symbol in the shape of a horseshoe, just like the pendant that hung around her neck.

Emery pondered over the images for a minute, unable to shake the thought that it was more than just a coincidence. She reached for her pendant, unclasping the hook from around her neck and laid it down on the image in front of her. It fit perfectly, almost as if it were a piece of a puzzle that had gone missing. She turned her attention back to the oversized monitor in front of her and pulled out her phone. Torin had been on mute the entire time. *Oops.*

"Emery? Emery, are you there?"

"Yeah, sorry, I'm here," she answered as a hologram of Torin appeared from her phone.

"Where are you?" he whispered frantically.

"I think I figured it out. I have the sanaré in gas form," she said as she re-clasped the pendant around her neck. "I'm in the control room now. Theo's body is here, along with the rest of the Federal Commonwealth. We need to disarm Dormance—this might be our only chance."

"You're in the control room now?"

"Yes, that's what I just said," she sighed, gesturing at her surroundings. "Do you actually listen to anything I say?"

"Sorry the connection is bad. Hold on, I'm hacking in now." The monitor in the control room flashed, numbers and letters scrolling up and down the enormous display. "I think . . . yep, I'm in," he confirmed. "The system is asking for something strange. It's asking for pod identification numbers."

Emery turned to look at Theo's pod, her eyes landing on a gold plate attached to the metal just underneath the glass casing. She scanned one after the other, realizing that each of the pods had one. Starting with Theo's, she read aloud each code, watching as the combination of letters and numbers appeared on the monitor.

"Okay, good," Torin said. "Now we just have to figure out the code to shut it down—"

Emery coughed, almost choking on her own spit. "We don't have the code to shut it down?"

"Every system is different," he explained, clearing his throat nervously. "We just need to figure out what works."

She watched as word after word, combination after combination appeared on the screen, followed by large blinking red Xs. Torin typed in another combination, but the same red X appeared.

"This is just great. Of course nothing is working," he muttered. "Any bright ideas?"

"Hold on," she said, racking her brain for answers. She gnawed on a hangnail, her eyes scanning the room for clues: first the door, then over to the pods, until her eyes settled on the text over the vault. *Everything's in Latin.*

Suddenly, a moment from her terrae training filled her thoughts. The green mist. Her mother. She'd said something. *What was it?*

Emery turned back to the monitor. "This is a total crapshoot . . . but try 'exarmet'."

"What does—?"

"Just do it." She watched as the words appeared on the screen, followed by an affirmatory message in green.

Disarmament Initiated in 30 . . . 29 . . . 28 . . .

"That's it!" he commended. "What in the world did I just type?"

She beamed, reveling in the moment for as long as she could. "My mom said it to me during my terrae training. It's Latin for 'disarm'."

"Only you would notice such a minute detail," he laughed.

"Looks like it wasn't so minute, was it?"

He smiled. "Okay, now what?"

"Okay, now teleport me back to the 7S world before the countdown ends," Emery instructed. "But first . . ."

She glanced over at the pods, noticing that each of them had a thick, silver wire connecting them to the control station. Emery rushed out of the room as an idea came to her.

The dagger.

She stepped over Rhea's body and walked over to the weapon, grabbing the handle with both hands as she tugged it from the wall. Emery ran back into the room and began slicing the silver wires that connected each pod to the main station.

"What are you doing?" Torin yelled as the countdown continued.

10 . . . 9 . . . 8 . . .

She slashed the final wire.

"Now! Do it now, Torin!"

Emery glanced back over at the control station one last time, her eyes settling on the two familiar images of the fish and the horseshoe. She suddenly realized what the symbols were.

Alpha and Omega.

Before she had a chance to analyze further, a tingling sensation overtook her body, hitting her legs first, then her arms and her neck. Emery kept her focus on the symbols, her fingers gripping the orange capsule, until her body was lifted and transported back to 7S Headquarters.

39

Torin watched as Emery's body appeared in segments on the platform—first her feet, then her legs and hips, followed by her abdomen, chest, and arms, and finally, her neck and head.

"The physics of teleportation will never cease to amaze me," he declared as he helped her off the platform. "Do you have it?"

She opened her hand to reveal the tiny orange capsule.

"And the device?"

Emery looked at him with a puzzled expression.

He sighed. "Check your other boot."

She reached into her right boot and pulled out another spherical golf ball shaped device. Emery handed it to him, her eyes wide with astonishment.

"What? I saw Naia put them into your boots—one in your right boot and one in your left," he bragged. "I had no idea what they were for. Until now."

Naia put them in my boots? Emery thought back to her training sessions. The orange capsule. The green capsule. The green haze. Theo *had* said that Naia was the one in charge of her training simulations. *Was she helping me the whole time? Where is she now?*

Torin's interrupted her thoughts. "Bad news. Right after you teleported back to Dormance, Theo and his soldiers came bolting down the stairs looking for you. Fortunately, they didn't see me, but I heard Theo tell his team to find you. And Mason."

Emery bit her lip, pushing her thoughts of Naia aside. "Did they say where they were going?"

"No, but the good news is, they're not on the roof anymore. And now I know what to do with this." He held up the device.

"Okay, here's the plan. You head to the roof while I go outside to look for Mason and Theo. When I give you a sign, release the bomb."

Torin tilted his head to the side. "What sign?"

"Hmm," Emery pondered this for a moment. "Are our phones still connected?"

Torin checked his phone, then nodded.

"I want you to keep me on the line and turn on your speakerphone. Release it when you hear me yell, 'Alpha'. Okay?"

He nodded again, his hands trembling slightly.

Emery reached out and placed her hands on top of his. "We've got this. I'll be back before you know it." She squeezed his hands before heading into the elevator shaft. She pressed her gun tightly to her side as the numbers above the elevator doors decreased with every passing second. She readied herself as the metal box landed on the ground floor, taking a deep breath as the doors opened. The lobby was still deserted like before, so she took advantage of the emptiness and rushed to the main entrance. She pressed the button on her headset to reignite the force field helmet, then burst through the entry doors, her eyes surveying the premises for any sign of Mason or Theo. She didn't have to look far because they were standing right in front of the building she'd just walked out of. And there was a gun.

Pointed at Mason's head.

Mason was on his knees, arms tied behind his back, his face bloody and beaten from a scuffle with Theo and his army. Emery gazed at Mason's terrified expression, her confidence wavering.

"Where is it?" Theo bellowed, his eyes blazing with rage.

"It's over, Theo," Emery asserted. "Let him go."

"The serum, Emery," Theo hissed, digging his pistol deeper into the back of Mason's head. "I know you have it. Give it to me. Now."

"There's none left," she lied, immediately wishing

that she hadn't.

"Funny," he chuckled, his finger on the trigger. "I never took you for a liar."

Emery's eyes widened. "Theo, don't—!"

Her words were cut off by a resounding boom. Her eyes ignited with fury as she watched the bullet leave the gun and enter Mason's skull, the remnants tearing through his forehead.

"ALPHA!" she screamed as she lifted her rifle, unloading a full round of bullets on Theo and his followers. The light left Theo's eyes, his body falling to the ground in a deafening thud. The others fell to the ground shortly after, their eyes wide open as their heads hit the pavement. It was then that the sanaré bomb lit up the sky, a flash of blinding white light followed by a vibrant orange haze.

Emery ran over to Mason and fell to her knees as the auburn haze drifted around them. She pressed her right hand underneath his skull, applying as much pressure as she could to stop the steady flow of blood. The haze quickly turned into a thick fog, her visibility of Mason's face fading until, eventually, it disappeared altogether. Emery remained still, her left hand on Mason's chest, hoping and praying for some type of movement. A flinch. A muscle spasm. Anything to tell her that he was still alive.

Time stood still as memory after memory flooded over her. The confusion she'd felt when her mom had given her the ring. The uncertainty when she'd first met her new roommate. The shock when Theo had told her about Dormance. The disbelief when Torin had told her it was all a lie. The heartbreak when Anthony had failed to recognize her. The regret when she'd rejected Mason. The anguish that had consumed her entire being when she'd killed Rhea. She could only remember the bad. There was nothing good left. And now Mason was going to die.

After what seemed like an eternity, the fog finally lifted and Emery's sight returned back to normal. Much to her surprise, something good started to happen. Through her tears, she could see victims of the battle lift themselves up off the streets. One by one, they rose from the dead. Everyone seemed to be coming back to life . . . everyone except for Theo and the eleven other FCW members.

It worked.

By some miracle, Mason's chest quivered. Emery immediately turned her attention back to him. *Oh, please. Please let there be one more good thing.* She watched miraculously as the orange particles healed the gaping wound in his head, the skin joining together again to make one cohesive unit. Mason's eyes fluttered open, his pupils dilating as he tried to regain focus.

He's alive. Mason's alive.

Emery bent over and kissed him on the forehead as tears formed in her eyes. "You're okay," she coaxed, stroking his bloodstained, matted hair. "Everything's okay. We're safe now."

Mason gazed up at her, a small smile crossing his lips. "I have a headache."

She laughed as happy tears streamed down her face. "I bet you do." Emery continued to stroke his hair when her eyes landed on a figure standing just a few feet in front of her. There stood Torin, motionless, his eyes locked on hers. In that moment, there were so many things she wanted to say to him. She wanted to thank him for reaching out to her. For telling her the truth about 7S. For trusting her, even in his moments of doubt, but the words wouldn't come. So, she did the one thing she knew he'd understand.

She nodded.

Torin nodded back, a brief smile faltering on his lips, before lowering his head and turning toward the doors that led to 7S Headquarters.

Their work here was done. Emery wasn't sure if or when she'd ever see him again. She wasn't sure what the future had in store. But one thing was for certain. Together, they'd freed the world from Dormance.

Together, they'd defeated The Alpha Drive.

40

President Novak watched from his office as specks of orange dust hit the window, a thick cloud hanging in the air. Bodies that were once immobile began moving again, waking up from their brief entry into Dormance.

He'd never doubted Emery. He knew all along that she'd be the one to get him to this point. True, his plans would be difficult without the assistance of his former colleagues, but he'd manage.

He had to.

Victor reached into his office drawer and pulled out a small tin box with a yellow bow plopped on top. He lifted the lid and ran his fingers along the fish-shaped ring, grinning at what was to come.

All he had to do was get Emery on his side.

Acknowledgements

I've always been a writer, but it's been a lifelong dream to become a published author. Now that it's here, I can hardly believe it. The child in me is freaking out right now . . . in a good way.

First, I'd like to thank God for blessing me in more ways than one.

I'd like to thank my incredible critique partner and newfound writing buddy, Vivien Reis. You catch things that I wouldn't, even after I've read my manuscript 10+ times. Your insight has been invaluable and has helped make me a better writer. I feel so lucky to have you not only as a CP, but also as a friend.

Thanks to my beta readers. You guys rock. Your comments are the first ones I go to when I need a little pick me up. Thank you.

I'd like to thank my parents, Barb Marvel and Ed Martin, for always supporting me no matter what choices I make. And for listening to me read every rendition of *The Christmas Monkey* every holiday season with full (terrible) illustration. I love you guys.

I'd like to thank my sister, Erin Martin, for being so incredibly supportive and excited to read this book. You were there from inception and stuck with me to the very end. I'm so lucky to have a sister who loves books and the art of storytelling as much as I do.

I'd like to thank my fiancé, Jonathon Bills, for sticking with me through every stage of crazy and for helping me come up with the concepts for the book covers. Loving a writer isn't easy, but you're always there, loving me and encouraging me every step of the way. I love you so much and cannot wait to call you my husband.

Lastly, I'd like to thank YOU, my readers. Without you this book would not be possible. So thank you. Thank you for taking the time to jump into the worlds of Emery and Torin and for choosing to read this book. There are so many incredible writers with amazing stories to share and it's so humbling to know that of all those stories, you chose to read mine. Cheers!

THE ORDER
OF OMEGA

Emery Parker must continue on her journey to save those she loves—all while coming to terms with her past and the terrifying power her family's secret holds.

Emery had all the answers to change the course of the future—or so she'd thought. The clarity of her situation diminishes as new things come to light during her quest for the truth. As she fights to maintain control, the grey area between betrayal and allegiance only grows larger. In a time of full-fledged uncertainty, Emery must fully embrace her past, even if doing so may mean losing everything, and everyone, she ever loved.

TURN THE PAGE
FOR A FIRST LOOK!

1

The sound of crunching glass beneath her blood-stained combat boots reminded Emery of a much happier time than this. Stepping out into the first Christmas snow in Northern Arizona, her family curled up by an outdoor firepit, watching as the blazing sun fell behind a wide canvas of mountains. It was one of her happiest memories, a time where she felt like everything had finally come together. Every aspect of her life had been perfect. Nothing had been missing.

But she was far from that place. And she wasn't sure she'd ever get to go back.

Emery broke her gaze from the shards of glass on the floor, focusing her attention on the blank faces staring back at her.

Torin. Mason. Warren.

They'd all survived the lethargum attack, thanks, in large part, to her. Their uniforms were still speckled with orange dust from the sanaré bomb that had lit up downtown Chicago just two hours prior. She never would have guessed that sanaré would be their saving grace. They'd sat in Torin's apartment since then, not moving or talking, stunned by the events that had just taken place.

Emery decided it was time to break the silence. "Well, that was eventful." She looked directly at Torin, mentally egging him on to respond.

Torin bowed his head to the floor and scratched at his scalp.

"Can someone fill me in on what just happened?" Mason interjected. "In case you failed to notice, I was shot. In the head. By *Theo*. By my own *team*." He twiddled his thumbs, his eyes flitting back and forth between Emery and Torin.

"I wanted to tell you when we were hiding behind the trashcan," Emery started. A flash of guilt crossed her face.

"Tell me what?" Mason asked through clenched teeth.

Emery sighed. "That we were fighting for the wrong side. Everything Theo told you about the Seventh Sanctum was a lie. The members of the Federal Commonwealth are the creators of Dormance, the ones who want to control all of mankind." She glanced over at Torin. "And had it not been for Torin and his impeccable timing, they probably would have succeeded."

Torin's cheeks flushed a rosy shade of pink. "That's not entirely true. It was all Emery's idea. I just did what I was told."

She felt her face burn with embarrassment.

"I hear what you're saying, but you can understand why it's hard to believe," Mason said. "I still don't understand what the hell is going on."

"It's a lot more complicated than you realize," she explained. "Trust me. I'll find more time to explain later, but first, there's somewhere we need to go." She walked over to Torin and grabbed him by the arm, leading him toward the fire escape she'd used earlier that day.

"You two stay here," she demanded, pointing her index and middle fingers at Warren and Mason.

Mason opened his mouth to object, but decided shortly after that it wasn't worth the hassle. He fell onto the couch, the toe of his boot knocking against what remained of a metal coffee table.

Emery climbed out of the window and slid down the fire escape, Torin's feet dangling just a few feet above her. When they'd both landed safely on the pavement, she turned to face him, lowering her voice to a whisper. "I left something behind in Dormance. Something important. At least, I think it's important."

"Well, that probably wasn't the smartest idea," Torin chided. "What was it?"

Before she could answer, a loud buzzing noise filled the space between them. Torin held up his hand as if to pause the conversation, and reached into his pocket for his phone. Disbelief crossed his face.

"It can't be . . ."

"What?" she urged. "Who is it?"

"It's a call . . . fr—from Dormance," he stammered. But before he could answer it, the buzzing came to a stop.

She rushed to his side, her eyes scanning the device. "What happened? Who was it?"

"I'm not sure. The call dropped."

It didn't make any sense. They had deactivated Dormance just short of three hours ago. The voice in the control room had confirmed it. How could Torin receive a call from Dormance when it had been terminated?

Unless it hadn't been.

"It didn't work," she thought aloud, kicking the pavement with the toe of her boot. She shook her head. "We didn't deactivate Dormance."

A wave of confusion washed over Torin's face. "Yes, we did. I was there—I heard the confirmation."

"No," Emery argued, her heart pounding. "We must have missed something."

Torin wrinkled his nose. "You sound mental, you know that?"

She waved her hand absentmindedly in the air, as if the insult had landed on deaf ears. She took a few steps forward in a zig-zag pattern, then back again in the opposite direction. Her eyes met his as a coy smirk crossed her face. "I need you to send me back."

Torin coughed as if he'd choked on a giant wad of his own spit. "I take back what I said. You don't just sound mental, you *are* mental! How can I send you back to Dormance if . . ." his voice drifted off as he caught up to her train of thought.

"You couldn't have received a call if we'd fully deactivated Dormance." Her eyes lit up like a child on Christmas morning. "That means it's still active. And you need to send me back."

"But what if something happens? What if you get stuck there?" Torin asked, searching for any reason that might change her mind. "What if there's retaliation? What if it's a giant black hole?"

Emery rolled her eyes. "Everything will be okay," she coaxed as she searched her pockets for the crystal dials. "I promise."

He shook his head, eyes wide with fear. "It's too dangerous. You know I can't let you go."

"Torin," she reprimanded as she extended her right palm. "Give me the dials."

He stood his ground, unflinching. After a few seconds of her seemingly endless death stare, he couldn't help but give in. He reached into his pocket and pulled out the dials,

5

watching as they fell from his fingertips into her open palm. Her hand closed securely around them.

Emery walked briskly across the street to the nearest platform with Torin hot on her heels. "Can you still connect to the holodevice in the common room?" she asked through hurried breaths.

"I'm working on it now." He fumbled with his phone, trying desperately to keep up with her swift pace. "If you'd just slow down a little—"

"We don't have time to slow down," she called over her shoulder. After walking another block, they finally arrived at a T-Port on the corner of 5th Street and Main. She hopped onto the platform and placed the crystal dials into her wrists, her foot tapping impatiently as she waited for him to catch up.

"Okay, I think I'm connected now," he panted as he approached the platform. "Are you ready?"

"Born ready," she teased. She closed her eyes, waiting for the familiar gust of air, the tingling in her legs and feet.

But it didn't come.

She opened one eye with caution. Her surroundings hadn't changed. Torin was still standing right in front of her, looking dumbfounded.

"Try it again?" she asked, noticing that her palms were starting to sweat. She wiped them on her pants and took a deep breath to calm her nerves.

"I can't," he muttered, looking up from his phone. "I'm getting an error message."

"What does it say?" she asked impatiently.

"It says that the portal is closed . . ."

As soon as the words left his mouth, Emery's phone buzzed uncontrollably. She didn't recognize the number, but history had proven more than once that she should answer it. She clicked the accept button, waiting for the voice on the other end.

"Hello?"

Static.

"Hello? Is anyone there?"

"Emery? Is that you?"

Her breath caught. She recognized the voice on the other end of the line immediately.

It was Naia.

Kristen Martin is the author of The Alpha Drive trilogy: The Alpha Drive, The Order of Omega, and Restitution. A graduate of both Arizona State and Texas A&M, Kristen currently lives in Texas with her fiancé, two rowdy dogs, and skittish cat.

CONNECT WITH KRISTEN AT
www.kristenmartinbooks.com
www.facebook.com/authorkristenmartin
Instagram @authorkristenmartin
Twitter @authorkristenm

CPSIA information can be obtained
at www.ICGtesting.com
Printed in the USA
LVHW11s1432071018
592735LV00002B/399/P